Shipwrecked at Sunset

Books by Jacqueline DeGroot

Climax
The Secret of the Kindred Spirit
What Dreams Are Made Of
Barefoot Beaches
For the Love of Amanda
Shipwrecked at Sunset
Worth Any Price
Running into Temptation with Peggy Grich
Tales of the Silver Coast, A Secret History of Brunswick
County with Miller Pope
The Widows of Sea Trail

To contact the author or find out about her other books,
please visit www.jacquelinedegroot.com

Shipwrecked at Sunset

Salvaged–Everlasting Love

American Imaging
www.americanimaging.com

© 2005 Jacqueline DeGroot

Author photo: Sally Neale
Jacket design: October Publishing

Printed in the United States of America

First Edition 2005

09 08 07 06 05   1 2 3 4 5

ISBN: 0-9747374-3-7

This book is a work of fiction. All characters in this book have no existence outside the imagination of the author and have no relation whatsoever to anyone bearing the same name or names.

I would like to dedicate this book to all the people who struggle to preserve their heritage. In a world bent on progress it's not always easy to set aside valuable land, but future generations need to see life as it once was, if only to appreciate what they now have. And to my sister, who has a passion for Civil War history.

Acknowledgments

I want to thank all the proofreaders who helped to make my story better:

Kathy Blaine
Arlene Cook
Bill DeGroot
Deanna Eirtle
Cliff Errickson
Lynn Errickson
Peggy Grich
Martha Murphy
Barbara Scott-Cannon
"V" from Shallotte

And Carl Wilson for his medical examiner's expertise.

Author's Note

The author made every attempt to maintain historical accuracy, and relied on a number of reference sources on this topic. Among the many sources used were: *Crime Scene: The Ultimate Guide to Forensic Science,* by Richard Platt; *Treasures of the Confederate Coast: The Real Rhett Butler and Other Revelations,* by Dr. E. Lee Spence; *The Civil War: Strange and Fascinating Facts,* by Burke Davis; *Graveyard of the Atlantic* by David Stick; and *Warships and Naval Battles of the Civil War.*

She also found the website www.usahistory.com to be very helpful with her research. The site at www.usahistory.com/wars/letter1864.htm has an excerpt from the Diplomatic Correspondence from Mr. Seward to Mr. Adams who was with the Department of State. The letter is dated February 5, 1865. It is page number 128 of the document numbered 833, and it discusses the case of the *Vesta* and the events that happened on January 20, 1864.

Shipwrecked at Sunset

Introduction

On April 19, 1861, six days after the surrender at Fort Sumter, President Abraham Lincoln mandated a blockade of the Southern coast from South Carolina to Texas. Just eight days later, he extended the blockade to include the coasts of Virginia and North Carolina–over 3,500 miles of coastline with many barrier islands and inlets.

For three years, the largest Federal squadron afloat was stationed at the bars on New Inlet at Fort Fisher and Old Inlet on the Cape Fear River at Smithville, now known as Southport. Their mission was to intercept specially-designed steamers whose captains were determined to bring needed supplies for the Confederacy into the port city of Wilmington. Their success was spotty at best at the onset, but their odds improved with time. The Federal net caught only one out of every ten runners in 1861, one out of eight in 1862, one out of four in 1863, and eventually, every other one in 1865. When Smithville and Wilmington fell to Federal forces in 1865, severing the lifeline of the South, the end of the Confederacy was inevitable.

The story of one particular blockade runner is rife with good luck, bad luck, meritorious victory, terrible choices, and ultimately horrible defeat; all of which occurred during the same fateful night.

Before securing the anchor, Captain R.H. Eustace probably wished he had never left Bermuda. For almost as soon as he had, his ship, the *Vesta* was the hunted. For seven days she was chased by avid Yankee cruisers. She finally managed to elude them and came over the horizon facing the southern coast of North Carolina. Being compelled to lay to before navigating the Cape Fear River, she was spotted by a Yankee cruiser, which immediately gave chase. Soon, eleven Yankee vessels were bearing down on the newly-discovered prey. Completely surrounded, the *Vesta* turned into harm's way and ran the gauntlet in one of the most stirring scenes the war had witnessed on water to date. She outmaneuvered cruisers that attempted to cut her off and was so fast she was able to sprint away from the cruisers that were firing their broadsides upon her. Five cruisers gave chase using their bow guns almost continuously as she neared the safety of a sandbar. Despite their constant volleying, no one on board the *Vesta* was hurt. The vessel raised her flag in defiance as the shallow waters of the shoreline accepted her and distanced her from her enemy. Although the ship had endured heavy fire, she suffered only one hit–a shot that had miraculously avoided flesh and machinery and landed well above the vessel's water line. The *Vesta* was victorious.

Unfortunately, Captain Eustace and First Officer Tickler began to celebrate their victory, and it is reported that they both became outrageously drunk soon after night had fallen. It was said that the captain was asleep on the quarter-deck, stupefied with drink, when he should have put to land. At two in the morning, he woke the pilot and directed him to take the ship ashore, telling him that the ship was above Fort Fisher, when in fact, the runner was about forty miles to the south of Frying Pan Shoals. Within fifteen minutes she had run aground so hard she could not be moved.

The *Vesta* carried valuable cargo, including a grand, honorary uniform intended as a present for General Lee from some of his London admirers. Three-fourths of her cargo consisted of badly-needed army supplies, among them very expensive English shoes. Ironically, it had been the *Vesta's* first attempt at running the blockade.

Passengers and crew were forced into lifeboats without their baggage even though one of the passengers was a paymaster for the Confederate Navy. The final affront occurred when the inebriated captain ordered the ship fired and burned at the water's edge with everything aboard.

Yankee cruisers did not happen upon the smoldering hulk until the afternoon of the following day when the smoke from the wreck drew their attention. Nothing of any account was saved from the ship. Official records show that the *Vesta* wrecked four miles south and westward of Tubb's Inlet, North Carolina, listing in just ten feet of water. She had been a fine looking, double propeller, blockade runner, just like her sister, the *Ceres*. Brand-spanking new in late 1863, she was worth about 300,000 pounds Sterling. With her long iron hull and modern elliptical stern, she was almost 500 tons, yet barely drew eight feet of water. At 165'x23'x13,' the *Vesta* was said to have been one of the finest steamers in the entire blockade running line.

Chapter One—Shelby
Figure Eight Island, NC

S helby walked along the shore eyeing the huge twenty-foot wall of sandbags snaked against the eroding beach. Nestled together, they were the prescribed six-foot-high barrier grudgingly permitted to minimize the damage caused by the buffeting waves. She shaded her eyes and looked up at the massive white beach house towering above her, and the tall pylons supporting it, not ten feet from where the water was lapping over the sodden sandbags. She counted the balconies on the three-million dollar house–nine, on four different levels.

Hurricane Glynnis had certainly done her job here. From the looks of her backlog of new appeals, they should have named this hurricane Griselda, after one of Cinderella's ugly stepsisters.

Shelby Laine worked for the Division of Coastal Area Management or C.A.M.A., enforcing the laws of the North Carolina Coastal Resources Commission, the NCCRC, or No Crack as she often thought of it. No crack—don't give in. Make a decision and stick with it, come hell or high water. And high water was exactly the reason her job was so difficult; the hell part came from the people she refused permission. Permission to shore up, wall in, barricade, or otherwise protect their homes from the ever-encroaching oceans and tidal waters.

Since the coastal engineers in power believed that hardened structures, such as groins, jetties, seawalls, and bulkheads actually accelerated beach erosion, she was forced to deny requested permits many times over the ones she approved.

She looked down at her clipboard, scribbled a few notes and then flipped the pages back to look at her workload. Twenty-seven requests still in need of determinations. Thirteen more than she'd had this time last week. Oh, what great fun hurricanes are!

Well, she'd better get busy; the tide waited for no one. Neither did time, she reminded herself as she looked at her watch and checked the local tide chart. High tide was in fifteen minutes. These sandbags were going to be breached even more within the next few minutes. She could envision the briny saltwater bashing the two dozen stilts supporting the back side of this paradise by the sea during a full lunar cycle.

For the owners, it was becoming a paradox by the sea. Whether to keep appealing for help, or bite the bullet and move their little "cottage" back several hundred feet; that was the question.

Moving the home would entail two to three hundred thousand dollars for a new lot, thirty thousand more to physically move the house, ten thousand for the architect who had to figure out how to adapt the garage and front door to face the street when it was moved to the opposite side of the road, and sixty thousand to make the necessary repairs to the new first-level design. And that didn't include the cost of all new landscaping, this time not only for a front yard, but also for a back yard that would no longer be the free and easy, eye-catching, and continually changing roll of the ocean.

Shelby continued walking along the shore, sometimes walking backward to look back up at the house. The owners were requesting permission to double the fabric wall of sandbags from twenty feet long to forty feet long and to layer them ten feet high instead of the current six feet. The prevailing thought, provided by a well-paid oceanographer and current Duke professor, was that the primary channel to the Rich Inlet would eventually begin shifting back toward Figure Eight Island, allowing the sediment that had been robbed to be replaced just in time to save the house from falling into the sea. The hurricane certainly hadn't helped things, and from the looks of it, neither would more sandbags. She put a check mark beside the project name and jotted down a few notes to incorporate in the report she had to write when she got back to her office. Hell, at least the extra barrier would give the owners a chance for the stock market to rebound so they wouldn't have to attempt a new mortgage. Generally banks weren't keen on loaning thousands of dollars to make a property less valuable on the marketplace. Beachfront was, after all, beachfront, even if the waves *were* at your back door. Second row was, well . . . it was second row.

Continuing to walk backward, she tripped over something and turned to see what it was. Squinting her eyes in the dazzling sun, she saw that there was a small piece of metal protruding from the sand. Realizing the potential danger to a jogger, she squatted and reached down to tug on it. It didn't give, so she dropped her clipboard. Using her cupped hands, she dug the sand from around it in small semicircles until she could see what it was.

It looked very much like the barrel of a gun. Digging deeper, she realized that was exactly what it was–a gun with a very long barrel. It took her a few more swipes of digging a trench into the sand to pry the whole thing loose. Finally, she pulled the mass of metal out of the sand, being especially careful not to touch the trigger area. She noted that it was a very old gun, similar to something you'd see in an old pirate movie.

Guns had always made her nervous and this one was no exception. It was heavy, cumbersome, and rusty. As she cradled it in one hand and turned it over with the other, she wondered what metal it was made of and if it would fire anymore. And why was it here? Why had it been buried in the sand next to million-dollar beachfront properties whose beaches were inaccessible to anyone not passing muster at the security gate leading to this barrier island? Looking out at the distant horizon, she reminded herself that this seashore *was* the eastern edge of America. Anyone owning a boat capable of navigating the ocean could feel free to drop anchor and come ashore if they so desired.

Placing the gun carefully on her clipboard, she stood and carried it in front of her like it was a cake on a serving tray. Cutting through what was left of the back yard to this erstwhile, deserted, Hampton-styled beach house, she found her way to the generous circular driveway and from there to the road and her truck.

Keeping her eye on the pistol, afraid that if she jarred it the wrong way it would go off, she maneuvered herself into the driver's seat and gingerly placed the clipboard beside her. She was especially careful to aim the barrel toward the passenger door. The gun had a Spanish flair to it somehow. Scrolly metal and dark, pitted wood that had petrified lent it that air; but for all she knew about guns, it could have been German or Italian-made just as easily.

Rationalizing that she had to go on site to Oak Island anyway, she decided to make a stop at the North Carolina Maritime Museum in Southport. Surely, someone there would be able to tell her about her find.

Two hours later, when she showed it to a man who could best be described as a very knowledgeable, laid-back curator, she watched as he whistled through his teeth. "Man, that hurricane sure has dredged up some interesting stuff. Never saw the likes of this kind of bounty coming in from the ocean. It's booty from the shipwrecks. This appears to be from the blockade runners' graveyard. You're the third one today with something from the late 1800s. This," he said as he picked the gun up reverently with a hand cradling each end, "is a Civil War Navy Colt. One of the newer models back then, with the fluted cylinder and navy grips, .44 caliber, 1860 percussion, if I'm not mistaken. Probably saved some Confederate's life a time or two against the Union boys. I doubt if it would fire now though, even with a good cleaning. See here?" he asked as he slid his hand around the barrel. "The trigger is locked, sort of melted on one side, the wood, too, but not on the other. It probably was laying down on something when a ship was set afire as most of the captured blockade runners were. The crews didn't want to surrender their cargoes to the Yankees. They were determined that their ships go up in smoke rather than be of any use to the North." His hand lovingly glided over the coarse, pocked metal and the concrete-like striate that had once been smooth polished wood. "This was an expensive gun in its day. A gentleman's gun. Definitely not government issue. Whoever lost it probably missed it, if he was given a chance to."

"No way to ever track the owner down, huh?"

"Nah." He turned the gun over in his hand several times. "These were handmade. Somebody could work on it, see if they could get to a manufacturer's number, but it's highly unlikely even with it, that it could be traced to the rightful owner. For one, they didn't keep all too good records back then; and for two, even if they did, they were probably destroyed during the war. Even if you found out who originally purchased it, there are so many ways it could have ended up in somebody else's hands, either by being sold or bartered, or used as collateral to settle a debt, even confiscation by the other side. No way to tell. And even if you had a name *and* an address, you still couldn't find the owner."

"Why not?"

"'Cause they'd be dead! This has probably been in the sea about 150 years. You'd be looking for somebody's great, great, great, great, great, grandson or daughter. I think you could consider yourself fortunate to be a finder's keeper on this. No one's ever gonna make a claim. Ain't no way to even tell which blockade runner this could be from. Why in six months alone, twenty-two were captured and destroyed around Wilmington. You got a piece of Civil War history here, little lady. I suggest you save it and give it to your grandson."

"I don't have a use for it and I don't like having guns around. Can't I just donate it or something?"

"Sure. We'd love to have it. I'll even make up a little plaque and put your name beside it."

"Oh, that's not necessary. I didn't do anything but dig it up."

"Well, that's mighty generous. Cleaned up and with the right buyer, I bet it would fetch nigh onto four thousand dollars."

"Really?"

"Change your mind?"

She thought for a moment and then vigorously shook her head. "Nah. If it's a part of history, people should see it."

"Well, if you change your mind, come on back and git it, we'll just consider it on loan."

"Thanks. And thanks for all the information. I'll come back when I have more time; this sure is an interesting place you have here."

"Don't I know it," he chuckled as he reverently carried the gun over to a display case. "Come back anytime."

"I will," she promised and then left the storefront building to trudge up the long hill to her car. The smell of Thai food at the Thai Peppers Restaurant around the corner tickled her nose. She wished she had time to sit at one of the outside tables and have some Lard Na or some Pad Thai noodles, but she still had two more sites to visit. With a quick look behind her toward the Cape Fear River leading into the Atlantic, she studied the coastline. She saw the huge gray rocks with white-tipped waves crashing over them that made up the Southport beach and the now-cloudy horizon that was quickly darkening. There were a few more hours of daylight left, but her jobs were so scattered about the county, she'd probably use most of the available time just driving.

She pulled away from the curb and a few blocks later followed an ambulance leaving Dosher Hospital. They were the only vehicles on the road until they reached the intersection leading to Long Beach and Oak Island. Normally busy, all these touristy towns were now deserted in the aftermath of the hurricane. While the locals were regrouping and the tourists were rescheduling, the municipalities were coping with each new crisis, all the while hoping that the state or the federal government would intervene and provide some badly-needed emergency funding.

The house she was going to see on Oak Island had previously been condemned because of encroachment; but the owners were now adamant that the state or F.E.M.A., the Federal Emergency Management Agency, do something for them, posturing as if this situation was all the hurricane's fault instead of their own.

There wasn't even a road to the house anymore, which made the idea of moving it unworkable. It should have been moved out of harm's way two years ago when the state had notified them of their intent to condemn the property because it no longer conformed to the required setback allowances. Hell, there wasn't a single dune, sand hill or even a clump of seaweed to keep the churning green waters from whipping against the rotting wood pilings that supported the rear deck of the cedar-sided house.

With each inward wave, precious grains of sand were being swept away from the very foundations that held it aloft from the licking, briny tongues. Soon, nature would weaken the structure and it would fall into the sea. Her job was to assess the situation and make a recommendation, if there was one. Unfortunately, in this case, there was none; nothing could be done. The owners should have moved it when there had still been a road to use. Now, they would lose everything–the house and the land. And unless they started to disassemble it immediately, they would also be getting a bill from the state for dismantling and carting away piecemeal what was probably at one time their cherished beach home. And no doubt it was mortgaged, which meant despite having nothing but air to claim as their own, they would still be obligated to pay the bank back for the loan; insurance just didn't cover this kind of loss.

It saddened Shelby not to be able to help these people. But really, what was she supposed to do? When you built a house by the sea, you had to know who was boss. The owners of the home on Figure Eight Island, where she'd been earlier today, had planned for their loss, instead of ignoring it. They had secured the necessary permits to install sandbags years ago before there was a moratorium on their use. Now they were only asking for a variance, not the ability to actually have the bags. The homeowners here had done nothing but fight the municipality when talk of relocation had come up three years ago. It was a shame when people lost their homes this way. She tried so hard to keep that from happening. But every once in a while, the ocean won and took what it wanted, regardless of the cost.

Her next stop was the pier at Sunset Beach where she was to meet with Mayor Cherri Cheek, Town Manager Linda Fluegel, and the pier's owner, Marc Kaplan. The hurricane had effectively ruined the emergency ramp to the beach, torn out the decking around the gazebo, and washed away yards of asphalt from the parking lot. In some places the parking lot had pot holes so deep and so wide that you could lose a car in them.

Cement structures beyond the dune lines were not necessarily a concern under C.A.M.A., the Coastal Area Management Act. In this case however, dunes had been compromised and it was necessary to bring in a backhoe to build them up again. This required permits, permits that were her job to recommend or deny. This one would be a no-brainer, but there were certain protocols that had to be followed and far be it from her to stand in the way of the red tape mongers. She would fill out forms, fax forms, and sign forms. She'd do her part to push everything forward from here. Still, it would probably be a few weeks before the damage could be reversed unless different channels, more direct channels, were utilized.

After seeing the breech and measuring the nearby swash, she phoned her boss and requested an immediate response. If the breech was not taken care of before the next storm surge, the town would have considerably more damage to contend with including unnecessary flooding, which in turn would cause unnecessary pollution. And since the local oyster and mussel beds still contained runoff bacteria from the last hurricanes, more flooding certainly wouldn't help things. At the rate the bacteria was building, without the added destruction caused by hurricanes, the local fishermen wouldn't be able to harvest these beds for at least another decade.

Satisfied that she had done everything she could, she walked over to where a large group of people stood looking down into what appeared to be a huge pit. Linda, having finished some paperwork of her own, followed her. "That's the Vesta. It was buried under the parking lot. In the sixties, it was visible at low tide through the slats at the end of the pier. That's how built up our beach has become over the years, it's way back here now, hundreds of feet from the existing pier."

"What was it?"

"A blockade runner with an unusual history."

A blockade runner, huh? Interesting, Shelby thought. *That man at the museum said the gun I found was probably from a blockade runner.* Although the gun she had found in the sand had been dug up three beaches north of Sunset Beach, it was still quite a coincidence to her way of thinking. "What's going to happen to it?"

"It'll be recovered when they dig all this up. The Senior Conservator has decided that they want it," Linda said as she indicated the parking lot that reminded

Shelby of craters on the moon. Where the asphalt wasn't completely missing, it was cracked or layered on top of itself. It was as if underground volcanoes had erupted here and there but left no lava or steam.

"The force of mother nature is amazing! I sure have seen some unbelievable sights this week." Shelby murmured.

"I'll bet you have," Linda commented. "We were lucky this time, this is all we lost. Thought for a while that the water tower might buy it. The guys in the fire station said it was groaning the whole night of the hurricane. Like to drove them crazy! But, the 'amazing wonder' made it through another one. Trees and flooding were our biggest problems this time. Water, water, everywhere. Miss Glynnis managed to hit just right on the lunar cycle, the surge was incredible. But we were still very lucky."

"How'd the evacuating go?"

"Oh, once they announced a category four was on its way, we had no problem getting people off the island *and* off the mainland. Glynnis was all alone and in the dark when she arrived. Guess she didn't appreciate the hospitality, so she left us with this big mess!"

"It's not too bad. At least you'll get to see the ship raised."

"Get us those permits we need and I'll save you a front-row seat."

"They're in the works. I'll bet they'll be here before you can find yourself an idle backhoe."

"You may be right about that. I guess I'd better go see if I can scare one up."

"When should I come back to see the *Vesta*?"

"I'll call you. Not inside of a week, I'm sure. Probably more likely two. These things generally take years to work out, but Cherri told the historians that if they wanted the ship, it was now or never. She told 'em we weren't waitin' for 'em. If they didn't get it out of here by the end of the month, it was going to be buried real good this time."

"She's a tough one, that Cherri. By the way, good job on the bridge."

Linda beamed back at her, "It's the reason my hair is gray. But what a party we're going to have when it's completed!"

∝

Two weeks later, Shelby stood beside Linda and Police Chief Kerr as the remains of the *Vesta* were carefully uncovered and lifted by crane onto the back of a huge government flatbed. The area had been siphoned out; but still, the muck the ship had been mired in for many years sucked against it and held it firmly in place for one last second before releasing it from its watery crypt. With one loud, sucking slurp, it was free. Up, up, and over it went as the tall crane lifted and deposited its dripping and oozing carcass on the back of the supersized truck. With loud, clanking and crashing sounds, it settled and tilted.

Men jumped from the cab of the truck and began securing it with heavy nautical chains. It was going to the navy shipyard in Wilmington where its fate would be determined. Everyone was hopeful that it would find its way to a museum or be set up as a memorial somewhere in the South.

Shelby watched, fascinated, as the men worked. There was hardly any wood left to speak of, but from the metal skeleton, you could tell that this had once been a very large ship. Her new friend at the Maritime Museum in Southport had provided her with a sketchy history of its past, but nothing had prepared her for the size of it.

Suddenly, a loud scream reverberated in the air behind her, and everybody turned to see what had happened. A woman holding a small boy by the hand was sucking in big breaths of air and letting them out as ear-piercing shrieks.

Chief Kerr and a few of his men ran over to where the woman and boy stood. One officer, Lisa, a young mother herself, gently took the woman and boy aside as the others looked into the hole from which the *Vesta* had been taken. The wide-eyed look of shock on their faces, along with their frantically pointing hands and their hastily-curtailed outbursts of obscenities, brought everyone else to their side.

There, in the middle of the muck, flattened and colored with mud, shells, and debris, was what appeared to be a man in uniform—no hat, no face, no flesh, but still identifiably a man. He wore a heavy jacket over massive shoulders, now threadbare in many places, a tattered shirt that once could possibly have been white or cream-colored, long trousers with stripes on the sides, and heavy boots where the thick-corded trousers ended. Everything was orangish-red from the clay in the mud except where it was gray from the sand. His light-colored hair was plastered to his scalp and tiny crabs were picking their way through it. His hands, clenched by his sides, were missing fingers.

Shelby's hand went to her throat as she gasped. Fascinated, she could not take her eyes from the sight. All around her, women were sobbing and men were cursing but she didn't pay them any attention. As gruesome as the scene before her was, she was morbidly drawn to it. Who was he? And how did he get there *under the ship?*

Chapter Two—Ben
University of North Carolina
at Chapel Hill

I can't believe you're making me do this! How this man died a 150 years ago can't possibly mean a thing to anyone living!" The man frantically waving his hands, compressing his lips, and furiously blinking steely eyes, managed to stay in control of his temper, but it was very obvious that he was extremely upset.

"Now that's where you're wrong, Ben. The town of Sunset Beach believes it has an unsolved murder on its hands. Historians agree that the entire crew of the *Vesta* waded no more than twenty feet to get ashore. Most of them didn't even get their pants wet according to a written record of the account, so there's no accounting for how this officer ended up under the prow." The man seated casually behind the huge desk was trying to hide a quirky smile behind the hand that cupped the bowl of his pipe. The wizened, austere professor kept the Dr. Graybow pipe filled with "Very Cherry" tobacco, but he hadn't lit it in over two years; just the smell of the familiar fruity tang was enough now. Running his tongue over the hard ridge inside his cheek, he was reminded of how close he had come to losing both his appearance and his health. As it was, he was one of the lucky ones. There was no visible scarring for his years of supporting North Carolina tobacco farmers, just a well-worn scar that his tongue refused to ignore. He was the Chief of Pathology, Professor John Clark, and he was secretly enjoying the hell out of getting a rise out of Ben, a pathologist and the forensic pathology professor who ran the Gross Anatomy Lab or as it was affectionately called, The Body Shop. Ben was his favorite, had been since his residency, and he loved him like a son. He had even encouraged Ben to go for his Ph.D. in histology after he had received his medical degree, but now he wanted Ben to slow down a bit. He wanted to nudge Ben out of the world of academia for a while, if only for a week, to broaden his horizons so to speak. He wanted to make Ben experience something new, give him cause to liven up his life. After his own recent scare, he knew there was more to life than just work.

The younger, agitated man was pacing now, still gesturing with his hands. "It's not likely there's any soft tissue left to even determine how he died, especially if he drowned or was sliced through by a bayonet. If he bled to death, I'll never be able to prove it! The only thing that's going to be left is his bones!"

"Not necessarily. The local coroner says there's still some skin and tissue."

"You can't charge anyone even if I prove it was a homicide!"

"No, but the citizens of this state, who pay your salary, will be grateful to know what happened to this man and why he didn't make it home with the rest of his company." He tapped the plug of tobacco out into a sixties-style, art deco ashtray and painstakingly refilled the bowl again with fresh tobacco. He had no idea why he did this, the ritual just seemed comforting somehow.

"There were lots of men who didn't make it back from the Civil War. Strange and incredible things happened back then."

"Well, we want you to tell us what 'strange and incredible' things happened to this man. We also want you to tell us who he was."

"And it can't wait?"

"He's not in terrible condition, considering, but now that he's been removed from under the ship and the muck that was preserving him, he'll deteriorate much faster. The sooner you get to him, the more you'll probably get out of the autopsy. Besides, in just two weeks the fall term will begin."

"I know that! And you know I have plans! You know how long I've been talking about having these two weeks off!"

"Yes, yes, I remember," the old professor said with a sigh. "Since mid-May you've been telling me about watching these girls from your living room window as they lounge around the pool at your apartment complex, bronzing their bodies. I know you've been waiting for the summer hiatus so you could finally join them and meet your new, uh . . . neighbors."

"I moved there specifically so I could meet some nice young girls who aren't off limits to me!"

"I can appreciate how hard it is teaching at a university and being unable to socialize with students or faculty, but I find it hard to believe that you can't find any suitable girls to date in Chapel Hill."

"Everyone I meet is associated with the University! I'm beginning to think people don't come to Chapel Hill unless it's for the school. All the waitresses, all the salesclerks, and all the bank tellers are part-time students! That's why I chose the Laurelton Forest Apartments. They're *outside* of Chapel Hill and they cater to singles, mostly nurses, attorneys, businesswomen. I hear from the super that there's even a flight attendant or two. I planned this all out—two weeks sitting by the pool, doing nothing but downing a few Coronas and getting to know my fellow apartment dwellers. Damn it, John, I paid for the privilege! The place costs a fortune. And the girls are looking so, mmm . . . " he sighed, then regrouped, "nicely browned. I've watched them go from creamy white to toffee-colored in six weeks. Now I want to check out some tan lines!"

"This will only take you a few days. A week tops. They'll be even tanner."

"More tanned," Ben said absently as he stared out the director's office window to the busy campus common beyond.

"You're not getting on my good side by correcting my grammar."

"Apparently I'm not on your good side anyway," he said as he spun on his heel and prepared to leave his boss's office.

"We're paying you to go to the beach for crying out loud! How bad can that be? I hear they have tanned girls in bikinis there, too!" the professor called out as Ben left the room.

"Yeah, yeah," Ben mumbled as he continued to walk away, "girls in bikinis who are geographically undesirable."

"Well, who says you're gonna find love in your back yard? Branch out a little!"

"Yeah, John. Work on a decayed corpse all day; then try to find someone who can stand the way I smell. Thanks, I'll remember this."

The loud clicking of Ben's shoes in the empty corridor

echoed off the walls. The forceful way he propelled himself along, his arms swinging purposefully, gave evidence of his heated temper.

It just wasn't fair. He had plans. For the next two weeks all he wanted to do was sleep until noon, drag himself and a cooler to a lounge chair by the pool, watch girls slathering their skin with lotion, and hope for the chance to see a few nipples puckering in the refreshing blue, chlorinated water. *But no!* Some stupid hurricane had to unearth a body, a really *old* body.

He left the shadowed wing of the Forensic Sciences Department. All the lights were out now and the halls were empty of students. It was the true summer break, the only part of the summer when the school was absolutely closed, the very short span of time between the end of summer classes and the beginning of the fall ones. He taught classes during all the sessions, so this was his only free time until the Christmas break. He felt like something had been stolen from him. He'd been cheated and he wanted to punch John right in the mouth!

He left the building and made his way to his car. He was stopped on the sidewalk just in front of his BMW roadster by Carla, one of his second year students.

"Dr. Kenyon, what are you doing here today?"

"I was called in. I guess there's some merit to having caller I.D. I'm definitely going to have to look into getting that. This was one phone call I sure wish I hadn't picked up."

"Something wrong?"

"No, nothing that can be helped. What are *you* doing here today?"

"I had to make some photocopies at the library and I left my day-timer in your lab on Friday. So, I came back to pick it up. I've been lost without it. I don't have a clue where I'm supposed to be."

"Did you find it?"

"Yup," she said, waving a black, leather-covered book in front of her face. "In fact," she said as she flipped open the book to the current date, "today's page is totally blank. Care to join me for lunch?"

"I'm sorry Carla, but I have to work. Some new research project we've been called in on. I have to pack, drive for three hours, and then perform an autopsy."

"Oohh, sounds interesting. Can I go with you?"

"No," he said firmly. "This isn't a field trip."

Her chin dropped and she pouted. Her puffy lips did look enticing and her sad, blinking eyes, that were all for show, were certainly beautiful. But hadn't everyone received the message by now? He was *not* going to date a student, or an assistant, an intern, an assistant professor, a full-fledged professor, or anyone who ranked the same or lower than he did on the food chain. And, since he had a Ph.D., only directors, chancellors, regents, and deans were above him, and they were all too old—way too old.

Ben was twenty-seven. He'd been on an accelerated course since graduating from high school at the age of sixteen and he hadn't slowed down yet. His goal was to head up his department by age thirty-five. Either that, or be the head coroner in a large, crime-infested city. Death was his business, and except for his much-deserved summer break, there usually wasn't enough work to keep him busy. He was passionate about his work and all that it entailed. He lectured, reviewed papers, supervised a handful of interns, assisted or directed autopsies, was an expert witness when called on, did research for the university, was a favored guest speaker all over the state, and he also wrote books published by national textbook companies.

He loved what he did. He just wanted two weeks where he didn't have to do it. Any of it. Was that asking too much? Two lousy weeks? Since he knew he would never let another woman get close to him the way Anna had, he really needed this time to have a few superficial relationships before buckling back down and living for his work. It had been a long time since his randy days in med school where he'd met Anna. And Anna . . . well, that hadn't lasted as long as it should have. Now all he wanted was a few late-night dinners with a sweet, twenty-something beauty who would laugh at his jokes as they polished off a bottle of wine, danced cheek-to-cheek, and maybe later, shared some pillow talk.

He looked down at Carla, who was still preening for him. "Well, I'd best get moving. The day is getting by me. See you next term."

"You bet, I've already registered for your course this semester. The one where you show us how to dig up a grave for physical evidence. Can't wait to get down and dirty with you this year, Dr. Kenyon."

"Yeah," he bit out, trying to keep his phony smile in place. God, she was so obvious. How the hell did he end up in a profession where beautiful young women were throwing themselves at him all day? Very sexy, beautiful, young women, the exact same type of women he was eager to meet around the pool at his garden apartment complex. Sexy, young, beautiful and not affiliated with UNC in any way. Maybe if he was able to get this job done inside of a week . . .

Chapter Three—Shelby & Ben
Sunset Beach, NC

Shelby sat at a small table at The Sunset Gourmet coffee shop. She was sitting against the wall facing the door so she could see him when he came in. *He* was Dr. Ben Kenyon, and according to Linda, this was the first place he said he was heading when he left the Sunset Beach Town Hall just a few minutes ago. Linda had managed to hold him up long enough to get Shelby on her cell phone and direct her there.

"If you want to meet the man who's working on that corpse you're so interested in, hightail it over to The Sunset Gourmet. He'll be there in a few minutes. You can't miss him—six foot something, as beauiful a human specimen as you're likely to see; hair dark as coal, blue eyes behind thick lashes, and a jaw like granite. I never saw him smile though, not once. And he wears way too much cologne. You'll smell him before you see him, trust me. Oh yeah, and his jeans . . . they're light blue, but they look like he washed them with something red. Hope it wasn't blood or anything like that!"

So, here she was, waiting for a crabby man who didn't know how to sort clothes and reeked of overindulgence. The image she conjured up as she sat there was almost comical, but when the door opened and Dr. Kenyon stepped inside, nothing was funny about his appearance. Nothing at all.

He was gorgeous! A lot like George Clooney only with more hair and sans the beguiling smile. She looked him up and down from the back as he walked over to the counter. She let her eyes wander from his thick black curls brushing against his collar to his broad shoulders stretching out a white polo shirt, and then on to his braided black leather belt and beyond. And sure enough, his blue jeans were almost lilac-colored in places. He sported Keds on his feet, no socks, but actual real Keds! She smiled and continued to ogle him as she lifted her iced mocha latté and sipped it through the straw.

Linda was right, everything he had made the human race look good. Big ears, crooked nose, unsightly scar, thinning hair, they'd apparently run out of all those before he'd made it to the front of the line. Instead he was given perfect, thick, wavy hair, smooth, bronzed skin and everything beautifully proportional. Other women in the cafe had noticed him too, Shelby reflected. Two groups of women across the room were staring at him the way men usually stared at attractive women. Only this time it didn't seem lewd. It seemed like admiration for living, breathing art. You couldn't fault them; he was damn good looking.

Shelby admired his firm, rounded butt as he leaned against the counter, ordered his coffee, and waited for his bagel to be toasted. Then he turned to look for an available table.

Her eyes met his and she waved him over. "Over here, Dr. Kenyon."

Briefly blinking his eyes and shaking his head, he walked over to her table and looked down at her, "Do I know you?" He was used to unsolicited attention from women at the college, but not in the "real world." The last time he'd really been away from the academic scene he'd had the awkward grace of an adolescent.

Shelby smiled brightly and lifted her hand up to him. The whorls of dark chest hair nesting at the vee of his shirt drew her attention and she forced her eyes up. "You do now. My name is Shelby Laine. We have a friend in common at the Town Hall. Please, have a seat."

He took a generous sip of his coffee before putting it down on the table along with his bagel. Then he gingerly pulled out a chair, still looking at her strangely. It was then that she noticed the smell—a sickeningly sweet citrus combination of lemon, cloves, and bay rum.

"Whew! Linda was right, you do announce yourself to the olfactory lobes."

"Ah, Linda. You're the phone call she made from the other office when she didn't think I could hear." He nodded as if everything made sense now and sat down in the chair. "Trust me, this particular odor, one I designed myself by the way, is far better than the odor that lingers long after my work is done."

Shelby sent him a puzzled look and said simply, "Clarify?"

"Something about old, rotting flesh seems to permeate everything around. Numerous showers with harsh soaps do very little to eliminate it." When he saw her scrunch up her nose and purse her lips, he said, "I assumed you knew what I did."

"I do, I guess . . . that is, I think I do. You do autopsies and try to figure out how people died."

He chuckled and said, "Well, I guess that simplifies it some."

26

Shelby tilted her head in surprise.

"Yes, I do smile. And I even laugh every now and then," he said, as if reading her mind. "Linda had the dubious honor of seeing me before my morning coffee," he said as he lifted his coffee cup in salute. "Cheers!"

After another incredibly huge sip, he whispered over to her, "And yes, I do know how to do laundry. However, my thoughtful niece does not. I should have checked these before I packed them, but who was to know she had a new red bandana in the pocket of her jeans when she washed these for me."

Her red lips puckered as she sipped her latte. He noticed dark lashes fanned over her tanned cheeks as she looked down her freckled nose at the frothy confection. Her short hair was every bit as dark as his where it wasn't streaked with auburn, and it was curly. It fell around her face in soft waves and was tucked behind her ears. It was a rather boyish cut, but it looked adorable on her. In her tiny ear lobes were small seashell studs. Her pert facial features accentuated her flawless, smooth skin and except for the lipstick, she didn't appear to be wearing any makeup; she had the healthy glow of a young, dewy teenager. When she looked back up at him, her eyes met his. They were blue like lapis, shimmering like icicles twinkling under lights.

"You like your morning coffee cold?" he asked.

"Yes. And apparently you like yours burning hot. I don't see how you can stand it right from the thermo pot like that. And you're not taking little sips, either."

As if to confirm her observation, he lifted his cup and took a lusty swallow. "Just used to it I guess. It has to be hot enough to burn a trail and start the thought processes churning. So, tell me, why did you lay in wait to meet me?"

"I was there the day they pulled the *Vesta* up. I saw

Captain Whatever-his-name-is before the coroner took his body away. I know this may sound strange, seeing how long he's been down there and all, but I somehow feel a connection, like he's somebody I should know."

"Well, first of all he wasn't a captain. He was a Chief Engineer."

"How do you know that?"

"From his uniform. That was one of the easiest things to look up. Don Troiani's *Regiments and Uniforms of the Civil War*. It was a simple matter of matching buttons, epaulets and insignias; even his suspenders were those of an officer. So, tell me about this connection you're feeling. It's a little odd since he's been buried at sea, so to speak, since the middle of the nineteenth century."

"I don't know. I just feel something for him. I need to know his story and not just the story that's on the surface, but the whole story." She didn't tell him that she was having dreams of a man in a Civil War uniform walking out of the sea with his arms raised, beseeching her to help him get home, because even she knew how ridiculous that would sound. But the dreams were quickly becoming nightly haunts, leaving her restless and unfulfilled upon awakening. A few times she had sat straight up in her bed, sweat-soaked and hearing the most awful moan, *"Where is my beloved? I did my duty, I want to go home."* No, this was not the time to reveal she had a nightly intruder who had instilled a covert mission in her heart: that she see him carried home to his beloved.

"Well, that's not likely to happen. The best we can hope for here is a quasi-I.D. and cause of death. Anything more than that is going to be out of the forensic realm, I'm afraid. Since the body was brought up, it has been quickly deteriorating. It's in cold storage now, being kept at twenty-nine degrees, but by the time I get it to

Jacksonville later today the breakdown will begin again in earnest. Quite frankly, if the ship hadn't run aground so close to an old inlet, I might only be looking at old, washed-out bones right now. Tannin in the water acts as a preservative. It's found where the waters of the sea meet the inland waters. Apparently there used to be a high concentration of it there and still is because of the oak leaves washing down from the mainland. Also, when the knee braces of the ship sprang, it created a hog hole under the belly of the ship. I think that's where he got sucked under. Then during the slack tides, the hole filled in with silt and he was buried. He was preserved in a manner similar to the Bog People of Grauballe, Jutland, only without the high level of acidity found in the peat. For the most part there's only skin and skeletal remains, some lower entrails maybe, and a chunk of the heart," he saw her starting to blanche so he stopped talking.

"Well, would you mind letting me know what you find? I'll even be happy to do any additional research you need. I'm into computers; in fact, I have a degree in programming."

"Really? What do you do with it here?" he asked, waving his hand to the area beyond the window. She knew what he meant. People from the *big* cities always thought of Brunswick County as plebeian.

"I work for the Division of Coastal Area Management."

"And what do you do with them?"

"Basically, I tell people whether they can stop the ocean or not."

"Powerful lady."

"Yeah, to some. To most, I'm just another kind of cop."

"Well, as much as I'm enjoying your company, I have to get back to work. I've got a few days of work here, then I have to arrange to take the body to Chapel Hill with me. They don't have the equipment I need here to do the tests that have to be done. Do you have a card? I may take you up on that offer to do some research. I'm used to an unlimited research staff, and here, I have none."

"Unlimited?"

"Practically the whole junior and senior class of Forensic Sciences signs up to intern for me. Seems they're just dying to get this peculiar smell I'm so enhanced by."

Shelby suspected there were other reasons that the students clamored to be one of his assistants and they were far removed from his clinical expertise, especially by the female population. She handed him her card and stood.

"My, you're a tiny little lady for such a powerhouse."

"Size is irrelevant in my job. It's my rubber stamp they fear," she said with a big grin.

"I'm sure you command their attention with those beautiful eyes," he looked down at the card she had just handed him and added, "Shelby."

"Yes, well . . . thank you," she murmured.

"I look forward to seeing you again. Is research the only thing I can call you about?"

"Uh, well, I'm not seeing anyone, if that's what you're asking."

"Yes, that was exactly what I was asking." He smiled and picked up his empty coffee cup and bagel wrapper. She was still sipping at her latte as she made her way over to the door.

Ben threw the trash into the container by the counter and went to hold the door for her. "Stay close to the phone. I *will* be calling," he whispered down to her as she ducked under his arm.

They both left the coffee shop and headed for their vehicles. He slid into his convertible roadster and she climbed up into her beat-up work truck.

Chapter Four—
Charles Edward Garrett
Jacksonville, NC

Standing over the decaying mass in front of him, Ben spoke to the corpse as if he'd known him all his life. He looked down into the bony face with its hollowed out eye sockets and the rictus grin that stared back at him. "So, Charley, what's the story here? Why were you under a ship you weren't even on?"

Receiving no satisfactory answer–in fact, receiving no answer at all–Ben continued his questioning as he picked up his instruments and cleaned the area. He put aside the moldy clothing and the sodden boots he'd removed during the initial exam. The boots had given him his biggest clue so far. Etched with fine, gold stitching onto the leather of the inside cuff, was the name Charles Edward Garrett.

"Well, I guess you've told me all you can, or all you care to. The rest is up to me. But I gotta tell ya, this isn't the best way to get in good with me, ruining my vacation and all. You're going to be damned lucky if I'm ever able to figure all this out, so a little help from the spiritual world wouldn't be frowned upon right now. So, why not just sit up and tell me your story? I promise not to run screaming down the halls."

The echo of Ben's words rang in the mostly metal and tile room belonging to the medical examiner based in Jacksonville. After a few moments of shrugging his tired shoulders, Ben mumbled, "Nothing huh? Gee thanks. But that's okay. Hey, no sweat, I'll do it myself. I'll find out what the hell happened to you and then, and then . . . ." Ben realized he was threatening a dead man, and he threw his head back and roared with laughter. *Lord help him, he was forever getting way too involved in his cases!*

Suddenly, the lights in the examining room flickered and the metal pan holding everything that had come from the dead man's moldy and frayed pockets fell to the floor. Bone buttons, a small knife, rifle bullets, a silver spoon, two glass marbles, a folded cloth, and a locket scattered across the floor. The clattering made Ben jump, and in the flickering light, he stared down at the items rolling and spinning on the tile floor below the table.

When everything had settled and all was still except for one slow-rolling marble, he bent to retrieve them. "So I'll haunt you, or you'll haunt me. Which one of us is the unlucky man now?"

The locket, which had caught his eye hours before, felt solid and somehow warm in his hand, which was terribly unusual. Rooms like these were kept very cold; any kind of metal was always cold to the touch. He turned it over and over, marveling at the condition. It had been in an inside jacket pocket, wrapped in an oilskin that had protected and preserved the finish. A ribbon had been tied around the small bundle as if it had been intended as a gift. Because of this care, the locket did not appear rusted, tarnished, or even scratched; yet he hadn't been able to open it since he had discovered it on the initial exam.

Now his thumbnail gently caressed the crease opposite the hinged side as he knelt on the floor gathering the buttons and marbles. One shiny, green marble had managed to hit the far wall and was slowly rolling back. Since the floor was sloped for easy cleaning, it finally made its way to the drain in the center. As Ben leaned forward to pick it up, the pressure of his thumbnail on the locket seam triggered the stubborn catch and the locket sprang open.

With the retrieved marble in one hand and the now-open locket in the other, he sat Indian-style on the floor in his scrubs, staring at both. His hands were just above his knees, his palms facing up like he was chanting to the god of lost causes.

"Okay, what's this?" he mumbled as he held the locket up to the light and stared at two sepia portraits, each in its own respective oval frame. They were facing each other. A rakish, young man, with untamed light hair and piercing dark eyes looked out at him from the left. Moving his eyes slightly to the right, he saw a dark-haired, dark-skinned beauty with just the hint of a smile causing her brown eyes to twinkle. And even though her skin was glowing with light and shadow, it was all too obvious that the dark shading had not been caused by the sun. She could possibly have been Polynesian or Tahitian, since she looked so exotic, but Ben didn't believe she had tropical origins. Something about the fullness of her lips and the texture of her hair belied that. Yes, she definitely had Negroid features, softened for sure, but still unmistakable. Above, and centered over the two folded-out pictures, on the underside of the locket cover, was an inscription. Engraved in Old English script were the words:

Everlasting Love

After staring at the two portraits for several minutes, Ben mumbled to himself, "Well, Charles Edward Garrett, it appears you have some 'splainin' to do." Ben carefully folded the pictures together and closed the locket. Then he gathered the rest of the items from the floor and stood with them. "Charley, ol' boy, I don't know what you got yourself into, but I'm going to do the best I can to find out." With that, he reached into his pocket and pulled out the phone number he had memorized within minutes of receiving it.

Chapter Five—Getting to know Chief Engineer Garrett Holden Beach, NC

Shelby toweled off her damp curls then used her fingers to scrunch them close to her head. Moppy curls, that was the look she was going for, a sort of Meg Ryan gone auburn style. She had the smile and pert nose to carry it off, but her eyes were a little too blue and dark-fringed where they would have had to be light-colored to fit the bill. Her dark eyebrows were just a bit too expressive, going up when she was challenged or surprised, meeting together when she was perplexed or miffed. She did have the same upturned smile crinkles at the corners of her mouth that made her smile seem so devastatingly sincere.

Looking into the mirror now, she wondered if she should color her lips with her Passion Berry Creme Lipstick or just coat them with Strawberry Kiwi Marshmallow Cloud Gloss. She opted for the clear gloss. On the off chance that he kissed her, she wouldn't have to worry about the dark plum-colored stain smearing both her lips and his, and wherever else they might possibly stray. *Why was she thinking like this? Her nights with men never went that way. She didn't know why, they just never did.*

The thought that maybe this man, this man whom she had actually daydreamed about, this man that she had met only a few short days ago, would press his smooth, firm lips against hers, sent a shiver through her. What the hell was the matter here? So what that he was handsome, and quite sinfully so? So what that he was muscular and tall, sexy as all-get-out and mmmm . . . . So what indeed. He was exactly her type. Sensual. Manly. Even in pink-shaded jeans he was all male. The vision of his face floated across her memory and she remembered that when he smiled, long creases hollowed out his cheeks. Those craggy channels, combined with his full, smiling lips were incredibly sexy and virile. Then her nose wrinkled. *I wonder if he'll have that unusual smell. I wonder if I'll ever come to like it.*

An hour later, when Ben knocked on her door, she knew without a doubt that it was him. That peculiar tang of citrus and spice was either going through the door or coming under it. Without using her peephole, she opened the door.

"Hey."

"Hey, yourself. Come on in." She opened the door wide and he strolled leisurely through it, eyeing her appreciatively. He then turned to take in the surroundings. Candles and hurricane lamps were on almost every surface giving the room an eerie glow.

"I knew when I pulled up that this was going to be a very special place."

She laughed. "Living in a purple and salmon-colored house has its advantages. No one ever has to ask directions twice."

"Did you paint it that combination yourself?"

"Nah. It's not my house. I rent it. But only from September through May, then I have to get out and it becomes a weekly rental for the season. This year I got in early because they didn't have it rented for the last few weeks of the summer."

He strolled around the living room, which connected to the dining room, and then to the galley-type kitchen. Bedrooms, he assumed, were off the hall to the right. "Gee, I can't imagine why not. It's so—"

"Cottagey," she chimed in.

"Yeah. Cottagey. Beach cottage circa 1940s." He was in the kitchen now, eyeing the huge old-fashioned porcelain sink that was at least two feet deep. It was more like a laundry tub. The stove in the corner was just one decade removed from having to be stoked with wood. There was no refrigerator, no microwave, no toaster, and no electric coffee pot. A large Rubbermaid cooler took up the majority of the floor space in the kitchen and he surmised that it was her makeshift refrigerator/freezer. "Don't you miss modern conveniences?"

"Hey, it's right on the beach; it's clean and it's cheap."

"Well, that's good to hear. I'd hate to think they were holding you up on the price just because it's beachfront."

"I like a simple life. It suits me. It's like camping only I do have running water and some electricity."

"Well, that's good to hear too, since I was planning on using your Internet connection to do some research. I didn't even think to ask if you had DSL; it never occurred to me that you might not even have electricity."

"I have electricity on the glassed-in porch. And believe it or not, I also have DSL. Where are you staying? Some of the newer hotels have Internet hookups, we're not third world, you know."

He shot her an arrogant look with one eyebrow raised skeptically as if he doubted what she was saying. "Well, the first night, after I checked out the 'scene of the crime,' so to speak, I stayed at the Sunset Beach Inn. The second night I slept on a couch at a funeral parlor while Charles and I waited for transportation to Jacksonville. The third night, I slept on a cot at Camp LeJeune. Tonight I'm staying here."

"Here?" she managed to squeak out.

"No! Not here, as in here with you. Here on Holden Beach. I booked a room at the Gray Gull on the causeway."

"Oh. Well, that's a very nice place. You'll like it there," she said fully recovered now from her errant thoughts. "Although, unless they've changed things, I doubt that they have DSL or even dial-up in the rooms."

"They didn't mention it when I called, but that really wasn't my first consideration. After two nights on a sofa and cot, I'd really like a comfortable bed. So, where do you live when the season's in?"

"Usually an apartment complex unless I can find a rental on the mainland that's fairly cheap."

"Saving your money for something special? Or don't they pay you a decent wage around here?"

"Oh, I don't know, I do all right. I guess I just can't see paying out a lot of money for a place when I'm hardly ever home. I do try to watch my pennies. One day I'd like to travel—see Europe, Australia, and the Greek Islands."

"Ah, admirable, sacrificing now so you can splurge later."

"Oh no, I never splurge. I'll take economy tours, maybe even stay at hostels."

"Oh. Well that still sounds like fun. Where can we work? My laptop's fully charged, but I need to hook up to your server."

"Follow me, the study's out here." She led him over to a sliding patio door. She unlatched it and slid the door to the right. Beyond it, all he could see was darkness until she flicked a switch on the inside wall. Then the room beyond lit up and came into view. It was an incredible incongruity for this clean, but ramshackle, clapboard house.

The room he was looking into had obviously been a well thought-out addition. The huge Carolina room was bright and roomy. It contrasted with everything he'd seen so far because of the modern decor and up-to-the minute furnishings. *And*, it had electricity.

He stepped down into the room and noticed the oyster-colored Berber carpet coming right up to meet the faded and peeling linoleum of the room he'd just left. His eyes scanned the oversized leather sectional sofa in the middle of the room facing the opposite wall where a huge fireplace was set into a stone wall. The mantle was of rough-hewn timber, polished and lacquered until it gleamed. One long wall had a combination curio, bookcase, and entertainment center. In the corner, set off by three separate sets of track lighting, was an executive-style computer desk along with a tall hutch filled with software books and storage cabinets.

"Nice, very nice. And so totally unexpected after seeing the rest of the house."

Shelby laughed. "The owners won a lottery. Not enough money to do this place justice, but enough to make some needed improvements. Now their son-in-law can get some work done when he comes to the beach with his family. The owners get to have their grandkids a little longer, the wife gets to stay and vacation at the beach she visited as a child, and the husband gets Internet and cable TV connections so he won't drag them all back to

Greensboro after just a few days."

"And you, what do you get? A half-and-half house?"

"I get an old-fashioned house that has gorgeous views from one incredible room, with a fireplace to keep me toasty while I'm enjoying it. Plus, I'm saving money. This place is a steal. I think the older couple who owns it just wants someone here to see after things while they winter in Florida. Everybody gets what they want, and the house *is* charming. I've never even considered looking for anything else."

"How many years have you been doing this seasonal moving thing?"

"Four. This makes my fourth winter here. Come on, I'll show you where the quick-connect cable is. Just set up over by the desk. I have to fish the cable out."

Before he could put the computer on the desk and unzip it from its case, she was crawling under the desk, her backside up in the air wagging back and forth as she inched her body into the tight corner. It was an enticing derrière, subtly beckoning his now-ardent gaze. Fine, tight little ass, he whispered to himself as she swayed her back and stuck her bottom even further up into the air. *Mmmm, mmm, mmm.*

He heard a muffled voice pulling him out of his reverie. Then he heard it again. He realized it was Shelby talking to him as she pushed a cable and a phone jack line up through a small circular cutout on the back of the desk.

"Here, take these," she called for what had probably been the third time. Finally she felt a tug as the cords were pulled through. She bent her head, flattened her body, and inched out from beneath the desk. "Don't know why they always fall through when somebody disconnects them. You'd think they'd take the time to wrap 'em around something or tape them up somewhere."

Still on her hands and knees, she looked up at him. He was looking down at her with an odd expression on his face. Had she smeared her face or tangled her hair in something? He put his hand out to help her up and she took it. Standing, she looked at him with a question in her eyes and her brows lifted, "Everything okay?"

"Uh, yeah. I was just watching to make sure you didn't hit your head."

"Thanks, I'm very careful to duck my head down low; there's a monster screw down there somewhere that just loves to pull out a hunk of my hair."

His eyes flew to the top of her head and his fingers itched to tumble through her silky curls. He just knew how wonderful they'd feel by the bounce they had. His eyes dropped to her smiling lips and he noticed their genuine rosy color. As far as he could tell she wore no lipstick. His eyes searched the rest of her face. He took in her cheeks, her brows, her lashes, and her lids. Remarkable. The lady wore no makeup whatsoever, yet she was pinked where there should be pink and naturally dark of brow and lashes. Looking closely, he noticed that there was even a tinge of lilac on her lids caused by the natural shading of blue veins shadowing through the thin, almost translucent skin over her big blue eyes.

Nervously, she ran a hand through her curls, shaking and fluffing them with fingers tipped with unlacquered nails that were clean, short, and squared-off. All natural. This woman was completely natural and so far as he could tell, unflawed. His eyes fell lower where they registered the sudden appearance of skin caused by her hand reaching up to smooth back her hair. Her white T-shirt was an abbreviated cropped style. He had a fleeting glimpse of smooth skin and unadorned-navel before she hurriedly lowered her hand, and in turn, the shirt.

His eyes roved upward and he noticed her breasts. And he was sure, absolutely certain in fact, that they were standing out on their own with no barrier between him and them but that soft cotton shirt.

Bubbles. He didn't know why, he'd never called them that before, but they were most definitely bubbles. Delightful, rounded, little globes puckered at the tip, standing erect and unapologetic for their slightness, as she arched her back.

"I'll uh, get us some lemonade."

"Lemonade?"

"Yeah, I got a whole bag of lemons for sixty-four cents: so, when life hands you lemons . . ."

"Make lemonade," he finished for her.

"Yeah, unless you'd rather have iced tea. I got two boxes of tea for the price of one at Food Lion. It's decaf though."

"Lemonade works for me. I'll just get us set up here."

She smiled brightly and spun on her bare feet as she headed back into the "old" part of the house.

He turned back to the computer, and as he made all the necessary connections, he thought about breasts, all kinds of breasts. Breasts that pushed up and out under soft sweaters on women seated in the front row as he lectured, breasts that bounced and settled as women ran on the university track, breasts that almost completely poked out of formal gowns at alumni events, and breasts that greeted him in all their naked glory on page after page of men's magazines. Most of those, he knew, were intentionally designed to conform to today's ideals. All the ones not initially bared for viewing usually suggested more than there was. They were molded and camouflaged by designer padding and gel cups. They were taped, wired, and pushed together to show maximum cleavage, but they never seemed to actually be all that they promised. Under all that impressive definition, once the padding and straps were removed, there usually wasn't all that much there–to his experience, never as much as originally thought, anyway.

With Shelby, there was no pretense. There actually was very little there. But what there was, was admirably rounded and peaked to perfection. He was all but certain that she had small nipples, and that they would be tight, firm buds, ever at the ready to tease and taunt his tongue. In fact, he recalled that standing there in front of her just a few moments ago, he had barely managed to stop his tongue as it had escaped his mouth, tip pointed and purposefully aiming toward the beaded morsel his eyes had focused on. He'd had to feign dry lips, back it up and detour it behind his teeth, where he forced it to adhere to the roof of his mouth.

No, she surely wasn't buxom, but what she had was real. And although her form was childish in appeal and almost waif-like, it was very sensual. It seemed to him that her innocence would always be around to replay again and again until wrinkles and gray hair came into play. Yes, most definitely, this woman would never show her age; she would always appear innocent. And what man wasn't incredibly turned on by the thought that the woman under him was untried? If just looking at her drove this fantasy so intensely, he knew that regardless of how many times he actually took her, he'd never tire of her.

For a man who had made the most concerted efforts to inure himself and shy away from the youthfulness of his students, he was struck by his baseness for the ingénue that was Shelby Laine. Nymph-like, she reminded him of a dark-haired fairy–an impish Tinkerbelle in tight jeans.

She was setting his loins on fire from just the hint of a curve appearing across the otherwise flat plains of her T-shirt. *Damn! He wanted to make it with Tinkerbelle!* He wanted to lay her back on her fluttering wings, strip the pants off her slender, trim legs and bunch her T-shirt so high on her chest that he could suck her tiny, cherry-like buds with abandon. "Aaarrghhh!"

"What? What's wrong?" Shelby asked as she came back into the room and handed him a glass of lemonade.

"Nothing. I just can't believe how long it takes to boot these things up."

"Oh, I know. I figure I've wasted at least a week of my life so far. By the time I'm forty, I'll have wasted months on foreplay."

The glass had made it to his lips; he had actually even tilted it. But now, he wasn't at all ready to accept the golden liquid running down his throat, so it went elsewhere. He held the dripping glass away, coughed to clear his airway, and wiped at the dribble on his chin. "Pardon?"

"You know, the time before you can play video games—like Tetris, or Taipei, or Solitaire."

"Booting up is known as foreplay?" he asked, definitely perplexed and suddenly not so sure she was the kind of girl he'd been thinking she was.

"It isn't?"

"Honey, please don't tell me you don't know what foreplay means."

She stood stock still as color instantly flooded her cheeks and neck. He watched as realization dawned on her and it was evident by her coloring that she wanted to die. Nobody could fake that kind of blush, he thought. She was genuine. Someone, somewhere, had fed her a line referring to booting up as foreplay and she'd fallen for it.

"Oh my God, that's what I said wasn't it? Oh my. I didn't mean . . . I mean–"

"Never mind. I'm glad the time you're wasting is for turning computers on, and not men."

Her hands went to her reddened cheeks and she closed her eyes. "What must you be thinking of me?"

"Trust me, right now, you *don't* want to know what I'm thinking of you. Come on. Pull up a chair, let's see what we can find out about Charles Edward Garrett."

An hour later, Ben leaned back in his chair and stretched his back. "You know, this blockade runner thing, it sure was bad news. If the North could have really hunkered in and kept those ships from getting ashore, the war wouldn't have lasted anywhere near as long as it did. Just think of all the lives that could have been saved."

"And all the subsequent lives that would have been changed, and the hundreds of thousands of people who would have been born because of those changes."

"You know the beginning lines of *A Tale of Two Cities*: 'It was the best of times; it was the worst of times?' Well, just forget about the best part, there was none. The Civil War was a hideous war–neighbor against neighbor, brother against brother; the lifeblood of a new country all but wiped out." He was in his professor's voice now. "Did you know that in Sharpsburg, Maryland, over 3,600 soldiers died in combat in a single day? It's still the record casualty count of Americans who've died in one place on any given day. For many years after the War, the proud people of the South, unwilling to acknowledge it actually was a war, one that they'd lost, had the audacity to refer to it as The Late Unpleasantness."

"I didn't know all that. Wow, that battle in Maryland

was catastrophic. The South sure made a lot of mistakes, though. I can see why they wouldn't want to own up to any of them. You said you couldn't find Charles Garrett's name on the *Vesta's* register. What made you think to even look?"

"Because I suspected that he was never there."

"What do you mean?"

"Look," he said as he highlighted a line in a long column of names printed on a page he'd taken from his computer case file section. "'Chief Engineer Edward R. Holmes.'"

"So?"

"Well, I read that a Chief Engineer made $2,500 a trip. That was a huge chunk o' change back then, and none of the other ship's registries that I looked into had listed two Chief Engineers. It made me think that maybe he wasn't even from the *Vesta*."

"Then where did he come from?"

"Don't know yet. That's what we have to find out. Hand me that page we printed from *Graveyard of the Atlantic: Shipwrecks of the North Carolina Coast*."

Their fingers brushed and he lifted his eyes to meet hers. He gave her a big smile, winked, and then took the sheet from her.

His fingers flew over the keyboard as he inserted new search parameters. Within minutes, his fist hit the desk in triumph. "I knew it! I just knew it! Chief Engineer Charles E. Garrett was from a different ship. He was from the blockade runner *The Bendigo,* which ran aground the week before, just west of the entrance to Lockwood Folly."

"Well, how in the world did he get from there to Sunset Beach and under the prow of another grounded blockade runner?"

"How indeed?" Ben mused. "This is beginning to

get very interesting."

"You didn't think it was before?"

"No, it was just a dead body taking me away from what I wanted to do."

"Wow, I can't imagine a dead body not intriguing me. What was it you wanted to do?"

He smiled over at her and ran his thumb alongside her jaw. "Exactly what I'm doing right now."

"Oh."

Their gazes locked and they found themselves staring into the depths of each other's eyes. Shelby, unnerved by the tension, was the first to speak as Ben reluctantly dropped his hand to his side.

"So, tell me about the autopsy. What did you find?" She'd had another dream last night, and now, more than ever, she wanted to find out where this man's body belonged. Not that the man in the tattered Civil War uniform scared her or anything, but he sure was compelling in his desire to get home. If she could somehow help him to do that, maybe he'd let her get a full night's sleep again. She thought about mentioning the dreams to Ben, but between the deep concentration lines furrowed between his brows, and the faraway look in his eyes, she doubted he'd give her silly dreams much credence right now.

Ben leaned back in his chair and began telling her about the examination and the theory he had about Charles' cause of death.

"Well, first off, I couldn't even make a proper 'Y' incision. It goes from shoulder to shoulder and then down the middle of the torso to the bottom of the abdomen. The tissue was very badly deteriorated. There was no lividity in what remained of the skin. No coloring or bruising. All skin tissue was pale and gray with no form or tension. When I tried to remove the breastplate so I could get to the organs, I found it in bits and pieces. The weight of the ship had crushed his chest wall and his heart and lungs had been squeezed out of place. The only part of the heart that was intact was the small part that joins to the aorta caps of the atrium. We'll run toxicology on that, but I doubt we'll find much more than some heavy metals and that he was vitamin deficient. Almost everybody was back then, especially seamen.

"The body odors of a corpse are usually very telling. The smells from the stomach digestion, the decaying of the liver and the gastrointestinal tract can tell a coroner a lot. But in this case, everything just smelled of dead fish.

"The heart was shriveled and split in two in its pericardial sac and was no help at all really. All totaled, it weighed half its normal 310 grams, which I attributed to expected decomposition. I tried to draw blood for toxicology, but only managed to get a paste-like film for testing. So we'll only test the part that was intact at the aorta caps.

"The lungs, a normal pink color, were tan, but they were also black in several places, which would indicate that blood was sucked into the air spaces, or what we commonly call drowning. So, that's the actual way he died, but it was not the reason."

She lifted a brow and he explained.

"For example, if a man gets shot on a roof top, then falls to the ground and breaks his neck, how did he die? It depends on what killed him first. Either way, it was the gunshot that killed him; but from a coroner's perspective, you have to read the whole body to find out the whole story. In Charles' case, he drowned."

"Ah, but the reason he was in the water to begin with was because he was already dying."

"You catch on quick."

"So as a coroner, what did you 'read' that told you that?

"After removing the organs, I noticed a nick in his spine. Working backwards, through the kidneys and spleen, I found corresponding nicks. Then I checked what was left of the stomach and found a tear. There were no contents in his stomach, indicating that it had either been a long time since he'd eaten or that they had seeped out through the tear. The tear was significant though. An adult stomach can stretch up to six inches to accommodate a meal. When his was slit, it was compact, the stomach wasn't distended, meaning that a one-inch knife blade would make a one-inch cut. If it had been distended, a one-inch cut would have been much smaller when the stomach shrank back, leaving a quarter-inch cut or even a little less. His was the worst type of cut, compacted as it was, more blood vessels were affected, and he bled to death. But he drowned first . . . even though he was knifed before he drowned."

"Wow. That's amazing."

"What's amazing is that whoever knifed him, and it was a clean cut, so I have to assume he was driven through with a blade, had enough strength behind the blow to drive it into his spine leaving a piece of it there. It's a rather large piece that actually shows cleavage or break lines. It was made of British steel, which was vastly inferior in quality to that used in the Asian or Arabic blades of the time. So, a rather bad piece of iron oxide was forced through the ribs and someone used a fair amount of effort jamming it in, unless of course Charles was supine, then it wouldn't have taken all that much effort. A downward jab goes in deeper on a thinner, elongated body."

"So, someone murdered Charles?"

"Yes it all points to that. I also cut through the

skull bone, removed the skull cap and brain and then did a cross section of several slices. He'd had some hemorrhaging from what appeared to be a very small aneurysm. I can't be sure, but I think he might have been a little out of his head toward the end."

"Someone knifed him and then threw him in the water?"

"Actually, there's no evidence that he had fallen or was thrown. His skin wasn't abraded or bruised anywhere. Except for the torso, there wasn't an abnormal mark on him anywhere. I did find some rope fibers around his wrists and on his coat, indicating he may have been dragged some distance, or that he forcibly reined in a horse tethered by hemp or rope instead of a leather bridle. The skin from his fingers was completely deteriorated. Every tissue had been broken down and sloughed off. His hands were just white bones."

"I remember that from when I saw him. Poor Charles."

He watched genuine sorrow shadow her face and he wished he could think of a way to cheer her. Then he remembered. "I forgot to tell you about the locket I found."

"Locket?" she asked, her interest piqued. "There was a locket?"

"Indeed, there was. All wrapped up nice and pretty with a blue ribbon and thankfully, in a waterproof covering. It was in his inside pocket. I've got it in the car. Hold on, I'll go get it."

She watched him open one of the French doors facing the ocean. Then he walked to the side of the house and down the driveway to his car. A few minutes later he returned, carrying a tiny bundle.

She held her hands out like a supplicant as he gently unwrapped the package and placed the locket in her waiting hands

"Oh, it's beautiful," she cooed, as she turned it over and over. "Still shiny, or did you clean it?"

"It was shiny, but I dabbed it with some cleaner to get some of the tarnish off."

"How do you open it?"

"It's a little tricky, plus it keeps getting stuck. Here, let me show you." He stood behind her and reached both hands around in front of her. He could smell her soft floral fragrance as his cheek brushed her hair. The sensation sent a shiver through him. With a flick of his nail, the locked popped open. He could have stepped back, but he didn't. He looked at the now-familiar, daguerreotype photo images over her shoulder. The images etched on metal were detailed against the dark hues, yet grainy on the lighter background colors.

"Oh my, he was a looker, wasn't he?"

"I wouldn't know."

She smiled back at him over her shoulder. "'Course not. And her, look at her. She was black, or at least part of her was. She looks too dark to be a white woman. Sultry, dreamy eyes. And the full lips, those lips and cheekbones; they're more like . . . Mmm mmm mmm. Interracial romance wasn't done back then, it would never have been tolerated. So what do you think this is all about?"

"I was hoping you could tell me. I can't figure it out either. Look at the inscription."

"Where?" From her angle, the light cast a shadow and she couldn't see it.

Ben reached around again and tilted her hand forward.

"Everlasting love," she whispered. "Oh my, oh my."

"Yeah."

She turned in his arms and looked up at him. "I want to know more, Ben. I want to know their story." The look in her eyes was almost a plea. He wanted to kiss her so badly that he had to purse his lips against the desire.

"What do you suggest?" he said smacking his lips together before giving her a sideways quirk of his lips, "even the Pinkerton Agency doesn't have files going back that far."

"You and I. Let's investigate it. Let's figure it all out. I promise I'll work hard. I'll do whatever you say, I'll track down every lead. Just tell me what to do. Teach me how to investigate and find the trail of these dead people, these people who had everlasting love, but rotten, deplorable luck."

"You're sure? This is a tedious business, lots of dead ends and blind alleys. And it could all be for naught. There may be nothing else we learn to matter how hard we work."

"I'm game if you are. How hard can it be?"

Oh, how he wanted to show her how hard it *was*. Right this very minute. For her.

"Okay, but we've done enough for tonight. The day after tomorrow, I have to get back to the university and I'll be swamped with work for days. We'll have to rely on e-mail, and then find time on the weekends to do some more research. *Sure, like research is what I'm thinking about right now.*

"That's fine with me. I'll make myself available."

Baby, you sure are saying all the right things. "Okay. Let's see if we can find out what their story was."

"More lemonade?"

"No, I think I'd better be getting over to the hotel before they give up my room. It was nice seeing you again, Shelby." He deftly took the locket from her and with the same hand he chucked her under the chin. Then he walked over to open the French door. Just before disappearing behind it he leaned back in and whispered, "Oh, and about the foreplay, it's never time wasted, trust me."

Chapter Six—Ben & the Dream Holden Beach, NC

Ben pulled into the parking lot of the neat little motel. At first it had bothered him that everything around this area seemed old. This old-time beach resort could easily have been one of many where scads of baby boomers were conceived right after the war. But now, after being with Shelby and allowing her simple life to sneak into his modern crevices, he saw it as quaint, very charming, in fact.

There was a heavy scattering of cars, the number easily more than the twenty or so rooms visible. He hoped he hadn't lost his reservation because he didn't feel like heading back to Chapel Hill tonight.

Optimistically, he lifted his small case out of the trunk and walked to the door marked "Office."

"Dr. Kenyon?" the man behind the counter asked before Ben could even close the door behind him.

"Yes?"

"Welcome. Been waitin' for ya."

"How'd you know it was me?"

"Only one room left, so it must be yours," he answered with a grin.

Ben looked back at him and smiled. "I reckon it is, thanks for holding it for me."

"No problem. I put you on the end on this side. There's three families with babies on the other."

"Thanks, I could sure use some sleep."

"I heard you was the corner who's takin' a look at that Civil War officer's body."

Coroner, he mentally corrected. "How the hell did you get wind of that?"

"Well, you was lookin' for some books today at L. Bookworm, wasn't ya?"

"Yeah . . ." he said with some trepidation.

"Well, Jim and Barbara Lowell own the store. He was the last mayor, you know."

"No, I didn't know."

"Well, anyways, he said you was looking for some Civil War books and at the time, he couldn't put his finger on the one he wanted to show you. So, since you asked him where to stay, he called to see if you took his advice to stay here. When we confirmed your reservation, he sent this book over for ya. He said you don't have to pay for it unless you want to keep it, but maybe it has what you was lookin' for in it." He produced a fat, dog-eared edition of *Treasures of the Confederate Coast: The Real Rhett Butler & other Revelations* and held it out to him, almost reverently.

Ben took the book and turned it so he could read the cover. Small towns, they never ceased to amaze him. "Thanks, I'll take a look at it."

"He said if you wanted it, just to leave $3.50, since it's used. Here's your key, we can settle up in the mornin'."

Ben took the key, tucked the book under his arm, and went to find his room at the end of the long row of doors. As he walked, he breathed in deeply. The breeze coming off the ocean had a salty tang and he could see pockets of mists rising. From the parking lot he had been able to see the tall, arched bridge leading to Holden Beach.

He opened the door to room seventeen, threw his bag on the bed, and thumbed through the book on his way to the bathroom. The book was filled with pictures and text and listed every shipwreck on the Confederate Coast of North Carolina, South Carolina, and Georgia, and according to the table of contents, had a nice, long chapter entitled *The War and the Blockade*. The book was written by Dr. E. Lee Spence, and this was an autographed copy. Surely a bargain at $3.50.

He tossed it on the counter and reached for a washcloth so he could wash his face. But even with the warm cloth over his eyes, the book seemed to have some kind of draw, and he found himself eyeing it around the edges of the cloth. While he walked around stripping off his clothes, he reminded himself how very tired he was, but in the end, it didn't matter. He went back over to the low counter, picked up the book, and took it over to the bed with him. Many hours later, his eyes bloodshot and his mind reeling, he switched off the light and slid under the covers.

What a fascinating war. The images from the locket floated in front of him and he could swear he heard strains from the song "My Everlasting Love" coming through the wall on the other side of the bed. He closed his eyes and fell fast asleep.

CR

A man and a woman were walking hand-in-hand through a grove of trees. The man stopped to pick a lily for the woman and as she turned to face him to accept it, you could see her beautiful, light mocha skin, unblemished and smooth. It was so inviting that the man had to rub the backs of his knuckles over her cheek and chin to assure himself she was real. "I am being called back into service on the coast. This time I should be gone less than three months. When I get back, we'll figure this out. I will find a way, trust me. I'll call for support from my brother if need be. He always stands with me against them."

"It will not matter, they will never let us be. It is not done. This is something they will never accept."

"Then we will leave. I will take you to Barbados where it is accepted. We'll make our own family of 'spices.'"

"You can't leave your home. You can't leave Beau Marecage."

"It would not be my choice, but I would gladly do so if that was the only way to make you my wife. It will tear out my heart to leave you tomorrow, but know that I will spend every moment away dreaming of making you Mrs. Charles Edward Garrett by springtime." He opened his hand and moved it to caress the nape of her neck. Then he bent low and pulled her gently toward him, his other hand possessively encircling her tiny waist. He pressed his lips firmly over hers, tilting his head for better access to breech her mouth. She dropped the lily she held in her hand as her arms reached up to grasp his shoulders. In the next minute, he crushed the lily under her as he stretched his body over hers on the tall, fragrant grass.

Chapter Seven—Beau Marecage Instant Messaging

Ben: Hey I spoke to a few people, plus I had an intern do some research for me. Found out a few things. That green-tinged, linen cloth that C.E.G. (for future reference, that's Charles Edward Garrett) had in one of his pockets originally had something akin to a bar of soap in it. Back then you had to carry your own. Soap was a precious commodity, and usually it was only home grown. Analysis of the remains from the linen shows his was made from the normal fireplace ashes and lard but had bayberries added for fragrance. Apparently this was quite a luxury back then. I will look at my bar of Zest quite reverently from now on. Anyway, only wealthy plantations made soap of this quality and as it's highly unlikely he was able to buy soap like this away from home, he must have carried it with him. So, we're looking for a plantation that made bayberry soap a hundred and fifty years ago. Your turn.

Shelby: Well, that's a lot of help! I imagine there were only three to four hundred plantations scattered around the South who made their own soap back then!

Ben: Just joking, but I told you that this wouldn't be easy. We already know the name of the plantation. Just wanted to see how hard you were willing to work on this. My sources say he was from Beau Marecage, about forty miles south of Charleston.

Shelby: You got all this from the soap?

Ben: No silly, I just looked his name up in *The Confederate Roll of Honor: Minutes of the Confederate Congress General Orders Number 64. Richmond August 10, 1864.* It's the only complete source of names of Confederate soldiers who were rewarded for bravery. I noticed one of the medals on his uniform was the Cross of Honor, a reward for exceptional service, so I knew he had to be listed in it. Then I cross-referenced it with *North Carolina Troops 1861-1865, A Roster.* With the genealogy records maintained by both the historical societies of North and South Carolina, pretty soon one of my interns will come up with the name of his parents, his siblings, aunts, uncles, cousins, you name it. Then we can trace the family tree and see who his closest living relative might be. I just thought you would like to know that C.E.G. was a nice, 'clean' man. Now it really is your turn.

The Next Day

Shelby: Okay. here's what I found out. Beau Marecage (pronounced Bow Marekaz) means lovely swamp or beautiful marsh. It is indeed just south of Charleston, in Beaufort County, AND, it's still there! While it's no longer a working plantation, it has been kept up and renovated over the years and is often used as a movie set. Chances are we've both probably seen parts of it in movies or in old TV shows. It was used a lot in the fifties and sixties, but now, there are other, more magnificent homes for Hollywood to choose from. I called for a brochure from the South Carolina Department of Tourism. It should be here tomorrow or the next day. Are you doing anything next weekend? Want to meet there and check it out?

Ben: I would love to meet you there. Let me know what the weekend hours are and I'll make plans to drive down. Did I tell you that I really wanted to kiss you before I left last week?

Shelby sat in front of her computer and read the last line over and over again. He *had* wanted to kiss her. She'd thought so. She brushed her lips with her fingertips as she stared at the word kiss. Mesmerized by it, as if she'd never seen the word before, she envisioned his face lowering to hers. Oh, how heady this feeling! This wonderful tingle that made her shiver in her seat. Nervous, and not knowing how to answer, she signed off.

The Following Day

Shelby: I received the brochure today. They have a museum in the old library and the family cemetery is on the grounds under a "gnarly live oak draped with mysterious Spanish moss, giving it an eerie yet comforting aspect at sunset." They have a walking tour so we can learn all about the "main house, the outbuildings, the slave settlement, and the day-to-day life of a working plantation in the 1800s." There's a $6.50 admission fee and donations to the Charleston Historical Society are graciously accepted. And no, I didn't know that you wanted to kiss me, but I suspected as much.

Ben: I'd like to say I'll meet you at the "gnarly old live oak tree," but since I want to pay your admission, how about we meet in the parking lot around eleven? Then afterwards, I'll take you somewhere for lunch.

Shelby: Sounds like a good plan. I'll look forward to seeing you Saturday morning at eleven. The jpeg attachment is a map. I scanned the one on the back of the brochure for you.

Ben: Thanks. Maybe Saturday, I'll stop thinking about kissing you and just do it.

Shelby smiled as she read Ben's last missive. Yeah, just maybe he would and just maybe she'd let him.

Chapter Eight—Martha & Plantation Life in the Late 1800s South of Charleston, SC

en sat in his roadster editing a section of a colleague's proposed textbook. He occasionally looked up into the rearview mirror for a glimpse of Shelby turning off the main road and coming into the parking lot of Beau Marecage. It was a beautiful summer day, the weekend before Labor Day, and tourists were pulling into all the available slots. If she didn't get here soon, she might have trouble finding a place to park.

He went back to reading the manuscript, his red felt pen at the ready, as he looked for grammatical as well as structural errors in the writing. He knew damn well that Lloyd wouldn't dare commit an inaccuracy in subject matter. After all, six of Lloyd's interns had already proofed this work for him. Ben's perusal was the last chance for something to be caught and fixed before Lloyd's editor got his hands on it.

But right now, he just couldn't get into it. His mind kept reverting to Charles and to the body that had followed him back to Chapel Hill. Ben knew that his mind was his greatest enemy; it never relented when there was a mystery to be solved. He wasn't as singularly possessed with this death as he had been with ones in the past, probably because time certainly wasn't a factor, but still, it irked him not to know all the answers.

Ever since he had been a kid, he had constantly challenged his mind with some kind of mystery or puzzle. He was an aficionado at those wooden peg games found at restaurants along the interstates, and the Rubik's cube hadn't kept its secrets from him for more than a day or two. He always managed to find the "secret" key to most video games within scant hours, allowing him to whomp his friends handily in scoring, and he read voraciously. He had started in elementary school with the Hollisters, progressed to the Hardy Boys by junior high, and in one summer, delved into the Sherlock Holmes series. By the end of high school he had read every book John MacDonald and Dick Francis had written and was working his way through Ed McBain's police stories. College had left him with little time for recreational reading, but by then he had focused on a career that offered him endless opportunities to challenge his fertile mind. Now, if he wanted to be honest with himself, he'd have to say he was practically obsessed with the mysterious case files that crossed his desk.

The glint of something silver caught his eye and he looked up to see a light-colored Ford Escort pull into the space two rows behind him. His eyes narrowed and focused on the glimmer of burnt red he saw through the windshield. Shelby's auburn tresses for sure. They not only bounced as they settled when she braked a tad too hard, sending off arcs of color, but they also shimmered in the morning sun filtering through the windshield. It was Shelby all right. What other woman's smile could make her face glow with such radiance? You just knew that if you gave this woman her choice of shopping at Tiffany's or a romp in the wilds of Africa, that pretty soon you'd be high in the air, seeing the world's most wondrous sights from the back of an elephant. He dropped the stack of papers he'd been holding and quickly exited his car.

"Hi! Sorry I'm late, it took forever to sign all the papers at the rental car company," Shelby called as she continued to roll up her window.

"Rental car? What happened to yours?"

"Oh, I don't own one. Never have. The state provides me with one, either a standard issue sedan or a 4x4 when needed. I get to take it home at night, but when I go on trips, I have to rent one. I find renting a car is much cheaper than owning one, what with depreciation, insurance, maintenance and all that. I got this beauty for the weekend for $49.95 plus $11.00 for the insurance and unlimited mileage. You can't beat that. And, so far, I'm getting close to forty-three miles to the gallon!"

He looked at her, at the sincerity in her face and at the excitement he saw there. *Man she did love saving money, didn't she*? None of the women he knew would consider a Ford Escort a "beauty," new or not, and they certainly would never think to track the mileage. *Had she really never owned a car*? It was like a rite of passage in high school to get your first car. What an unusual woman. He didn't think he'd ever known anyone this frugal and it amused him to listen to her prattle on in such a practical vein.

"So, the drive down was pleasant?" he asked as he watched her carefully lock the car.

"Oh yes, it was delightful. I saw some neat places I'd like to visit, and I learned a lot about Civil War history. Yesterday, I stopped at the library and got two books on tape. I learned things I never knew before and the man reading one of the books has the dreamiest voice ever. I was practically swooning with each sentence."

He was unprepared for the stab of jealously that speared through him. "Oh, really? Who is he, maybe I've heard of him?"

"I don't think so, he's not famous or anything. The back of the box says he's in a soap opera in New York, but boy, the timber of his voice . . . mmm. He makes it a pleasure to learn history, I'll tell you that!" She hefted her bag onto her shoulder and from there, effortlessly inserted the opposite arm into the other long strap, wearing it as a backpack. You could tell by the smooth efficiency of her actions that she'd done this many times before. From a quick glance at her shapely legs, he knew she was a woman who was no stranger to exercise.

"Well, you'll have to educate me."

"Boy, that'll be a first. A last row student lecturing the prof."

"My field of expertise is forensics, not American history. Enlighten me."

They were walking toward the impressive wrought-iron gates that were wide open and beckoning. They mingled with the crowd lining up to pay admission.

She noticed a pleasant sandalwood fragrance hovering in the air and drew it deeply into her lungs. Then, pleasantly surprised, she realized it came from Ben. "I'll have to educate you later on the war between the North and the South; it's not just a quick tale, you know. By the way, what's that you're wearing? It's not your usual smell."

"It's English Leather. It's what I use when I'm not forced to use my own concoction."

"I like it. You know, you don't have to wear

something to cover up unpleasant odors."

"Something tells me you haven't been around rotting flesh before. Or liquified remains."

"As pleasant as that sounds, no I haven't. But I have had to deal with putrid fish odors, noxious swamps, an occasional leftover skunk marking, dead turtles and once, a beached and badly infected dolphin that I had to bury until the university could come get her remains and do a necropsy. But I've found that no matter what I manage to get myself into, the 'steel' gets me out."

"The 'steel?'"

"Yeah. Even when I'm unlucky enough to get a truck from the motor pool that reeks of cigarette smoke, all I have to do is shower with the 'steel' and the odor's gone."

"I take it you mean stainless steel?"

"Yes. So I gather you've heard of it?"

"Only once. Years ago someone mentioned you could use a stainless steel spoon to rid your hands of the smell of crabs after eating them."

"So, you never tried it?"

"Nope, never did."

"Well, it works. You just take something that's stainless steel, it won't work with anything else, and you rub it all over the area while rinsing with water. Usually thirty seconds'll do it. The steel leeches whatever odor is on you, off of you and down the drain. When I cut onions or shell shrimp, I reach for my stainless steel bar instead of the soap."

"You really believe this?"

"It works, Ben! I'm telling you, it works!"

"Well, it won't work for the smells I get on me."

"I'll bet you it will. I'm serious, I'll just bet it will."

"Just for you, I'll try it next time. Where do I get one of these stainless steel bars?"

"You can find them in any kitchen store, but you can use anything that's stainless steel. I just like my bar because it's shaped like a bar of soap and it's easy to rub all over my skin."

His mouth had gone dry at the thought of her rubbing anything over her naked little body. They arrived at the main house and the small booth at the entrance where tickets were purchased. Absentmindedly he took out his billfold, removed the requisite bills, and handed them to a smiling lady sitting at a table who handed him two small brochures in exchange for the fee. He took Shelby by the arm and led her into the house.

Why did he feel like a perverted cradle robber? Was it because she looked so young? Or was it because she seemed so incredibly different from the sophisticated and aggressive women he was always exposed to?

Chapter Nine—The Tour
Beau Marecage Plantation, SC

Shelby smiled at him as he handed her one of the brochures. He was mighty rakish looking today in his soft-brushed denim jeans, all blue this time, with a navy blue polo shirt. Birkenstocks were on his tanned feet and she couldn't help but notice that he had nice feet. To be fair to the rest of the male population, he'd have to be sporting one hell of a huge, ugly, hairy mole somewhere beneath his clothes. She wondered why he hadn't become a male model instead of a college professor. If he was at all photogenic, he had the men in the Sears and Penney's catalogues beat all to hell.

As she walked beside him, following the crowd into a large foyer, she picked up their conversation again. "It's the reason you're never supposed to cut fresh herbs with stainless steel scissors. The flavors jump right off the herbs like they're magnetized or something. So always tear your herbs, never cut them."

"I'll remember that," Ben said gravely, as if secreting away a key to one of the universe's most wondrous mysteries.

She jabbed him in the arm for mocking her and then pointed excitedly at an oil painting displayed above the huge fireplace. "Look! Doesn't that look a little like C.E.?"

His eyes followed hers and took in the image created by mostly dark shades of paint. Either this was the art world's early imitation of sepia or the bright and light colors of the painting had faded to gray or brown. The young man's unmistakable tawny hair rang true with that of the man's in the locket.

"Yeah, the hair and something about the eyes. Intense but somehow mischievous. His lips are even quirked in the same fashion. It could be him or any number of relatives who came after or before him."

"There's the tour guide. I'll ask her." And before he could say anything or accompany her, she left his side and squeezed through the crowd to the woman wearing colonial-styled clothing and sporting a gold "Tour Guide" badge.

He watched Shelby talk to the flush-faced, rotund woman who appeared to beam broadly, as if finding someone genuinely interested pleased her greatly. Shelby and the woman talked animatedly for a few minutes as more people crowded into the formal parlor, then Shelby made her way back to Ben as the woman began her practiced spiel.

He felt Shelby's warm breath fan his ear as she whispered excitedly that the portrait they were staring at was of Charles' younger brother, George, taken two years before the war, and that a portrait of Charles, taken at the same time, was hanging over the fireplace in the main dining room. He didn't know whether he was more excited by this connection and discovery or by the feeling of Shelby's breath tickling and awakening his skin.

Martha, the tour guide, was explaining plantation life, defining each job and the people who were assigned to each task. "This plantation had many exports. There was of course, rice the premium Carolina Gold variety, desired the world over. Indigo, used in the mills; cotton, shipped in huge bales from the port of Charleston; and tobacco, primarily grown for their own use and then converted as a cash crop when the demand rose. Upon reaching his maturity, George Garrett, the youngest son by eighteen months, was sent to a huge tract of property just west of Brunswick Town owned by his father, Lucas Garrett. There, he oversaw not only the mill business, but was also responsible for the harvesting of pine tar and the production of turpentine. These naval stores were in great demand in England, as well as in the States. Business had never been better, and then the war started and demand tripled. Eight hundred slaves had to be relocated to work the pine forests.

"Lucas bought Charles, his oldest son, a commission in the Navy, hoping to keep his first-born son from fighting on land should the need arise. He believed that if Charles was aboard a naval vessel, he would be far safer and that his return would be guaranteed. The war Lucas had feared came and with it irreparable damage to the South. The Yankees eventually captured Wilmington and with it the mill and tar fields in Brunswick Town. George was taken prisoner and most of the slaves freed. The mill and tar fields fell into the hands of the enemy.

"When the war was over, George, battered and now a pauper, yet young and whole, returned home and married a young widow from Charleston. Toward the end of the war, Charles became an officer on the blockade runner *Bendigo*. When it was run aground at Lockwood Folly, just south of Wilmington, he sent a message to his brother in neighboring Brunswick Town, asking that a horse be sent so he could return to the plantation. Unbeknownst to him, his brother, now a prisoner of the Union Army was no longer in charge at Brunswick Town and unable to attend to his needs. A Union officer, intercepting the missive, sent a small troop to find the man. Knowing that the successful interrogation of a Confederate naval officer would greatly enhance his career, the officer was furious when the soldiers returned without Charles Garrett. A slave, supposedly familiar to the Garrett family was enlisted, given horses and the necessary traveling pass. He was instructed to find George's brother and bring him back to Brunswick Town. The slave never found Charles Garrett, or if he did, they disappeared together, for neither the slave, nor Charles, nor the horses were ever seen again.

"After Lucas and his wife Emily died, the plantation was left to their remaining son George, and his bride Annabelle. George had four sons and two daughters; one son and one daughter died in childhood and the others grew up on the plantation as the first generation without benefit of slave labor. Oh, they had help. Lots of slaves stayed on to help. But now the slaves were free to leave or paid to stay.

"Beau Marecage was one of the few plantations in the South that wasn't destroyed by the Yankees. Some say that the swamp that partially surrounds it saved it. Walking through dry fields was tiring and tedious enough. No regiment really cared to slosh though the wetlands, braving mosquitoes and snakes. So the beauty that is Beau Marecage's survival is truly due to its 'lovely swamps.' Follow me and I'll take you into the dining room and give you an idea of what a typical meal was like in the late 1800s."

As the crowd pushed to follow her through the

narrow hallway, Ben grabbed Shelby's hand and held her back. "Let's stay in the back, I want to take this all in without all those other people in here."

Shelby looked down at their joined hands and then up into his face. She thought that if she acknowledged the fact that he was holding her hand, as if he hadn't noticed the sensual connection, that he would drop it. Not that she wanted him to, but she felt she had to react somehow. Instead of pulling away, she smiled and squeezed it tighter.

They both turned slowly around the formal parlor, drinking in the furnishings and the general condition of the home. They tried to absorb the atmosphere and imagine what it must have been like living here in the late nineteenth century.

"Smells a little peculiar, don't you think?" Shelby asked.

"You and your nose. But, yeah, it does have a pungent, outdoorsy smell. Must be the old wood. Think a giant-sized stainless steel bar would help?" he joked.

She laughed, "Too bad there's no way to get the magic of stainless steel in a spray can!"

They caught up with the group and listened as the guide described a typical Sunday dinner, or supper as it would have been called.

"In peacetime there was an abundance of food. The hunters were always able to provide meat for the table. There was goose, duck, wild turkey, venison, wild boar, rabbit, turtle, and the occasional 'gator. Fish were plentiful and oysters, shrimp, scallops, and mussels were practically a staple. Beau Marecage had its own dairy cows, so cheese, butter, and milk were kept in the larder all year 'round. Slaves harvested potatoes, ten varieties of squash, and every kind of green bean imaginable. In the good times, it would not be uncommon for the family to sit down to a meal consisting of six to eight courses. However, once the war was in full swing, the army required vast amounts of food to feed the troops. Soon the homeland stores were badly depleted. Breads, grains, and vegetables harvested from small, scattered gardens, along with herbs and plants found in the fields or forests became the primary sources of food. It has been said that Emily Garrett was quite fond of working in her gardens. In fact, Emily Garrett's mushroom soup was said to have saved the household when a group of five Yankee soldiers captured the house one early autumn morning.

"As the story goes, Emily was sick in bed with chicken pox when one of her maids burst into her room telling her that some Yankees were coming through the swamp. All the men from the plantation were in Charleston delivering their long-overdue cotton crop. Emily, unsure of what she should do, took her old nanny's muttered advice, 'Lordy, we best hide and take the good food with us. Let them eat the pig's swill.' Immediately, Emily sent the young women and children to hide in the forest, telling them to take as much food as they could carry. Then she instructed her cook to hurry and prepare a big pot of beef broth for the soldiers while she slipped outside to harvest some mushrooms—some very special mushrooms. By the time the Yankees came through the door, their thoughts of pillaging were distracted by the rich aroma of the beef and mushroom stock simmering on the kitchen hearth. They forced the cook to ladle out the soup and ate heartily before going about their mayhem. They were forcing themselves on the cook and her maids, sparing Emily their attentions because of her obvious pox marks, when the poison overcame them. One-by-one they clutched their cramping sides, held their pounding heads, and fainted dead away onto the floor. The women, abused but still fighting, finished the job by banging pots and pans on the soldiers' heads. Then they dragged the bodies into a fallow field where everyone gathered to bury them.

"So, Miss Emily's mushroom soup saved the day. Had she not known all about the local mushrooms, or not thought to pick them and steep them in hot water to make them more deadly, this plantation could have ended up like a lot of the plantations in the South, with nothing more to show than a split-rail fence surrounding a series of charred chimneys. Now, let's continue on to the library, shall we?"

Ben, still holding Shelby's hand, leaned over and whispered in her ear. "The femme fatale. You don't cook though, do you?"

She smiled up at him. "No, I wouldn't know one mushroom from another."

"Good."

"But I am pretty good with a bow and arrow. You know there's just something more menacing about holding a knocked arrow against a taut bow. I think it's even more effective than a gun. I mean, you can definitely see that it's loaded!"

"Whatever happened to the docile woman, the damsel in distress who's afraid of a mouse, the woman who needs a man to protect her?"

"She's a myth. Women don't need men to protect them. They need men to . . ."

"Yes?" he prompted when she hesitated.

"They need men to fix the cars and clean the fish."

"Is that all?"

"Carry the luggage?"

He leaned toward her and kissed the side of her neck, little nibbling kisses that sent fire racing through her veins. "Anything else?" he huskily breathed, letting his hot breath fan her ear.

"Uhhh . . . ." When his tongue slashed around her tiny whorl, her knees buckled and had he not been there with his arm around her waist, she would have collapsed into a heap on the wooden floor.

"Maybe later, a different use will come to mind." Abruptly he released her and moved to stand behind her as they lined up to walk single-file into the library. It was just as well, as he needed a place to shield the center of his body. That tiny taste of her had made him hot, hot in wondrous ways that had nothing to do with the heat of the day.

Shelby licked her dry lips with the tip of her tongue. *Ahhh, what had just happened there?* She had felt a jolt go straight through her body, a heat so quick and so thorough that now she was chilled from the lack of it.

The droning voice of the tour guide brought her attention back around. "Charles always had a fondness for ships. At the age of fourteen he was apprenticed to a captain of a schooner, and for two years he was at sea. He came back to the plantation when George was sent to the mill and tar fields, shortly after Lucas' brother, who had previously managed them, died. When the war broke out, Lucas knew that George was needed in Brunswick Town to produce supplies for the South more than he was needed to fight for the South. But Charles was chomping at the bit to join the fray. Lucas finally consented, but only after Charles agreed to serve in the navy. The navy, as it turned out, was desperate for qualified sailors. The South was determined that the blockade the North had implemented not succeed.

"Companies were formed, many of them with English partners, with the sole purpose of breaking through the blockade. Steamers belonging to the British merchant fleet came from the British West Indies, their cargo holds filled with supplies that would bring incredibly high prices. Despite the Federal picket boats, the steamers ran the blockade and took shelter under the Confederate gun batteries.

"England, in complete sympathy with the Confederacy's cause, was quick to make blockade running a big business. People eagerly put their money into the stock corporations that were building the specialized steamers and also the companies that owned them.

"Fast, gray-hulled, shallow-draft, side-wheeled steamers of rakish designs were built and launched from the great shipyards of England for the express purpose of running the Federal blockade. Charles was sent to man one of these. His designation was Chief Engineer. Even though his father thought this to be the safer venue for his son, it was still a very risky business.

"For two years he ran the blockade, coming home for a brief respite whenever his ship sailed into the Port of Charleston. The last ship he was known to be on was the *Bendigo*, which ran aground just after the New Year in 1864. Other than the missive he sent to his brother, requiring that a horse be sent, he was never heard from again. It's assumed that he ran into a regiment of Yankees and was killed. His personal effects are in that showcase on the right. Emily's favorite perfume bottles are in the one on the left and a few of Lucas Garrett's hunting knives are in the one at the front of the room. Please feel free to walk around but please don't touch anything."

Shelby and Ben inched along in the line until they arrived at the showcase, then they bent to study some of Charles' early childhood toys and spoons, along with a wooden board game with marbles.

"I found a marble similar to that one in his jacket," Ben stated, pointing to a large green marble.

"It must have been very special to him," Shelby whispered as she moved along the showcase, practically bent in half so she could see into it better. "I had a special aggie many years ago; don't have a clue where it is now, but I was pretty unstoppable with it."

"Tomboy, huh?"

"No, the girls' games just weren't all that much fun, and nobody except the boys ever bet real money."

"Have you always had this thing about money?" he asked with a grin.

"Just like to keep what I got and add a little to it now and then, that's all," she said as she stood up. "Hey look!" Her hand snapped out and pointed to a small glass case attached to the wall. "I have one just like that!" Displayed in the case was a Navy Colt, like the one she had found.

"You have a gun?" he asked somewhat surprised.

"Well, I did. I found it. Then I gave it away. But I swear to you, it's exactly like this one." She leaned into the wall and read the small card under the box. "Part of a set, this Navy Colt was given to Charles E. Garrett by his father on his sixteenth birthday. It is believed he took the matching gun with him when he went off to war. It has never been recovered."

"I recovered it!" she practically screamed, alerting the tour guide and commanding the attention of everyone else in the room.

When she realized that everyone was staring at her, she said in a lower voice, "Well, I did. I found a gun just like this."

The tour guide came over and looked at the gun in the case. She was silent for a few minutes. Then she said,

"No reason why not. The mate is out there somewhere for someone to find. You should check with the Historical Society, someone there ought to be able to verify if it's the gun missing from this set."

"I just know it is," Shelby whispered. "I just know it is," she repeated as she turned back to the box and stared at the Colt.

After a few moments, Ben touched her lightly on the shoulder.

"I have his gun, Ben. You have his locket. We're supposed to find something else, Ben. I just know it."

A bit somber, they continued the tour, taking quick peeks into the bedrooms upstairs, wandering through the massive kitchen and relaxing on the shaded front porch. They took a breather before going down to the slave quarters at the end of a long dirt road behind the house. There were hay wagons and golf carts for people to use, but Shelby and Ben opted to walk down the dry, dusty road, trying to envision life as a slave on such a magnificent plantation.

"We could be walking in the same footsteps as Charles."

"Probably are," Ben replied.

For long minutes neither of them spoke and then Ben said, "You know, more than likely, we're also walking in the footsteps of the woman he loved. She was probably one of his slaves."

"What makes you say that?"

"Well, for one, it's only likely. You saw her skin tone. The only other thing she could have been was Cajun, and that's still part black. Also, I had a dream. I think I saw them here in my dream." He told her about the dream, not bothering to tell her that he'd awakened from it hard as pig iron, and thinking of her.

"Okay. So maybe she was a slave. You're right, that's

very likely. Where else would he have met her? White men took women slaves as lovers all the time, but they didn't marry them. That definitely was not done. Hell, it wasn't done openly and without censure until the middle of the twentieth century. My mom used to tell me about Sammy Davis, Jr. and a woman named May Britt, and the scandal they caused when they got married and I think that was in the *nineteen* sixties."

"But he loved her and he wanted to find a way. Besides, from her coloring, she wasn't all black. She must have been the offspring of a white man and a black woman. So maybe she was a white man's daughter, not a slave."

"No, she was light, but not quite light enough to pass. And if you give your dream any credence, what would he have been talking about when he said, 'they had to work things out,' and that they 'would never let us be,' that they'd 'never be accepted?' No, she had to be a slave."

"You *do* know that was just a dream, not an actual recollection?"

"Yeah, but I believe in dreams. Don't you?"

"Believe that I have them?"

"No, believe that they're real sometimes. That they can come true."

"Oh, come on Shelby, you can't possibly believe all that you dream is real?"

"Oh, you want me to just believe the nightmares, not the good stuff?"

"I'm not sure you should believe any of it. It's just part of your subconscious trying to work things out."

Shelby began to sing, "And the dream that you dream will come true." He recognized the song as being from Cinderella. She had a lovely voice, so he didn't stop her. What surprised him was that she knew the words to the entire song.

"All right, apparently you feel that dreams *can* come true. So I guess I won't mess around with this anymore. But regardless of how you are interpreting *my* dream, I think Charles' lover was a slave."

"Okay. Let's go see where she lived. Just for the record, I've had a few weird dreams lately, too. And if I didn't know any better, I'd swear Charles is using us."

His questioning face turned toward hers. "In what way?"

"I don't know. He wants to go home, though. And I guess he can't get there without help."

"This is so odd."

"Yeah, tell me about it," she whispered sotto voce as they caught up with the tour group.

While the tour guide was waiting for the rest of the group to join them, she was answering questions posed by the group. A question had occurred to Ben, so he sidled up to her and asked her.

"These stories and recountings, I assume that they are handed down knowledge, a form of folklore as it were?"

"Yes, actually that's quite true. Some of the stories were written down and logged in journals, but most of the events, while verified from history, are embellished by the locals. Tales that have been told over and over, from generation to generation; whether they're factual or not, they are pretty much fact to the people living now."

"Is any of the current generation still around?"

"From the slaves, yes. But not from the Garrett family. The only relative we know about lives in Baltimore, Randall Garrett. He would be one of George's son's great, great, great, great grandchildren. Two World Wars, Korea, and Vietnam practically wiped out the line, the family being so patriotic over the years. Randall's parents didn't live here on the plantation though, nor did his grandparents. The last generation that actually lived here was his great grandparents'."

"So, who owns all this now?"

"Randall Garrett is the owner, but The Historical Society has a fifty-year lease. In exchange for the use of the property the Society has been paying the taxes and taking care of the day-to-day maintenance for quite some time now. I understand that within the next few months, the lease needs to be extended or the property reverts back. If that happens, the feeling is that all this will end up being sold and subdivided so the estate taxes can be paid. The lease was a way around that for the last two inheritors. They'll come due when the lease is up, so they'll have to be paid. It'll go like most farms are going now. Part of the plantation will be sold to pay the taxes, the rest will be subdivided and sold for new housing."

"Wow, what a shame."

"Yes, but we see it all the time. We're slowly losing our heritage. The past is just too expensive to keep."

Shelby jumped into the conversation just then. "Are there any descendants of the slaves that you know about?"

"Oh, Lordy yes!"

"Really?" Shelby exclaimed, and Ben could see a fresh twinkle in her bright blue eyes.

"Yes. Not too far from here actually. Ever hear of the Gullahs?"

"Mmmm. No, can't say that I have," Ben answered.

"I have!" Shelby piped up.

"Well good, now that everyone's here, I think that's a good place to start." She raised her voice and gestured with her hands for everyone to circle up. "Everybody come gather around this cabin. I know to most of you, this wouldn't be much bigger than your tool shed, but believe it or not, six slaves used to live here . . ."

An hour later, Shelby and Ben had learned more about slave life in the South than they could have if they'd read volumes on it. Ben had to hand it to Martha, she knew her stuff and she made her tour very interesting. She even sauntered with them through the family cemetery pointing out the less prominent tombstones, ones that said simply "Mary" or "John" or "Sassy," ones that belonged to some of the family's revered slaves. Sassy had been nanny to Emily and Lucas' children and her gravesite was situated in a place of honor, against a hill and under a huge weeping willow.

"Now, this isn't the same tree that was planted when she died, but legend has it, there has always been a weeping willow over Sassy's grave site. It's been rumored that she cried every morning when she awoke and found that Charles still had not come home.

"Sassy had been a child when the Gullah tribe was granted land on Sea Island. She had been one of the first children taught to read and write at the only school for black children, now known as Penn Center. When Lucas saw her in Charleston one day making sweet grass baskets to sell at the market, he was so impressed with her manners that he invited her to come live at Beau Marecage and be the nanny to his young boys. As a Gullah, she was a quasi-free woman. He could not buy her, except from her family, who agreed to take yearly wages for her. Soon, Lucas found that she was worth far more than he was paying for her. He hired more Gullahs, finding it cheaper to pay a wage and board to willing workers than to buy slaves at auction who were unskilled and always looking for an opportunity to escape. Lucas and Emily, as many other slave owners, were concerned with a smooth-running plantation and tended to look the other way when their overseers disciplined belligerent slaves. But being Christian and opposed to the horrific beatings and grueling back-breaking labor, they were extremely happy to be able to replace indentured slaves with free slaves whenever they could. That's how they came to run this huge plantation so efficiently, and still managed to, well after the war was over. The innovation of paid labor at Beau Marecage was gradual, so that by the time the war was over and all slaves were free anyway, they had loyal and trustworthy hands already in place. They experienced a smooth transition from slave labor to paid labor instead of the desolation neighboring plantations experienced as first they were bereft of menial laborers and then plagued by carpetbaggers offering to 'extricate' them from their dilemmas by showing them new ways to rebuild and run their plantations.

"Beau Marecage survived because of the Gullahs and the trust and loyalty they found here with the Garretts. They stayed because they felt they were part of a huge, caring family. To this day, you can go to the Gullah settlement and mention the name of Garrett and there will be those who will tell stories about the time Beau Marecage was graceful, prosperous, and beautiful beyond imagining. Thank you for visiting us today. Please take a step back into the past often. Feel free to walk around and explore on your own."

The crowd began to disperse, a few walking up to the tour guide with questions, others to hand her a tip.

"Well, shall we walk around and see what we can see?" Ben asked.

"Yes, but first I would like to ask Martha a question," Shelby answered.

"Okay."

They waited until they were the last ones and she turned to beam at them. "You seem to be more into this than most."

"Yes, well . . ." Shelby started."We'd like to know more about the family, the family that came after."

"The family Bible is in the little chapel at the bottom of the next hill. It's locked in a display case, but it's open to the page where the family tree is diagrammed. Every birth, death, and wedding was recorded until the late 1940s and then either no one cared to do it, or they didn't know how to record the first divorce and remarriage and gave up. The relatives are spread out all over the country now, but the direct descendant, Randall Wyatt Garrett, the heir, so to speak, is living in Baltimore. He's a photographer, I believe. He comes here two or three times a year, mostly for promotional events, to hand out awards to the staff, and to help with fundraising for the Society."

Shelby cleared her throat and charged forth with a question she'd been harboring for some time. "If we were interested in more stories about Beau Marecage, do you know any Gullahs we could contact? We're particularly interested in what might have happened to Charles Garrett, even if it is just supposition or folklore."

Ben gave Shelby a queer look, then turned to face Martha for her answer.

"You've heard of hoodoo and the storytellers, haven't you?" she asked Shelby intuitively.

"Yes," Shelby whispered. "I know that some Gullahs have the gift of storytelling, and that it goes way back. The stories themselves having been told over and over again to the point that no one really knows what's real and what's not anymore."

"That's part of the tradition," Martha said with a

generous smile.

"Well, I've read that some of the stories have a germ of the truth in them. I'm just wondering if we can find someone who may be able to spin us a tale that may have a hint of some discovery in it for us."

"Could be. Could be." She eyed Shelby and Ben, looking back and forth between them. Then she harrumphed, crossed her hands over her large bosom and said, "I'll tell you what, you wander around for a spell and I'll send word to Mareesa at St. Helena's Island. Mareesa knows all the stories. Can't vouch for any of them myself, but if there's a story to be told, she's the one to be tellin' it. It'll take her about an hour and a half to get here though, if she can come, and it'll cost you fifty dollars, but you'll get your story."

"Oh that would be wonderful!" Shelby exclaimed, practically jumping up and down and clapping her hands.

Ben looked at them both like they were crazy. "Would you mind telling me what you two are talking about?"

Shelby touched his arm and smiled up at him. "Yes, I will, but first do you have fifty dollars you could loan me for Mareesa if she can come?"

He put his hand into his pocket, pulled out his money clip, and handed her a fifty-dollar bill. Knowing how dear money was to her, he knew that this had to be important. "Okay, so what's the explanation? And don't tell me I just signed up for some kind of séance or something. Just what is this voodoo thing?"

"Hoodoo!" Both women corrected.

Shelby handed the fifty to Martha and asked her to please try to contact Mareesa. Martha said she'd go send her a message now and that she'd arrange for a time they could meet later that afternoon. Ben handed

Martha a twenty and said, "That's for you, you make this place come alive."

"Thank you, but you haven't seen anything yet. Just wait 'til you meet Mareesa. Come back up to the main house when you're through walking around and we'll see what the afternoon will bring for you."

Martha ambled away, trudging up the hill to the main house so she could use the telephone to call her brother, who would in turn call his friend the policeman, who would drive over to Mareesa's house on the island to see if she was up to coming to the mainland today.

"Well, what was that all about?" Ben asked. "It was like you two were in a secret club or something."

"It's Gullah. And Hoodoo. It's all so mysterious and otherworldly."

"Care to fill me in?"

"Well, sure. Come on, let's walk down to the pond. I see some ducks."

He took her hand, tucked it in his arm, and started walking with her down the old rutted road.

Chapter Ten—Mareesa
Beau Marecage Plantation, SC

Gullahs are very spiritual people. They believe in signs, especially signs from the past. Magic isn't scary to them because it's done for good, not evil. They don't make an effigy doll and stick pins in it or sacrifice animals like they do in voodoo. But they are likely to make a potion and believe it will protect them from something or do any number of strange things that we would attribute to being plain superstitious. Anyway, hoodoo is an ancient practice. You either have the art, or you don't. If you do, sometimes people from the past speak to you. I'm hoping this Mareesa has talked to someone who knows something about Charles or his lady friend."

"You don't really believe this, do you?"

"Not any more than you believe everything you dream. But there must be a reason we were led here. There must be something more we're supposed to find out."

They were at the pond now and the ducks were

gliding across the water. You could see their little feet paddling and pushing them through the shadows under the trees. A little dock jutted out from the other side and a few yellow chicks were swimming beneath it, looking like yellow cotton balls floating on the water.

Ben helped Shelby down and together they sat at the edge of the water on patches of cool clover. He settled himself close beside her, her left thigh touching his right.

"Maybe Charles and his 'lady friend' sat on that dock, or one similar, dangling their toes in the water," Ben whispered in the quiet summer breeze.

"No, that wouldn't have been proper back then. Ladies didn't show their feet."

"I thought you said she was a slave. Slaves didn't even have shoes, did they?"

"Well, they must have had something to wear in the winter. Summer wouldn't have been too bad, if you were careful where you walked. But still, they wouldn't have sat side by side anywhere. What if someone had seen them?"

"He was practically the master here. What would anyone have been able to say to him? Besides, didn't you tell me just a little while ago that the masters took their slaves to bed all the time? What would have been wrong with a little getting to know each other?"

"Well, they didn't actually take them to bed. They just took them. Wherever. A barn, a little hideaway shack, against a tree. And I don't think they 'romanced' them. They just threw them down, tossed up their skirts, and had at it."

Ben looked at her out of the corner of his eye and smiled sideways at her. "Just had at it, huh?"

"You know what I mean. It was all for the man."

"You know this to be fact?"

"Well, doesn't it stand to reason? If you owned twenty young women who had to do your every bidding, would you waste time on foreplay if you didn't have to?"

"There you go with the foreplay thing again. What do you have against foreplay? I told you it's not time wasted."

She turned beet red and started to stammer, "I . . . I don't h-h-have anything against it."

"Good." His right hand went around her waist while his left cupped her cheek and he turned her to face him. For one fleeting second their eyes met and she read his intent. Panic flared in hers, but he didn't let it deter him. His mouth crushed hers and took full possession. He ravished her lips with a profound curiosity. He had to know her, at least this part of her, for now.

His lips moved over hers molding and capturing them with his as his hand moved from her face to the nape of her neck. With his hand he drew her closer, trying to give his lips more of the taste of her. When she gasped from the sensations, he inserted his tongue and plundered greedily. His tongue darted everywhere, feeling her teeth, the soft undersides of her lips, her smooth gums, all on its quest to find her tongue, which thankfully was now eagerly searching out his. At the touch of her tongue to his, he moaned and the sound filled the quiet little glade.

Desperately, his demanding tongue dueled with her timid one as he coaxed her and teased her and finally drew her into his mouth. His sigh was one of bliss as he ever so gently laid her back on his arm in the soft, sweet, summer grass. His hand stole from her neck to her cheek and then to her shoulder as he took one kiss after another, covering her face with hot kisses and repeatedly returning to lick and suck on her soft, smooth lips. His other arm was under her, supporting her and allowing him to prop himself over her. His free hand caressed her chin and stroked her neck. When he felt her hands splay in his hair, he took it as permission to touch her more intimately and brought his hand down to her breast, his hand open and eager to palm her. Her nipple seared the center of his palm through her ribbed cotton shirt as she arched to fill his hand. And amazingly, she did fill his hand. While her breast was fairly flat, and not at all meaty, it was a rather large circle on her chest wall. Ah, but it was the nipple that intrigued him. The nipple was delightful–tall and hard as it drove into his palm. He commanded his eager fingers to pinch it and gently pull at it through the meager fabric.

Oh! My! God! This was incredible. His kiss. His kiss. It was . . . well, it was . . . hell, there were no words for this! Heat flushed her and coursed through her and she thought at first that it would completely disintegrate her. She was hot, incredibly hot. And surging, surging. Oh, his lips. His tongue. She could not get enough. He tasted all male and he felt all male lying practically on top of her. Her tongue in his mouth circled and lapped and then she just had to draw him back into hers. Yes. Yes, she wanted him in her mouth, plunging over and over again. And then his hand covered her breast, and she liquified. Every cell, every pore melted into the heat of his body and she arched to feel the delicious sensation over and over again. When his fingertips grasped her nub and pulled, she thought she would die. Ohhh. Ohhh. Lordy, this must be what necking and petting was supposed to feel like, but yet never had. She moaned something unintelligible even to her own ears and continued to kiss him, this time faster and more feveredly.

As he continued to taunt and tease her nipple, she

found herself involuntarily thrusting her hips and when one of those upward thrusts was returned, there was a large, firm ridge jutting into her belly. She could feel him prodding the curve of her hip through both his jeans and her shorts. The urgent press matching hers made her want to reach for his zipper. But she knew that they had to stop, that they couldn't do this here. For for the very first time in her life, she wanted to complete this, to have everything culminate with "the act." She wanted to go forward, when every other time this was where it had all halted.

She marveled at the thought that flew through her mind: I want to be taken. I truly want this man to slide himself into me and show me what this having sex thing is all about. But she could already tell from the way he was kissing her and the places he was kissing her, that he was calling everything off. His lips were kissing their way back up her neck, to her jaw and then lightly nipping at her lips while his thumbs stroked her temples in tiny circles. Slowing down the burn, he was turning off the flame.

He kissed the tip of her nose, her eyelids, her cheeks, and took gentle nips on her lips again. "Foreplay," he whispered.

"Good stuff," she whispered back.

"Very good stuff."

"You're amazing."

"I haven't even begun."

She shivered at the thought. For the first time in her life, she wanted to find the nearest motel, pay whatever it cost, and drag this man inside so she could be pleasured by him. *Was this what other women felt all the time? Was this what it was all about?*

Growing up she had never been anywhere near this desirous, ever. She'd been curious just like any other teenager or young woman, but she'd always been a daddy's girl, and the last thing in the world she wanted to do was disappoint her daddy. As close as they were when she was growing up, she just knew that if she'd let any boy have her, her daddy would see it in her face and he'd know, and she'd just die from shame. Those same feelings came to her every time she was alone with boys and then later, with men. By itself, it would have dampened her ardor had there been any. But no one had ever turned her on like this.

Now, using perfect teenage logic, she realized that since her father didn't even recognize her anymore, it didn't matter if she gave in. That special part of her was now only hers to give away. It was no longer the precious treasure that it once had been. Now, it seemed more of a burden than anything else.

Ben's fingers brushed against her cheek and she lifted her eyes to his. "I'm thinking we'd better get up to the main house," he murmured against her cheek.

"I'm thinking we need a bed, too."

He laughed out loud and rolled off of her. "No, nitwit. We need to go find Martha, remember? But I'll take you up on your offer later if you're still in the mood."

"Still in the mood? How long does this feeling last? I've never had it before."

He was standing up and straightening his clothing and at the same time extending a hand down to her, but he stopped short at her words.

"Pardon? You've never been in the mood? You've never . . ."

Embarrassed by what she had just said and certain she had turned him off of her forever, she stood on her own and faced away from him.

"Ahh, no. Never," was all she said.

"Any particular reason? Are you waiting for marriage or something?"

"No. Just waiting for the right reason."

"Ah, love then?"

"No. To be honest, I just never wanted to. You're the first man to stir this kind of desire in me. You could have gone all the way with me a few minutes ago, and I wouldn't have dreamed of stopping you; it felt that good."

He walked over to where she had stepped away from him and gathered her into his arms, his hands overlapping around her waist as he pressed her back into his chest. "Well, that's nice to know. But if you don't mind, I'd like our first time to be someplace private, and maybe on something a tad bit softer." He kissed the back of her neck and felt a frisson of heat go through her.

She turned slowly in his arms and he looked down into her face, at her lovely flushed face, and kiss-swollen lips. He bent and kissed her gently on her sweet, sensuous mouth. "Yes, indeed, definitely someplace softer. You're so tiny that I'm afraid if I drive into you like I want to, unless you're on something that gives, I'll break your pelvis." Her eyes blinked wide, but she said nothing. Silently she turned toward the water.

She looked around for a moment, taking in the peaceful summer day in front of her—the vista of the swamp unfurling as far as the eye could see, the tiny pond with its lily pads and ducks, and off to their left a massive, gnarled live oak tree. "You know this looks a lot like the place you described in your dream."

"You mean the place where Charles took his 'lady love,' on the cool, green clover?"

"Mmm hmm."

"I'm beginning to feel some of that connection you've been talking about."

"You mean you can identify with Charles?"

"I can identify with any man who has a beautiful, sexy woman in his arms. It's universal. We all want to lower her to the ground and as you say, 'toss her skirts over her head.'"

"I'm not wearing a skirt."

"You keep pressing up against me like that, and you won't be wearing those shorts much longer either." He kissed her on her forehead then slowly turned her away from him and said, "Come on, let's find Martha and find out what kind of mess you've gotten me into. I just know there's gonna be a doll with pins in it somewhere in all this."

He took her hand in his and they started walking back up the hill.

"No, no, no. Hoodoo isn't evil. Gullahs were and are Christian. We're just going to take a journey back into the past. Think of it as reading a chapter in Alex Haley's *Roots*. We're going to see about Chicken George and the 'massah' of the plantation."

"You're looney."

"And you're going to be open-minded, right?"

He looked down at her as they walked up the drive to the house. "The only thing I'm guaranteeing that I'm going to be today is horny. You are definitely doing a number on me little lady."

She blushed and smiled broadly as they entered the house to find Martha.

Chapter Eleven—
Waiting for Mareesa
Beaufort, SC

They found her just as she was getting ready to start another tour. She excused herself for a minute to meet them in the hallway. "Mareesa is on her way. Why don't you grab some lunch in Beaufort and come back in about an hour or so. She said to have you meet her by the old cemetery. I told her you already gave me the money for her storytelling."

"Thank you. We appreciate it." Ben said.

"No problem. I hope it helps. I hope you find out what you want to know. Worst case though, you're going to meet one heck of a character. Mareesa may be old, but her memory sure ain't. I'd best get back to my tour. Good luck to you." She turned in her big, swishy skirt. It was very hot in the house now and Shelby wondered how Martha stood the heat with all those heavy clothes on. It must have been awful not to be able to wear something akin to shorts and tank tops in the heat of the summer. She wondered how the women of yesteryear kept from passing out from the sweltering heat.

"Well, are you ready to go find a place to eat?"

"Yeah. I'm starving. That Sausage McMuffin I had on the way down wasn't quite enough."

"I had coffee and a sweet roll. I could go for just about anything, how about you?"

"I could go for a nice, juicy cheeseburger."

"I was hoping to take you someplace nice."

"Even if you do, I'll probably still ask for a cheeseburger. What do you feel like eating?"

No, no, no. Don't go there. Definitely don't go there, he thought. "Let's just drive until we see someplace that looks interesting."

They were back in the parking lot now and he was walking her toward his car. "I'll drive so you can enjoy the scenery."

"Wait! Let me get some money from my car so I can pay you back for the storytelling."

"Not a chance. I feel exactly the opposite about money as you do. My mission in life is to get rid of it as fast as I can. Can't stand the stuff!" he said with a smile. "There's no need to pay me back; besides, I couldn't stand watching you cry as you counted it out to me anyway."

"Thank you," she said smiling back, her blue eyes glinting in the sun. She lowered her sunglasses from where they had been stuck in her hair, and said, "You're just too funny, you know that?"

He helped her into his car, noting her smooth, tanned legs. Yes, this woman exercised. While he was normally attracted to feminine-wiled women dressing with the height of fashion in frivolous girly things, this woman in her khaki shorts and plain cotton T-shirt was the most wanton thing he'd beheld in years. He closed her door and walked behind the car so he could adjust his suddenly too-tight jeans.

A few miles down the main road they found a restaurant called "The Little Mermaid." It was at the end of a strip mall in a converted church. The high steeple was decorated with tiers of Victorian scales painted to resemble the scales on a mermaid's fin. The mermaid's three-dimensional body was attached just as a masthead would be. The glittering acrylic paint, shining in the sun was what had caught Shelby's eye.

"There. Let's try that place. There's lots of cars parked out front and I just love the name. It was one of my favorite movies."

"Really? One of your favorites?"

"Yeah. She loved him so much she wanted to live in his world. She wasn't a woman just sacrificing her career, she became an entirely different creature and gave up her whole way of living for the man she loved. Great movie," she said wistfully and starting humming "Under the Sea."

He pulled into a slot and put the car in park. "Sounds like you're quite the romantic."

"Aren't you?"

He thought for a moment, his hands still on the wheel. "No, not really. Not any more."

"Uh oh. Something happened. You must have been in love once, am I right?"

"Mmm, not sure anymore just what love is. At the time, she was comfortable and fun, and I needed her; but I wasn't ready to settle down. We were living together when she died suddenly. I had put off defining my feelings because I thought there would be lots of time for that later. After she died, I had to accept the fact that she meant more to me than I realized. The pain of losing her totally engulfed me. Somehow I had become obsessed with her without even knowing it. I died with her. For months I was inconsolable."

"Tell me more."

"After she died I found a grocery list she had left under a magnet on the refrigerator. The items she had listed were: bacon, bread, eggs, sour cream, orange juice, and Wilton clear vanilla extract. I had no idea what the last item was, but every time I went to the grocery store, I searched out the manager and inquired if they had any. I wanted to have it for her when she came home. She had put it on the list and I wanted to get it for her. But no one ever had it.

Then one day I chanced upon a woman in a Super Wal-Mart in the baking section. I asked her if she'd ever heard of it. She nodded and said she knew exactly what it was. She led me up and down aisles and around displays until we arrived at a cake decorating center in the craft department. Then triumphantly, she reached down to a bottom shelf and stood proudly holding a tall brown bottle declaring it to be 'Wilton Clear Vanilla Extract–Artificial. Will not change icing color!' I wanted to hug her. I bought six bottles. I took them home and put them away, along with the collection of bacon, eggs, sour cream, bread, and orange juice I was amassing. But it didn't help. She still didn't come home and I continued to lose more of myself with each passing day.

I soon came to realize that I had to give her up or lose myself completely. I threw out all the groceries and poured all the vanilla down the drain as sort of a cleansing ceremony. It was about that time that I was given a very challenging murder case. My focus shifted and my work became everything to me. It saved me."

"That is so sad. You'll have to tell me all about her and the case."

"Maybe one day. It's too heart-heavy of a tale to have over lunch though. The murder case, too. Especially right before you're going to make me go back in time with someone akin to the famed Marie LeVeau."

"Oh, I saw her grave in New Orleans! But Gullahs' storytelling is not about witchcraft, and hoodoo is not voodoo, although it is a type of sorcery, I guess. The Gullahs are an awesome people."

"You seemed to have settled on a topic that I am completely unfamiliar with. Would you care to enlighten me while we dine?" He walked around the car to open her door and they walked together, hand-in-hand up the white wooden stairs to the old sanctuary.

"Sure, I'd be more than happy to 'educate' the teacher."

They waited to be seated, then as they settled into a booth made from old church pews, he muttered, "Just don't expect me to take any notes."

"Well, the word 'Gullah' actually describes the conservative black English spoken by a settlement of slaves who were originally from Liberia, Sierra Leone, and Angola. In some places it's referred to as 'strange speak.' When they came to the Carolina colonies, they were isolated on the sea islands off the coast of South Carolina and Georgia. That sheltered them from the changes other slaves were exposed to that gradually influenced their speech. They were not exposed to the prevailing language of both the colonists and the Americanized slaves; hence, they did not lose their heritage or their flowing creole language. Have you ever been to the Caribbean? Jamaica? The Bahamas?"

"I've been to Jamaica and Freeport."

"Well then you've heard the flourishing banter of the natives there. They talk fast, often dropping consonants and running words together, changing the pitch up and down. It's melodic, sort of singsong and mush-mouth, similar to what we would call 'jive.' Outsiders don't readily understand it or even identify it as English, but it is. It's part English mingled with a West African dialect and grammar. The word 'Kumbaya' is actually Gullah. It translates to 'Come by Here.' As the Gullah communities became less isolated, they yielded some of their African linguistic characteristics over to American English. Even today, the language of the slaves' ancestors carries on where the black English was the thickest and purest—on the sea islands south of Charleston and inland, near the old rice fields along the Cooper River."

"How do you know so much about this?"

"I came to Charleston a few years ago and was fascinated by the city. I spoke to some of the native women in the straw markets and discovered the dreaded benne wafer."

"Benne wafer?"

"Well, it's actually a cookie. A cross between a shortbread cookie and a molasses cookie topped with sesame seeds. They're incredible."

"Why dreaded then?"

"I always eat the whole package in one sitting. Calories off the chart."

"You look like that wouldn't be a problem."

"One cookie leads to ten, ten to twenty . . . . No one can burn all those calories."

"I'll have to try one sometime."

"Take my word for it, try one, and you'll try twenty."

"You'd make a good salesman. You've got me salivating for one."

"I'm sure one of the gift shops in this center sells them. Just promise to keep them away from me!"

He smiled over at her and reached for her hand that was idly stroking the condensation on her water glass. "I can think of some ways we can burn off those extra calories."

The huskiness of his voice sent trills through her. She visibly shivered, and then blushed when she saw he had noticed.

"Well, uh . . . anyway, back to the Gullahs. The Charleston Colony was founded in 1670. Though legally enslaved–some lived independent, sometimes autonomous lives. During the war, some were bonded, some had liberty, and some were halfway in between. They experienced something like quasi-freedom, the ability to come and go as they pleased, providing they did their jobs or made sure others did theirs.

"Their lives revolved around family, spirituals, and storytelling. The songs of the slaves were heavy spirituals with much care for pronunciation, even though you and I would probably have to work really hard to understand them, we'd get the gist because most of the words would be somewhat familiar. They coined a lot of their own words too, though, like: yam, benne, cush, goober, buckra, cooter, okra. We've even adopted some over the years. Cooter is a turtle, buckra is a white man. If Mareesa speaks Gullah, you're going to think you're on the set of *Gone with the Wind* with Hattie McDaniel. But if we tried to speak it, they'd think we were making fun of black people from the South."

"Well, what's all this have to do with good ol' Charlie?"

"The storytelling."

"Come again?"

"The Gullahs are renowned for their storytelling. Generation after generation passes down its history through storytelling. If we're lucky, someone who was a slave on Beau Marecage at the time Charles and his family were alive passed on some interesting stories, something that the history books don't have. I'm counting on a good story, Ben. You know how dear fifty dollars is to me."

"It was my fifty dollars."

"I tried to pay you back! And it doesn't matter, I'm counting on getting a story worth the price and worth the trip."

The waitress came and took their order. While they waited for it to be served, they took the South Carolina trivia test on the paper place mat. Ben proved to be more knowledgeable than he'd let on, especially about the State capital, motto, flower, bird, and tree. When their meal came they both ate ravenously.

"Must be all the fresh air. My appetite is never this strong," Shelby commented as she popped the last bite of her cheeseburger into her mouth.

"If you're finished, we have just enough time to check out one of those gift shops you mentioned for dessert."

She gave him a wry grimace. "Wish I'd never told you about those things!"

They both stood up and he carried the bill to the cashier. "I must say you manage to peek my curiosity about things. A lot of things," he whispered as he bent to her ear.

Ben's breath on the back of her neck was warm and it was all she could do to keep from turning, reaching up, and pressing her lips against the column of his throat. *Oh, how this man could heat up her insides.*

To Shelby's chagrin, Ben bought two packages of the benne cookies in the kitchen specialty shop. It was like he was buying popcorn before the movies. He smiled at her as he paid for them and she softened. She hoped this Mareesa would be entertaining enough to keep his attention, because, if she had her druthers right now, the idea of a motel room sounded pretty appetizing indeed. What was it about him other than his stunning good looks that made her heart do flip flops?

As she paid for her own purchases, she realized exactly what it was about Ben that turned her on so. It was the idea that he was masterful, masterful in the art of seduction. And smug. He was purposefully keeping her on edge. To what aim? Well, now, wasn't that obvious? To get her in the sack and have her submit to him. Smug and masterful. Well, tempting as that all sounded, he was going to have to work a lot harder than this, she decided. Maybe he was thinking she was going to be easy because he was so good at "foreplay." *Well, we'll just see about that!* She grabbed the bag off the counter and stalked out of the store.

What had gotten into her, Ben thought as she pushed past him and made her way to the car. She couldn't be that upset because he bought a few cookies, could she?

When they arrived back at the plantation, Martha met them and told them that Mareesa was waiting for them down by the cemetery beneath the big weeping willow tree.

Ben took Shelby's hand as he led her down the road and across the field. "You okay?"

"Yeah, just getting tired I guess. I'm liable to fall asleep in the middle of the cemetery, just sitting in the sun."

"I have the feeling that you're somehow mad at me."

"No, not at all." She squeezed his hand. "Thanks for lunch, it was really nice."

"Thanks for the lecture. It was first class."

Chapter Twelve—
Mareesa, the Storyteller
Beau Marecage Plantation, SC

They walked up a little rise and saw a huge black woman sitting on a pile of pillows, propped up against the trunk of a gigantic willow. She looked up at them, grinned broadly, and waved them over with her big hand.

When they approached, she muttered, "Ain't gwine tuh be gitting up agin, not tuh easy, nomo'. Hab a sit wid me down here by the grabes."

"Mareesa?" Shelby asked as she put out her hand.

The big woman took it and shook it hard, smiling and flashing beautiful white teeth between thick brown lips.

"Sho, I am. My Lawd, ain't you a pritty one, yo' is." She turned to Ben and motioned for him to sit on the grass in front of her. "Una be bery good look'een yo'self!"

Ben gingerly sat on the cool grass, bemoaning the fact that he'd have to sit here and try to understand this woman's hard brogue and indistinct dialect for however long this took, or at least long enough to be polite, or to satisfy Shelby's enthusiasm for this storytelling stuff.

They introduced themselves and discovered her name was Mareesa Ball, a descendant of Jonathan Ball, who came to America as a slave aboard a great wooden ship in the late sixteen hundreds. She proudly listed a name for one person in each generation, descending from Jonathan Ball's and ending with her own. There were over twenty names and she hadn't faltered with a single one. It was like listening to someone spout their heritage from the Mayflower on down. She couldn't have been more pleased with herself. "Not tuh sweet mouth myself none, but I's is from the 'riginal Balls, we da goin' nigh on ta fo' hundert yars naw."

"Ms. Ball, thank you for meeting us today. Shelby has an interest in the first family here on the plantation, especially in Charles Garrett. We were wondering if per chance you know any stories from that time."

"Deah Lawd I do! We da go back in the time. Ta the day clean o' da age dis fambly mek Balldem."

Ben looked over at Shelby with a raised eyebrow. It was clear he hadn't understood a word Mareesa had said.

"She said, 'Dear Lord I do. We'll go back in time. To the dawn of the age where this family make Ball and his ancestors.' "

"Would you prefer that I didn't speak Gullah?" Mareesa asked in perfectly pronounced and perfectly enunciated, standard English. When Both Shelby and Ben just stared dumbfounded at her, she added, "People expect the native tongue. I try to set the stage, but really, if you'd rather have an easier time understanding . . . "

Both Shelby and Ben grinned broadly, and then nodded vigorously.

"I just do this for fun, and for my grandkids so they'll stay in touch with their heritage. They're both up at the house driving Martha crazy at present."

"Why, you don't even have a Southern accent," Shelby noted.

"No. After high school I went to school in Massachusetts. I worked very hard to keep people from finding out where I came from. Although why, I don't know. I went to high school with Clarence Thomas, and he didn't do so bad for himself."

Shelby inched closer to the woman, putting her chin in her hands with her elbows on her knees as she sat Indian fashion, transfixed.

"And you," she looked over at Shelby, "where did you learn Gullah?"

Shelby smiled up at her. "I just know a little. I like the music and the culture. I'm especially fond of the spirituals like, *I gonna lebe yuh een duh han' ob duh Kine Sabior*, and *Jesus gwine mek up my dyin' bed*. I've been fascinated with the language and culture ever since I found out that George Gershwin came here to James Island when he was working on *Porgy and Bess*." Shelby turned to look at Ben, "It's not commonly known, but he was so impressed with the language and the spirituals of the Gullah people that he called the time he spent with them the most euphoric and inspired moments of his life."

Ben shook his head in amazement and watched for the next few minutes as both women sang low and sweet of *anguls in de heben dun changed muh name, and laying down in de watry grabe*. He had to admit it was beautiful, moving music.

Then both women broke off laughing as they both tripped over the words about *don' wan' nobody tuh moan, wan' tuh die easy*.

"Miz Martha told me you wanted a story about

Charles Garrett, the one who went off to the war and never returned."

"Yes, we'd like to know something of his life if you know any such stories," Shelby ventured.

"Only one story about Charles I know of. And I can't say it's factual because of the many times of the tellin'. But the story goes that one day a man from one of the ships Charles was on came to the plantation. He did not know that Charles had not come home. The war was over and the man was looking for work. He remembered Charles told him about Beau Marecage and how many men it took to run it. Charles had invited him to come visit anytime. Well, the man couldn't offer anyone an explanation for where Charles was or what had happened to him, but he did tell George and his wife, Annabelle, that Charles had told him he left something valuable back here on the plantation, something worth more than gold. Something he was going to come back for and take care of. Charles wouldn't say what it was, only that he couldn't wait to get home to tend to it. Well, the rumor spread and soon everybody was digging with shovels and picks trying to find the treasure Charles had left behind. The story of the mysterious secret cache he left before going off to war has become a legend, and to this day, people often wander onto the plantation with metal detectors hoping to find the buried treasure. The park security people have to shoo them off all the time, 'cause if they didn't, this place would be nothing but gopher holes!"

"What do you think the treasure was Mareesa?" Ben asked.

"I don't think it was a thing. That's all I think."

Ben eyed her with a bit of suspicion. "What makes you say that?"

"Well, what's worth more than gold?" she asked

philosophically.

Ben nodded at her sage observation.

"That's the only story I can tell you about Charles, but I got others . . ."

They settled in and Mareesa told them old slave stories combining mercy, prestige, patience, greed, wealth, strength, success, honor, and sexual prowess. One particular story that seemed eerie in its candor of time past, touched on the heavily-burdened heart of a gentle slave man.

ଊ

"Olney Ball was a slave employed in the Dismal Swamp. He was hired from Beau Marecage Plantation by the Dismal Swamp Land Company to fashion shingles from cypress trees cut by timber slaves. His owner, one of the Garretts, was paid a hundred dollars a year to hire him out. For ten months the hired slaves lived and worked deep in the swamps. They made crude huts atop accumulated cedar shavings and whatever debris they could find. Great gangs of a hundred or more worked from February through November as 'shingle getters.' The life for this type of lumberman was not particularly hateful as far as slave drudgery went. The swamp workers had passes that allowed them to wander through the swamps when they were not working so they could hunt, fish, and collect pelts for trading. They were free to eat, drink, play, and sleep as much as they pleased, as long as the work was done.

"The men lived in shanties wide enough to accommodate three to five burly men. They made beds out of discarded cedar shavings and found warmth with a peat fire kept stoked throughout the night. It was not bad work, knowing that the alternative was the back-breaking labor of picking cotton.

"Olney didn't mind the work at all, but he did mind the time he had to spend away from his beautiful young wife, Leitha. Ten months was a long time to be away from her. Each time the ten months was over, he was given two months of vacation time when he tried to make it up to her before leaving her again.

"It was never known which day in late fall he would finally make it back to the plantation and to the woman whose warm, supple body he dreamed of during the long, cold winters and hot, humid summers. So, it shouldn't have come as a surprise to anyone that one year he showed up at Beau Marecage anxious to find Leitha, a week earlier than he'd been expected.

"When his heavy boots found purchase on the old wooden planking of their front porch, he savored the familiar creaking sounds and boisterously kicked open the door of their ramshackle cabin.

" 'Leitha!' he called as he cleared the doorjamb and strode into the one-room shack.

"His eyes damned near bugged out of his head as he watched the twin, white moons of a white man plunging down and raising up as the man rode his wife.

"At the sound of her name, the man's head spun around and his face paled.

"Olney stared at the plantation overseer's face, unable to believe what his eyes were seeing. A rage such as he had never known filled his body until he was shaking with the unleashed fury.

"Fortunately for the overseer, news of Olney's sudden return to the plantation had spread quickly. Olney had been spotted coming across one of the fields by the hands and the overseer's men had been alerted. They all knew where the overseer was and what he was doing, so they hightailed it to the slave encampment and to

Olney's cabin. Before the overseer could lift himself off of Leitha and close his trousers, his reinforcements were holding the big black man at bay reminding him of his lowborn status.

"See, in those days, a white man could take a black woman just about any time he wanted, but it wasn't thought to be couth to take a slave woman if she was married to a slave living and working on the same plantation, especially if he was a young buck who loved his woman as much as everyone knew Olney loved Leitha.

"As seven men held Olney back, the overseer took his time buttoning up, not once sparing a glance at the sobbing woman he had left naked from the waist down on the bed behind him.

"Safely cordoned off and carried away, Olney could hear the overseer laughing with his men as they rode up the dirt path and crossed the ridge leading back to the fields.

"Leitha cried in Olney's arms and finally confessed that this had been going on for quite some time, that the overseer was always more than delighted to see Olney pack his satchel and head back into the Dismal Swamp during the coldest part of the winter.

"Leitha even told him how the overseer had bragged to his cohorts that he was keeping Olney's bed and his wife warm for him. Olney seethed as rage poured through every pore of his body, screaming for some kind of release, some way to set things right. But there was nothing he could do. For if he killed the overseer, they would surely kill him.

"A few months later when Leitha grew big with child, Olney, beside himself with a new rage and insane jealousy, didn't even wait to see the color of the child's skin. He packed his bag and said he was going back into the swamp. He told Leitha he was going hunting, but he didn't tell her for what.

"Two days later when he returned, he told Leitha to let it be known that he was gone for good. Gone for another ten months, deep into the swamp. Then he hid Leitha in a tree house he had fashioned for her at the edge of the swamp. Returning alone to his homestead, he dragged a huge canvas bag behind him. Then he prepared the cabin.

"When the overseer heard that the beautiful Leitha was once again available to him, he wasted no time getting on his horse and riding to her shack.

"He ran up the uneven steps and across the weathered wood of the front porch, shoving his way past the open planked door with a reckless air of propriety. He was smiling in triumph when he saw Leitha's form squirming under the covers.

"'Your lusty lover's back, Leitha. And you know how much I love it when you fight me,' he added as he pulled the coverlet off and down to the floor.

"His loud scream reverberated and joined with the echo of a bolt being thrown from the outside of the cabin door. Olney had reversed the door on its hinges and now, the overseer was trapped inside. Earlier, Olney had nailed both windows shut and crisscrossed the animal membrane that let light in with wires wrapped and cinched around wooden pegs.

"No one heard the overseer's screams, except Olney, who was not about to put him out of his misery. When his screams died out and even the mournful whimpering subsided, he went to tell Leitha that she had been avenged.

"Later that evening when a search was underway for the errant overseer, Olney snuck back and waited until just the right moment to open the door wide.

"The men who found the overseer, couldn't help him. He was quite obviously dead. His body was swollen twice its normal size, his tongue and lips cracked and bluish-black in his distorted face, his eyes frozen wide open in terror. The reason he was dead became quite clear as they all had to scramble to get out of the way and run from what appeared to be at least fifty snakes of various colors and sizes. Also in the oppressive night air were swarms of angry wasps, the low drone of their anger escalating as they found new targets for their venom-laced fury.

"'Jaysus!' one man screeched as a snake went for his boot. His partner tried to shoot it, but missed, instead blowing off the end of the man's foot. As the man screamed and hopped up and down on the other foot, the other men ran from the cabin cursing and pulling at their clothing.

"The man who was hopping finally managed to get out of the cabin but tripped down the steps falling flat on his face. The snakes and wasps followed, crawling and swarming all over him. There wasn't a man left to hear his cries for help, as they were all floundering in the nearby swamp.

"Olney took a stick and carefully pulled the snakes off of the hysterical man. Then he dragged him over to the swamp and threw him in with his friends.

"One week later, Olney went back to shingle gettin' without a single worry that Leitha would be visited in his absence."

CR

Mareesa finished with, "And so, de po' man lib an' de rich man died, and de road beyan de moon was a hole 'he light when a bleck, bleck chile was born to Leitha."

There was silence for many minutes as Shelby sat transfixed. Ben was reclining on his elbows chewing on a blade of grass, and Mareesa leaned against the trunk of the tree, her eyes closed as if in sleep.

Out of the blue, Ben stood up, stretched and said, "So, Ball dem were very bexed with the buckra and scattered was nests an snekes in da bayd that meked it de buckras time obdyin'?"

Both women turned to look at him, stared for a minute, and then burst into wild laughter.

"Lawdy, I never had no one listen like you!" Mareesa chided.

Ben smiled and reached his hand down to help Shelby up. Just then two little children came running down the hill, screaming and laughing.

"Oh, my. Those two could wake up the dead. I'd best get them away from this cemetery. There are some folks here I wouldn't be happy about seeing again."

Ben and Shelby laughed with her, then they thanked her for coming out to see them. Ben snuck her a generous tip as he helped her up.

Mareesa acknowledged it with a big grin and said, "I'm sorry none of my stories dealt with Charles Garrett. But I'll tell you what," she held up the two twenties Ben had just given her. "I'll give one of these to Janeel, the dream lady, with specific instructions to send you a dream about him."

"I think I already had a dream about him," Ben said.

"Then you must be a good receiver, or something you touched that was his triggered it. Go to sleep by midnight every night next week. Janeel will send you a dream."

"Is this hoodoo?"

"Now what do you think, professor? Are you tellin' me you believe in this stuff?" she asked with a smile. Then she took each child in hand and started walking up the steep hill.

"Quite a lady," Ben commented as they also began the long climb, purposely lagging far behind. "So educated, yet so unwilling to give up the culture that sprang from a time when educating blacks was against the law. It's like she's encouraging the Gullah people to strive for more and to take advantage of every educational opportunity, yet still reveling in hearing their sassy baby talk."

"It's all about remembering where you come from and the people who came before you. She just doesn't want anyone to forget the hard lives her ancestors led to get them to this time of freedom and choices. Can you imagine not having the choice to live where you wanted, or do the work you were born to do, or to marry your own true love?"

"No. No, I can't. I can't imagine not teaching. And I certainly can't imagine bending over all day, everyday, picking cotton or rice."

"And I can't imagine not being a steward of the coastline, not being able to make a difference for the future. Sowing seed, picking beans, and harvesting tobacco seems like such a mundane way to waste a life. I'm glad I wasn't born black a century and a half ago. To have all your choices taken away from you . . . "

"Enough morose thought, let's get a motel room."

Her head swung around quickly. She had just bent to tie her shoe on a stump. *Oh the smug bastard*! Now, she looked up and examined the leer on Ben's handsome face. It was a put-on lecherous look that was almost comical in its exaggeration.

"I can see from the look on your face that intimacy

is the farthest thing from your mind right now," Ben said with a lazy sideways grin.

"Well, it's not exactly the farthest, but I've decided your good looks have made things a bit too easy for you. You're going to have to pass a test before I check into the No-Tell Motel with you."

"A test, huh? Did I ever tell you how good I am at true or false and multiple choice? What's the subject and format?"

"Make it an essay. Two hundred words on why you're the one to take something away from me that can never, ever be replaced."

"Great. You're a virgin. I should have known. I thought when you indicated no one had gotten the foreplay right, that they had still run the bases and made home plate. Just left you without a score of your own. I had no idea you'd stopped the play."

"Had to. It never seemed right. I never felt comfortable."

"Well then you've made good choices. But I think you're going to be way out of my league. I need something simpler."

"You need somebody easy?" she asked astonished at his cavalier attitude.

"No, not easy that way. Easy, as in uncomplicated."

"Just for fun then."

"You make it sound so tawdry. I *am* looking for much more than that, just not something with the permanence that taking a woman's virginity normally entails. I can't get involved with anyone right now, and I certainly don't have anything to give back to a woman who gives me an irretrievable part of herself. As much as I want you, it wouldn't be fair to you. Award-winning essay or not, I feel I have to curb my urges where you're concerned so you don't get hurt."

"You can't hurt me unless I let you. So we don't go to a motel. Take me to the beach and I'll let you get to second base. There's nothing says we can't just neck like teenagers."

"Teenagers don't neck anymore. Even they run the bases and slide into home. But I would be more than happy to sit with you on the beach and feel you up."

"That's second base?"

"Yes. Kissing is first, necking which includes petting, is second; clothes generally stay on. Touching the genitals is third; clothing is either off or out of the way, and penetration is all the way."

"I've never actually had it broken down like that before."

"I've never actually gone into this much detail about it verbally myself. But I can tell you, it's certainly setting the tone. I can hardly wait to get you alone on the beach." He stopped walking beside her and faced her. His hands reached out and cupped her head. His eyes bored into hers and she saw the heat building in them. "This is a mistake. I know I shouldn't be doing this." But his words had no effect. He brought his lips down over hers anyway; the moment they met, his heat turned to flame and he fairly consumed her.

Chapter Thirteen
Beau Marecage, Just Outside the Cemetery

Slanting first one way and then the other, his lips took full possession of hers. Opening her mouth to his deeper onslaught, he took siege of her tongue and forced it to follow his while he backed her into the shelter of a stand of pear trees until she had one at her back.

Her quiet, mournful groan acted like a magnet to his hips, and he frantically slammed into her, molding his blatant hardness into her pelvis. While one hand captured the back of her head and his fingers delved into her thick curls, his other dove under her T-shirt and ran up her back. His splayed hand moved along her soft, warm skin until he was reminded that she was braless, then his hand quickly worked its way to her front and slid up to capture a naked breast.

So small, yet so firm and so sensitive. The nipple was already beaded and begging for the attention of his thumb. He flicked it back and forth mercilessly, abrading it roughly. Overcome with passion he plucked, pinched, and pulled on it as his tongue went concave in his mouth in anticipation of licking the tantalizingly sweet nubbin.

The completion of some kind of circuitry she had not known existed in her body caused her knees to buckle and her center to throb. She began to join in the gyrations that were pressing her into the tree. When the circling motions weren't enough to satisfy and give her the relief of pressure that she so desperately sought, she stood on tiptoe and pressed her straining vulva against his hard, throbbing ridge. She rode his length up and down, pressing feverishly to produce more sensation through the material of her shorts. When he reached down and grabbed the back of her knee and lifted her leg over his hip, she keened. Through the crotch of her shorts, her blossoming center opened and pressed very deliberately and suggestively against him. As she repeatedly arched and rubbed into him, he lifted her leg even higher.

"We're way beyond second base here," he breathed against the side of her neck, and then as if sensing her frantically contriving to reach something, he pressed her fully back against the tree and jammed himself hard against her, making the connection bold in the center of their bodies. Deftly, he ducked his head, pulled up her shirt and suckled on a pink-tipped breast.

He felt her convulsive spasms followed by a series of remarkably strong, rhythmic pulsations. His mind alerted himself to his own extremely fragile state; it instructed him not to move even a hair closer into her. With all the strength he could muster, he forced his body to heed the panicked warning. Instantly he stopped thrusting against her swollen and distended lips. The abrupt discontinuation of the contact through their now-dampened clothing banked his desire and began to draw away some of the sensation from his engorged shaft. In order to stifle his need to roar from the frustration, he bit lightly into the side of her breast.

Shelby leaned her head back against the tree, her eyes closed as she savored the incredible things her body had just done. *Who would have thought?*

She was floating in and out of some sort of delirium, astonished with what her body was capable of; a high she never dreamed possible, caused purely and naturally from touch. Her body fought with her mind to come back into control. *She was still a virgin, wasn't she?* All this had been achieved simply by being with Ben and responding to his wonderful touch. With her eyes still closed she listened to the quiet of the late afternoon. She heard birds twittering in the tree above them and wondered if they were talking about what had just gone on at the base of their home. She listened as Ben tried to get control of his raspy breathing.

"Damn, I can't believe I just did that."

"I do believe that my clothes and your clothes are still on. According to your definition, we didn't even get to third base, so why is it that I feel like something climactic just happened?"

"Because it most certainly did." His head was now resting on her shoulder, her shirt bunched between them. "Or at least from what I can gather, it did."

"Did I miss the part where we talked about past partners, communicable diseases, and birth control?"

He sheepishly nodded. "Yeah, you did. Didn't you notice when I surreptitiously donned a condom?"

"No," she chuckled.

"Would that I had, I could have used something to deaden the effect of you rubbing against me." He moaned as he pulled away from her, and using the tree trunk as a brace, he tried to stand on his own. Once stable, his fingers plucked at the denim fabric covering the long bulge that was still quite prominent. It started just below his belt and went down to the crotch of his jeans. *This is going to be a fun way to drive home.*

Shelby tugged her cotton t-shirt into place while she watched him. Then he looked up and his eyes met hers.

There was such a softness and an entranced look to her that he stilled. Her face and neck were flushed, her lips puffy and rosy from his kisses, but it was her eyes that held him. They were the eyes of a woman who had just learned about the power of her body. A woman in awe of her feminine nature. A virgin in more ways than one, he realized and leaned over to caress her cheek and to softly kiss her. "Welcome to Oz," he breathed against her cheek. Then softly into her ear, he murmured, "And thank you for letting me be the man to take you on that first journey."

Shelby met his eyes as he pulled away from that sweet, lingering kiss. She thought she heard the notes from the song "Part of Your World" from *The Little Mermaid* soundtrack wafting in the breeze high above the tree. If she didn't know better, she'd think this was the beginning of something remarkably corny, like love or something.

They straightened their clothing, glanced over at the cemetery, and then back again at the tree.

"I'm tempted to carve our initials here," he said rubbing his hand over the bark, "giving a permanent marker to this significant and momentous occasion."

"Our initials as in B.K. and S.L. with a heart around them?"

"You're pushing it, but okay, I'll give you a heart. But

it's B.K. M.D., Ph.D., if you don't mind," he teased.

"Okay Doctor. But as much as I'd like to see you spend the next hour chiseling with your Swiss Army knife, I don't think we should deface private property."

"Do you think there's a tree somewhere around with Charlie and Miss X's initials on it?"

"No, I'm almost sure that there couldn't be."

"Why's that?"

"Well, for one, the tree would probably be dead and gone by now; and if for some reason it survived, scarring would have grown over it. Two, carving initials into a tree did not become popular until the early twentieth century. Sometime along the time of 'A Bicycle Built for Two,' I believe. I think I read that some movie in the thirties popularized carving initials or names into trees."

They walked arm-in-arm up the long hill, enjoying the silence and the waning energy of the day.

"You don't wear a bra."

"What would be the point?"

"I guess I just wasn't expecting you to be so easily accessible to my hand."

"I don't have enough to worry about. It's not like I'm ever going to droop or sag."

"I like your size. I can't really explain it, but I think your body is just perfect. I like that you're tiny and petite. I like that I can span your waist with my hands."

"Thank you."

"So, do you think Mareesa is right about the dream?" Ben asked.

"She knew Charles left something here that he dearly cherished. If I'm not mistaken, I think she knew it was a woman. I think she even knew her name."

"Then why didn't she tell us?"

"Maybe she doesn't trust us. These were her people's

people," Shelby said waving a hand around to encompass the plantation and its surroundings.

"Maybe she'll have Janine tell me in my dream."

"Janeel. And you'd better get on the road. It's going to be your bedtime soon," she chided.

"Midnight is not my bedtime. You don't expect me to go along with all this do you?"

"I don't believe in the supernatural, but I do believe there are forces that control our destiny. I'd try not to make anybody mad one way or the other, just in case," she whispered.

As they walked onto the deserted parking lot, Ben took Shelby's hands in his. "I had a wonderful day. This has been extraordinary. I wish we didn't have to part like this. I don't feel like I've had nearly my fill of you."

"It *has* been pretty wonderful. You're fun to be with."

"You are incredible to be with," he said as he bent to kiss her on the cheek. "When can I see you again? When can I try to make it to third base the right way?"

She smiled up at him and just about drowned in his dreamy dark eyes. "I'm free every weekend, just name the day."

"How would you feel about coming to Chapel Hill the weekend after next? I'll show you around and take you to a show or something."

"That sounds nice, but where would I stay?"

"With me."

"Oh."

"Not ready for that yet?"

"I don't think so."

"Then I'll get you a room. Don't worry about it, I'll take care of everything."

"Sounds great."

"Well, have a safe drive back."

"You, too."

He took her keys from her hand and opened her car door. When he handed them back to her he bent and kissed her lightly on the lips. She slid in, attached her seat belt, and he closed the door. He listened for her to start the car before heading over to his roadster.

Opening the door, he slid into the seat and turned the engine over. Then, decisively, he gunned it, pulled out of his slot and beat her to the entrance gate, blocking her from leaving. He put his car in park, got out, and strode over to her. Then he opened her door, reached in to unhook her, and pulled her into his arms for a masterful kiss. Possessively, his arms wrapped around her as he practically lifted her into the air. His mouth crushed hers and his tongue delved deeply while his hands moved to her bottom to pull her hard into him.

When he released her, he was breathing harshly. "I couldn't let you go without tasting you one more time. Here, something for the ride home." He tossed a can of the benne cookies onto the passenger seat. "I promise to help you burn off the extra calories whenever you're ready." With one final thrust of his pelvis against hers, he released her. "I wish I wasn't committed to a book signing tomorrow morning. I'd like nothing more than to follow you home and show you a few more foreplay techniques."

"You have a repertoire of these?"

"Oh, yes. Believe it. Over the years I have learned how to study, and I have studied the art of foreplay extensively."

"My loss."

"Mine, too." He ran his finger down her cheek and turned to head back to his car when he heard her say, "Here, I have something for you, too." He turned back, and Shelby handed him a bag from the kitchen store they'd been in that afternoon.

He took it and opened it. Then he put his hand inside and drew out a stainless steel bar. Embossed on the front was a picture of an onion inside a big circle with a line intersecting it like a No Parking sign would have. Boldly the packaging proclaimed that this product would get rid of onion smells, among other things.

"Thanks, I'll give it a try. I'll let you know."

He bent and kissed her lightly on the cheek and then went back to his car. What an imp.

Shelby climbed slowly back into her car and after fidgeting with the seat belt, she managed to pull through the gates without hitting anything. All the way home, she kept pressing her fingertips to her lips, savoring the memory of his last kiss. It had been a kiss of abandon, almost a kiss of surrender. He'd seemed out of control somehow, like he was a man coming under the spell of a woman. A man fighting not to lose control, but not about to deny the inevitable, either.

If fairy tales did come true, hers was unfolding and she couldn't wait to turn to the next page.

Chapter Fourteen—Savory and Sage
Chapel Hill, NC

Ben arrived at his apartment a little after nine Monday night and try as he might, two things he could not deny. One, was that he could not stop thinking of the woman he was mentally calling "ma petite" in his head, and the other was that he was incredibly fatigued. He could not remember being this tired–not during undergrad finals, post-grad thesis deadlines, or even when he had stayed up four days in a row polishing up the dissertation for his doctorate. By 10:30 he stopped fighting it, stripped off his clothes, and slid under the covers of his king-sized bed. He'd had serious intentions of finishing the editing on Lloyd's book, but now even the thought of reading one single line forced his eyes closed. His last cogent thought was *midnight, bah!*

CR

The black man and woman were talking in low whispers, but their voices were anything but friendly.

"You have to rid yourself of it!"

"I cannot. Even the hoodoo woman says naught can be done. I have gone past the time. It has been five months since he left. He told me he would be no longer than three!"

"Savory, he is a white man! Why would you trust his word? And even so, he is not obligated to you in any way. Just because he bedded you, that does not speak of his matrimonial intentions. No one will believe that you are betrothed. I don't believe you!"

"He told me we'd go to Barbados," she sobbed.

"Well, little sister, he is nowhere to be found. I told you two months ago to take care of this babe. Now you have put me in a very bad position. I will have to promise you to Alred."

"No! No! I will not become Alred's wife! He is blacker than ebony and he sweats like a pig!"

"He is a farrier Savory. The bellows are hot!"

"I do not care. He always smells of filthy horses and putrid smoke. I will not wed with him."

"You have no choice. There is no one else. He is the only simpleton unwed who cannot even count the months. Even your rounded shape will not phase him."

"I will not!"

"Then what do you suggest we do?" Sage asked snidely.

"I could tell Charles' sire. Mayhaps his father will want to be guardian to Charles' babe. Or Ida! Ida has the lady's ear. Surely as fraught as the lady is over Charles being missing, she would welcome his child."

"You are tetched in the head! They will not

consider a white man's blow by on a black slave their grandchild."

"Sage, you have always been more than a brother to me. We have always been so close, why are you not standing with me on this?"

Savory's twin visibly steeled his anger. "You were always more than just a sister to me also," he gritted out. "Even though we are blood, I have always wanted you. Wanted you in ways that shame me. So I have no compassion or caring in my heart for a man who has taken you as I so often wished to."

Savory gasped at his words and took a small step back, her hand at her throat.

"I do not wish you any harm Savory, but neither do I wish you with another man. I never have. Alred is a simpleton. He can provide for you and this," he waved his hand at her midsection, "bastard you're soon to whelp. If you tell him it is his, he will know no different."

"I cannot," she wept. "Not Alred . . . . No, no, no. Please. Please. Oh Charles," she cried. It was obvious that her heart was broken and her spirit crushed. She fell to the ground sobbing uncontrollably.

"The anger that is seething in my heart is boiling over. If anybody had a right to take you, my beautiful Savory, it should have been me. Brother or not, I have lusted for you since you attained womanhood. I am even more angered by my own stupid hesitancy. I should have taken you years ago. Instead, a white man plowed you and filled your belly with his seed! Charles will not be returning. We must make plans. I will inform Alred." He turned his back on her and stalked away.

Chapter Fifteen
Instant Messaging

Shelby: I can't believe you had a dream last night. Just like Mareesa said. This Janeel must be a very powerful storyteller or dream giver or whatever she is. And this Sage . . . man, what an awful brother. He was despicable.

Ben: That he was. I'm so glad you were up early this morning so I could get your reaction. I've got to tell you, I'm spooked as all get out by these dreams. Think there's anything to this or do I just have one hell of an imagination?

Shelby: This is just too weird to be coincidence. There must be something to it. I guess the only way we'll know is to find something that corroborates your dream. We could go back to Beau Marecage and find out if there ever really was a Sage and Savory.

Ben: There was. First thing this morning I ran

129

to the library. There's a book called *Slaves in the Family* by Edward Ball. It's a compilation of slave listings from all over the South. They're in it. They were fraternal twins. When I saw their names in print, I just about passed out sitting there at the reference table.

Shelby: Maybe you have some kind of ESP or something?

Ben: You're just like me, not willing to believe all this hocus pocus stuff.

Shelby: Ben, I will believe anything you tell me until you give me reason not to.

Ben: I forgot to tell you that, in the dream, you and I were making love in the picture-in-picture corner.

Shelby: Okay, now you've given me reason not to.

Ben: You have an incredibly lovely body.

Shelby: Okay, I'll believe you again. Hey, I gotta go. Time to get to work.

Ben: I don't see how anyone can call walking on the beach all day work.

Shelby: I don't see how anyone delving into greasy, grimy, grizzly guts all day calls that work either.

Ben: Touché. And I'm on my way out, too. Later.

Shelby: Before you go, how's the steel working?

Ben: Remind me to ask you next weekend. I can't tell. I think I'm immune. But it is a lot cheaper than using soap.

Shelby: You're still supposed to use soap!!!

Ben: I know.

03

Shelby steadily worked her pile of requests and requisitions down. Every day she made some headway toward getting the coast back in balance. She worked long hours the week she got back from Beau Marecage, then on the weekend she volunteered to help the locals in Calabash pick up trash along the road. It was Labor Day weekend and even though they had just had one hell of a hurricane, the tourists were in full force to send the summer away in grand style.

The aftermath of a hurricane on the coast is an odd time for emotions. Amidst gung-ho rebuilding there are dispirited avowals to rethink policies about development on the fragile sands; so naturally, Shelby was spending a lot of time in meetings lately. She thought back over her week trying to find a situation or circumstance she had been able to improve, for either the petitioner or the environment. Mentally she ticked off each day of the week and its significance.

Well, she had seen to the implementation of some monitoring wells in a wetland restoration project, and then there was that Sargassum debate she'd participated in with the National Marine Fisheries Service. It looked like a decision would be coming soon in their favor, prohibiting harvesting of the brown Atlantic seaweed anywhere within U.S. jurisdictional waters, except off the coast of North Carolina, where it would be limited to 2.3 metric tons per year. That was something. The fact that her office now had a dispute with a homeowner regarding securing a permit to repair a seawall, and that it was going all the way to the State Supreme Court hadn't been good news, though.

The Commission was reviewing permits for stone riprap groins less than twenty-five feet long in estuaries and public-trust waters, and that was looking pretty good. The current C.A.M.A. law only allowed permits for wooden ones now, and those were woefully inadequate. An oceanographer from the Office of Coastal Resources Management had congratulated her on the report she wrote about the house in South Carolina. The one where the erosion point was moving so fast that now the state's regulatory baseline of control, dictated as where the ocean's highest tide line reached, had moved right up under the house, practically condemning it. She smiled to herself. She *had* written a good report. Then she frowned. The three-quarter of a million-dollar house *was* going to fall into the ocean. She was saddened by the waste and angered by the clod heads that had allowed it to be built there in the first place. Then there were the hearings being held by the N.C. Division of Coastal Management discussing incorporating new, long-range average annual erosion rates into the state's oceanfront development rules. Those meetings were always spirited to say the least. Yes, it had been a busy week, that was for darned sure! Sometimes she wished she could just do her job and not care so fervently about it.

As she rode her bike on the beach Sunday morning and watched a group of pelicans soaring in line across the water, she wondered what Ben was doing on this holiday weekend. The gentle, lapping waves ran under the wheels of her bike as she peddled and free-wheeled on the packed sand. Monday she went to a pig-picking and entertained her friends with some of the storyteller's tales. Driving home that night from Shallotte, she realized she was lonely and anxious for the weekend to be over so that the week could begin, and the following weekend would arrive. Next weekend she would go to Chapel Hill and see Ben.

Each day she found herself wondering what his day was like; what his office was like; what his apartment was like; and what the young coeds were like. Occasionally, she thought of the woman Ben had loved who had died before he realized he was in love. Then at night, she would lay in bed and remember his kisses, and the way his hands had felt on her. She was beginning to have strange feelings, at the oddest times. And her body, once so familiar, was now new to her. By the end of the week, she finally conceded to the feelings and acknowledged just what they were, what they stemmed from. She was in lust. Full-fledged, heat-up-your-body lust.

Chapter Sixteen—Ben's Dream
Sage at Ida's Deathbed
Beau Marecage,
late 1800s

*I*da. *I have done one bad thing after another. I do not even know where to begin, but as you are dying here, I will tell you all. You will get the full story and I will purge my black heart. Do you mind, my faithful Ida? You, my great aunt who has always cared for me. And Savory. Do you remember Savory, Ida?"*

The old woman's eyes opened and she smiled, "Savory . . . . Is Savory here?"

"No, no," he hushed her. "She will never come back. Wherever she is, I hope that she is finally happy. But she will never come back. And I am the reason why."

"You, Sage? Why would you not let her come back?"

"Oh, Ida, would that I could find her, I would beg her to come back! She hates me, I fear, and with good reason. But the reason she has, is not the true reason. If she knew the true reason, she would come back and plant a dagger in my heart."

"Sage? What are you telling me? What have you

done?" she whispered hoarsely up at him.

Her rheumy eyes were already watering with tears and he knew when he had confessed all, that she would run out of them.

"Three months after Charles Garrett left to run the blockade, Savory came to me to tell me of their love affair. It was hard for me to believe then, and truth be told, I am not quite sure I believe all she said now. But I should have. She had never lied to me before.

"She said she was with child. That they were to be married on his return, but she was worried because when she was up at the house, all she heard was that no one knew where Charles was. Then a month or so later she told me that a slave had been dispatched from Brunswick Town with a mount for him. But no one knew who the slave was, since there were so many new ones there, and neither the slave nor Charles was ever seen again."

Ida nodded and her eyes had a faraway look in them. "Yes, I remember that time. It was a time of intense worry. Many soldiers were being killed by Yankees on the southern roads outside of Richmond and Wilmington."

"I was that slave, Ida."

"You?" she asked, trying to get up on her elbows to look at him better.

He helped her back against the pillows. "Yes. I was that slave. I had been sent to Brunswick Town as a courier for Master Lucas. He needed to tell Master George that according to the monthly tallies on the barrels of tar and pitch there was enough to pay the taxes on both the mill and the plantation, as the plantation was now doing so poorly. He was instructing Master George to pay all the taxes they owed for the last year. I got there and went to find Master George so I could give him the message. I was told Master George no longer ran the mills, that it was the Yankee's now and Master George was their prisoner. I was escorted into the camp mess to quench my thirst and fill my belly. I was in the mess when a messenger came from Charles instructing his brother to send a horse for him. The Yankees sent some soldiers, but when they returned that night and said they couldn't find him, the officer in charge was furious. I raised my hand and volunteered to take a horse to Master Charles. I told them I knew what he looked like and where he'd likely be. No one there knew me; but as none of them had the desire to go because it was bitter cold, they gave me a pass, two horses, and sent me. They said if I didn't return with him, they'd come looking for me and then I wouldn't have nothin' to worry about 'cept picking my frozen fingers and toes out of the Cape Fear River.

"Two mounts were saddled and side bags packed with provisions and then I was off. I found Master Charles right where I knew he would be, waiting for a horse so he could speed his way home. Home to my sister. I decided 'twould be better not to tell him about Master George and the Yankees, as I wanted to go home, back to Savory, and they was only going to kill us anyway. So, I pretended everything was all right while I tried to decide what to do. But I could not get the thought of him layin' over my sister out of my mind. I was growing more and more incensed with each mile that took us further south.

"In idle conversation, I let it slip that Savory was becoming huge with child. The smile that lit his face sealed his doom in my eyes. He was ecstatic that he had ruined my darling Savory and left her with child.

"I can still remember his words to me, 'I am going to be a father. I can hardly believe it. How is she? Is she *faring well? Oh we must ride faster! I ache to be with her.'* Then he began a gallop that was so fast, I could hardly keep up. And of course, no further conversation was possible, so all I kept hearing in my head was, '*I ache to be with her.'*

"With each sound of the hooves pounding in my ears, I envisioned him rutting with my sister. When in my mind's eye I saw him arch and throw his head back when he spilled his seed, I collapsed.

"His mindless, breakneck pace was broken when he sensed that I was no longer accompanying him. He slowed and came back for me; and that was a mistake we both sorely regret.

"He had returned to me and tried to revive me. Just then we both heard the horses, and turned to see a group of Yankees approaching. My foggy brain cleared quickly and we remounted and broke for the trees.

"We urged our mounts forward through thick stands and underbrush until we came to the river. Riding the bluff we looked for a place to cross so we could escape the Yankees. A few miles further south, we chanced to find a series of fording ropes attached to sturdy trees. Later, we would discover that they had just been used by the crew of a blockade runner that had run aground on the island in front of us. The wind was biting and the water chilled our bones, but we grabbed hold of the guiding ropes and urged the horses across. Once on the opposite shore, Master Garrett tossed me his knife and instructed me to sever the lines. That done, we made our way to the interior of the island and to safety. Collapsing on the dunes, we noticed a ship burning down by the beach. It appeared to be a blockade runner and that explained the chance encounter with the Yankees. Union ships must have signaled them from the inlet. They were now looking for the stranded crew.

"I, no longer afraid of being captured, remembered that beside me on the sand was my enemy. I became bold and with the knife I still had in my possession, I turned and surprised him as he lay there recovering on the ground. I drove the blade well into his midsection and watched as his eyes became wide with shock. Blood was already staining his coat when I pulled the blade out. It had broken inside him. I know that had I not had the jump on him, he would have been far more than a fair contender. But, trusting me as he did, he did not realize how vulnerable he was to a man who loathed him.

"I screamed at him that he should not have taken Savory, that she belonged to me and always had. That I knew her in her nakedness long before we were even born, that she was to be mine one day, not his. He staggered to his feet and came at me. The action caused more blood to flow and I saw him becoming lightheaded. He shook his head as if to clear it, then started mumbling about how cold he was. He saw the ship burning at the edge of the beach. I was backing well out of his reach when he turned on me and spat out, 'It is not you that she loved, it was me. That is how it always will be. You have not killed our love, you have just killed me.'

"Then he tripped and stumbled down the long beach until he came to the water's edge. He waded in, his hands high in the air as if warming himself from the raging fire. I watched as he approached the burning and smoldering hulk as if he planned to climb aboard. He pulled out his gun, tossed it onto the ship's deck, then just before he reached the ship's ladder, he lost his footing and fell into the water.

"I waited for several minutes, and when he did not surface, I gathered both horses and made my way south.

I lost one horse when I tried to cross a monstrous inlet. It was the Master's, the one with all the provisions.

"It took me five days to make it back to Beau Marecage. I had a fever and chills that rightfully should have taken me. No one ever knew that I was the slave sent to fetch Master Charles. They just thought I was coming back from taking the tallies to Brunswick Town. Savory nursed me back to health. The woman who carried the seed of the man I had murdered, kept me from dying. Had she known what I had done, I do not doubt she would have finished me off herself.

"I recovered physically, but my mind would never let me forget my grievous deed. When I forced Savory to marry Alred, I compounded my sins. Then I raped her and I lost my soul. When she ran away and left me forever, I lost my heart."

"Why have you told me this?" Ida croaked.

"In hopes that someone can say I am forgiven before I die."

"It cannot be me."

Sage watched her as her eyes closed and she shivered. Assuming she had passed, he left the room.

Later, when her granddaughter checked on her, she found Ida staring at the ceiling above her. "Grandmother?"

Ida turned her head and smiled faintly at her young grandchild. "Selma, fetch me the storyteller. Make it quick, I have to set things straight before I go."

೧೩

Ben awakened from the dream perspiring and agitated. He had only meant to take a quick afternoon nap before his lecture this evening, but looking at the clock, he saw he had slept through the dinner hour. He would have to hustle if he wanted to get to the hall in time but he realized that he desperately needed a shower. He picked up the phone and called the coordinator for the lecture series and asked if things could be arranged for him to be the last speaker instead of the first.

Hanging up the phone, he hung his head between his bent knees, his hands thoroughly mussing his hair. Standing and stretching tall, he picked up the phone again and dialed Shelby's number. For some unknown reason, he felt compelled to call her. This was something he wanted to talk to her about now, not in e-mails over the course of a week.

As soon as he heard her voice, his body relaxed. The tenseness left him and he actually sighed. She was comforting, calming. And he wished he could hold her right now.

"Hey, babe," he said, loving the way that sounded and the attachment implied as to how he felt for her.

"Ben! How are you?" her voice was soft and silky, yet he noted there was an element of surprise at his call.

"You are not going to believe this, but I've had another dream since the one I told you about just two days ago."

"Wow. That's three so far."

"This one was by far the most revealing. And the scariest. But I think I found out what happened to Charles."

"Really?"

"Yes." Then he proceeded to tell her about the dream.

CR

"So somewhere there's a storyteller who's been handed down the tale of Savory, Sage, and Charles?" Shelby asked.

"Possibly."

"Someone who might even know about Savory's baby? From what Sage said, did you get the impression that Savory took the baby away with her?"

"Listen to you. 'From what Sage said . . .' as if all this was real. But no, I didn't get that impression at all. Then again, I didn't get the impression she'd left it behind either."

"Then that's the next step."

"What's the next step?" he practically croaked out.

"Finding out what happened to the baby. That's the next step."

"Ugghh," he groaned. "My head is splitting and I've got to take a shower and get over to the lecture hall. You figure out what happened to the baby!"

"Okay, I'll work on it. You go get ready. Are we still on for next weekend?"

"Of course. My headache will be long gone by then. If not . . ."

"If not, what?"

He smiled as he talked into the phone. "I guess you never heard of the cure-all for headaches?"

"Aspirin?"

"Not exactly. This cure is a little more . . . physical."

"Oh. Does that really work?"

"The theory is that the pressure of the blood reversing and heading south, relieves tension in the brain. Makes sense but honestly, I don't know. In my experience, it's usually the woman with the headache."

"So, you're not exactly a Fellatio?"

"What???"

"I meant Romeo!" she quickly corrected.

"Good God, woman! Are you doing this on purpose? Now I desperately need a shower! But keep that thought and I'll sure as hell try to keep this damned headache 'til you get here. G'night, Shelby."

"'Bye Ben. Pleasant dreams."

"Yeah, that'll be a switch."

Chapter Seventeen—Alred
St. Helena Island, SC

The fatigue Ben felt was so foreign to him he didn't know quite how to handle it. He was beginning to question whether he needed to start taking vitamins or some kind of supplement. He decided that exercise was probably what he needed, so he gathered his workout clothes and went over to the apartment complex's workout room. He warmed up on the treadmill, then pumped weights and used the universal equipment for an hour. Finally, feeling like he had invigorated his body as much as it was willing to take for the moment, he limped into the sauna.

The cedar walls and benches were quite cold to the touch. Apparently it had been some time since the sauna had been used. He set the temperature dials on the brazier to the highest settings and tossed two large ladlefuls of water from the bucket onto the briquettes. Then he stripped down to his jockeys and lay down on the lower bench, stretching out his long body before placing a towel over his lower torso in case someone else came in. He grabbed another towel, mopped his brow with it, and carefully folded and placed it under his head. A minute later, he was fast asleep.

CR

The shadow of a hysterical woman, sobbing and shaking, floated in front of his eyes. Then the image shimmered into full view and there was Savory standing beside a huge, dark black man. She had a fully distended belly that she cradled from the bottom as she wept uncontrollably. Savory and the hulking black man stood side-by-side in front of another black man. This man was in a long black robe and he appeared to be praying and blessing the couple. The towering behemoth of a man gripped her arm tightly and led her away from a small gathering of people. Around them young and old women alike sniffed into handkerchiefs while the men huddled around congratulating the oafish man. All but one man was smiling. The handsome man's good looks were marred by the look of intense anger and jealousy in his eyes. The man was Sage. The injustice of the forced marriage was mirrored in the eyes of the bride, the beautiful, young Savory. As the bridegroom pulled his new bride down a long, dusty path, she whimpered and turned back to appeal to the man with the hard, ebony eyes.

"What's your hurry Alred?" a man yelled after him. "Seems you've done the deed and been on her already!"

The men standing around laughed out loud at this and Alred turned to glare at them. The look on his face told them that he truly didn't understand what their banter inferred. He gave them an indistinct grunt and continued on his way, pulling his very reluctant bride in his wake.

The moment after Alred dragged his new wife over the threshold, he barred the door and turned to her. Reaching for the laces covering her bosom, he fumbled with the ties. She fought his hands with hers, but was no match for his huge, rough hands. He bared her heaving bosom and before she could turn away from his hot gaze, he grabbed her and pushed her toward the bed.

"Up, your skirt," he grunted.

When she cringed and turned away from him again, he reached out and slapped her. Then he threw her onto his grimy bed. His hands roughly kneaded her breasts while he worked at insinuating his knee between her thighs. One hand groped her while the other lifted her skirts over her thick waist and tore her undergarment aside. Then he alternately fumbled with his breeches and groped her sex.

She squeezed her eyes tightly closed and turned her head from side to side trying to block out the view of the horrible man kneeling over her. But she didn't need to see him or feel his clumsy hands grabbing at her to know he was there. The stench of him filled her nostrils. His breath was unbelievably vile. When he breathed near her face, she felt bile rise in her throat. His body odors, rife on both him and the bed covering under her, were apparently no better. When she continued to turn her face away from his sloppy kisses, her facial features showing the horror of her disgust, he slapped her hard across the face. Her hands followed and fought with his as he grabbed first one breast and then the other before assaulting her nether parts. When the moment came that he finally managed to loosen his trousers, he brought his fat belly down until it touched hers. When his hard maleness touched her, she screamed. He forced himself down on top of her and entered her before she had finished her scream. She continued to scream and pummel his sweaty chest as he thrust into her over and over again. Her eyes wide with fear, she looked up into his contorted face. The moment he pumped his seed into her, she let loose with an ear-piercing scream. The revulsion in her eyes was unmistakable, but in the event it could possibly have been misinterpreted, her actions could not. Savory gave one great heave of her huge stomach and vomited all over both him and herself. Alred, oblivious to anything but his newly-discovered pleasure, grinned broadly and lifted himself off of her.

A moment later, Savory's water broke and leaked out onto the bed. Through her terrible cries of agony Alred was finally alerted to the fact that Savory, his new wife, was birthing his child. A midwife was brought and while Savory labored to deliver her baby, Alred crowed to the men who had gathered around his hut about his virility. He put a baby on her their very first time. The men did not bother to correct him.

But Alred was not as stupid as Sage thought. The moment he saw the baby, he knew that it was not his. The skin was far too light to be a child of his. Dense as he was, he finally got a glimmer of what had gone on. While the midwife attended to his wife, he took the child and carried her deep into the forest. Savory, frantic with worry, yet unable to go after him, waited as the small village community hunted for Alred and her baby girl.

By dawn of the next day, Savory managed to climb out of the bed and crawl through the forest. A baby's cry that no one else could hear led her to her abandoned daughter. Savory succumbed to her frail condition and passed out on the floor of pine needles holding her babe *in her arms against her breast. When she awakened many hours later, raindrops were pelting them. She knew her child was not safe here, that she had to take her baby and run.*

ଔ

Ben awoke with a start, the loud hiss of the brazier arousing him. It took him a few moments to recall where he was. The sound of the water sizzling sounded like the rain pouring down in the dream. The sweat soaking his body and the towel at his waist were an instant reminder of what he had been doing before dozing off. The sheen on his arm as he wiped at his face was a clear indication that he had been in the sauna for longer than the prescribed time.

He sat up, instantly sorry he had moved so suddenly; he swayed a little from lightheadedness. You know you've just had a bad dream when the feeling of dread accompanies your waking thoughts. But this time, there was more than a feeling of dread, there was a terrible sense of doom. And knowing that the fate he was concerned with was Savory's, he knew that no matter what he did, he'd be too late to do anything to alter it.

Chapter Eighteen
Chapel Hill, NC

The next evening, Ben was previewing a video for a class lecture. It was one he'd already seen, but he needed to match a few scenes up to the notes he had organized. He was in the library in a private screening room. Normally, he would not have dozed off, even for a boring film, but he'd missed out on some sleep and it was catching up to him. He was watching two doctors compare the results from slides taken of brain tissue before and after embalming procedures. His head jerked and he blinked his eyes and refocused on the screen.

CR

Savory was lovingly holding a silver baby's cup in her hands. She was thumbing the initials engraved on the front of it. C. E. G. "You gave me this the day you left," she was talking to herself as she walked through the woods. "You wanted me to have something special of yours and you filled it with tiny tea cup roses before giving it to me," she said on a sob. "'One tiny little rosebud for each tiny little baby you shall have for us,' you said."

Walking in a trance, she kept talking as if there was someone there to hear. "I kept your precious cup, wrapped in corn husks, in an old hollow tree by the swamp where we made love. Now I'm taking it, along with our baby, to Charleston to find a buyer of silver. Surely someone at one of the many shops on the waterfront will want this lovely, sweet treasure," she said wistfully.

The dream faded in and out; and then just like an old newsreel, scenes sped up in short clips. A woman holding a child was walking up a gangplank. But before she was able to board the ship, authorities came and arrested her. Then the dream went even faster. The woman is seen being dragged to a carriage. She is driven to Beau Marecage where the Garretts, standing in the massive foyer, are identifying the cup as their son's. The woman is seen pleading, unwrapping the baby and holding it up for them to see. She is gesturing from the baby to them and is seen mouthing the word 'Charles' over and over again. The Garretts are shaking their heads in disgust and pushing the baby away. She and the baby are taken upstairs and locked in an attic dormer room. The Garretts take their supper with a magistrate who repeatedly snaps a leather thong over his wrist, indicating punishment by flogging as he sits at the table.

A man is seen stealthily climbing stairs in the dark. It is Sage, coming up a back staircase, anxious to see his sister. After checking to make sure he's alone, he enters the deserted hallway. He quietly removes the hinges from the locked door and moves it aside before creeping into the room and discovering his sister sobbing as she nurses her baby. His evil lust for her is again awakened. He walks over and stares down at her. He reaches a hand down and wipes the tears from her eyes and smiles. She cringes and shrinks farther back into the chair. His smile disappears and abruptly he removes the baby from her breast and puts it on the floor. Then he pulls Savory from the chair until she is standing in front of him, and he takes her bared breast into his own mouth. With his other hand, he rips her gown from bodice to hem. His mouth covers hers as she starts to scream. He throws her to the floor and gags her with the tatters of her torn skirt. Holding her down he pulls her clothing aside and forces himself on her.

After he has raped her, he kneels beside her where she sits on the floor sobbing. He tells her he is sorry, but it is not a sincere apology. It is obvious that he is not sorry for taking her. He is only sorry that she is not happy about it. He stalks out of the room leaving the door gaping open on the broken hinge. Coming to her senses, she ties her dress together, grabs the baby and the silver candlestick that is lighting the room. She wraps them both in the baby's blanket and flees.

She takes a pig cart that was left harnessed in front of the stable and rides to the river. There she begs passage on a barge, ultimately finding her way to St. Helena's Island where she asks for sanctuary in the Gullah Praise House.

Explaining the baby's parentage, she leaves her baby with church patrons asking that the candlestick be used as the baby's dowry. She begs them to entreat Macie, her baby daughter, to name her own children after spices. Should Charles ever come home and learn of them, he would have a way to find them. Many times they had spoken of their children and many times they *had laughed about calling Mace, Curry, Basil, Anise, and Ginger to the dinner table.*

With the help of the islanders, she went underground and eventually found her way to Barbados, and from there, to a tiny village nestled in a valley.

CR

"I wish you were here. In fact, I really need you to be here," Ben spoke into the phone. It was almost midnight but he had phoned anyway, knowing he would awaken her.

"I wish I was there, too," she whispered.

"You know, we're only an hour and fifteen minutes away if we both get in our cars and drive towards each other right now."

"This nightmare, you've yet to tell me about. It was that bad?"

"Yeah, it was pretty bad." He told her about Savory's sham of a wedding, her dreadful wedding night, how the stupid brute who only cared about his own physical needs used her, and then the latest dream where she had tried to run away and got caught, ending with her running away again, only this time, without her baby.

"Shelby, in less than a year, this woman went from being a virgin to being taken by her lover, abused by her despicable husband, raped by her brother, and giving birth to a child. All this while she worried about and then mourned the loss of her beloved. I hate that for some unseen reason I am being made to live her most traumatic moments as if they were my own."

"You should feel privileged that she's coming back from the grave to impart all this to you. She must feel, as I do, that you're very special."

Her words touched him, but he had to let her know he really didn't believe in all this. Yet, he couldn't for the life of him explain any of it.

"I think you're special, too. I'm sorry I woke you."

"Hey, that's all right. I'm glad I was here for you."

"I wish you were *here* for me."

"Just what would you do if I *was* there right now?"

"I'd show you some of my more aggressive foreplay techniques."

"Aggressive?"

"Yeah. I'm in a strange mood. If I had you beside me in this bed right now, I think I'd have to fuck you silly."

"What!"

"You heard me."

There was silence on both lines for a few moments.

"I'm sorry, I guess I shouldn't have said that, even though I certainly was thinking it."

"Don't apologize, you'll ruin it."

"You're not mad?"

"No."

"Slightly pissed?"

"No."

"Then what? You're awfully quiet."

"I guess I'm thinking about where I can get a car right now."

"Ah, Shelby, you're killin' me honey."

"Maybe we'd better say goodnight."

"No, not yet. I still need you, if only to talk to you. Ask me some questions. About anything, except our dearly departed dysfunctional family."

"What was your lecture about?"

"The odd things people do to the dead."

"Interesting . . ."

"Yeah, the coeds have dubbed it 'Fifty ways to show a corpse you care.' They made a bulletin board entitled, 'A New Hallmark Tradition,' stapled I don't know how many 'Sorry about your divorce' cards all over it, and inside each one, they've graphically pictured each scenario I touched on in my lecture."

"What a great bunch of kids," she said sarcastically.

Pretending not to pick up on her sarcasm, he said, "Yeah, I think they all deserve an 'A,' don't you?"

She laughed and just hearing it on the other end caused him to smile.

"I love hearing you laugh. It's musical."

Flustered, it took her a moment to gather her thoughts. She quickly thought of another question. "So, tell me what the weirdest thing was that you've ever encountered while doing an autopsy."

He laughed, and she could almost envision his bed shaking from his hearty laughter. It was all male and delightfully sexy. She wanted desperately to kiss the broad grin that she knew was plastered on his face.

"Oddly enough, there are many that qualify, but the one that instantly comes to mind was truly unique. Made me wish I'd known the woman before she died."

"Really? Why?"

"Well, she was quite the socialite, I can tell you that. She was here, in Chapel Hill, about two years ago, visiting her daughter."

"And?"

"And she died suddenly from a heart attack."

"So, what's so unusual about that?"

"Well, I was using X-ray to identify her because I didn't want to subject her daughter to a visual confirmation unless I was absolutely sure this was her mother. The victim supposedly had several metal pins and screws in one of her legs from a car accident. Before sending the body to be X-rayed, I ran a metal detector wand over her body. It went crazy when I ran it over her lower pelvis. I mean it went berserk! Well, naturally I had to investigate. My sense of curiosity would not allow me to let that pass. So I decided to do an internal exam. Lo and behold, no sooner had I spread her legs and opened her labial lips then out came a silver ball, followed by another, and then another. They clicked against each other between her thighs as they rolled down the table, gaining momentum until they fell to the floor. I stood there in shock until I realized what they were."

"What were they?"

"Ben Wa Balls."

"What are they?"

He cleared his throat a few times as he tried to think of a way to explain them. "They're uh . . . they're . . . Well, they're put there to . . ."

"Ben, just tell me!"

"They're put there to give a woman pleasure."

"You're kidding."

"No, honest to God, I am not. They're inserted up into the vagina and the action of them rolling around is supposed to be pleasing to some women."

"And she was wearing them to a social function? How did they stay in?"

"Yes, she was wearing them out in public. I think that part of the pleasure is derived from being out in public places with them inside you. And as to keeping them in, the muscles contracting and working to keep them up is known to cause orgasms. Multiple, I'm told."

"Wow. That is truly strange."

"I can go one stranger. A few days after we released

the body, I had a call from a man who wanted to know if I'd found his Ben Wa Balls in this woman's vagina and asked if he could have them back. They were some kind of antique, turn-of-the-century cloisonné, brightly colored enamel inlaid between thin metal strips. I guess that's what set the metal detector off. I asked if he was her husband and he said 'No.' So I told him he'd have to check with her husband as the body had been released to him. I told him I had reinserted the balls. He groaned and told me how expensive those things were and asked why I would do such a thing."

"What did you tell him?"

"I just told him that I had no idea they belonged to someone else and that I thought as long as she was dead, she might as well go to heaven."

"So the jerk just wanted his sex toys back, he didn't even care that his lover had died?"

"He was probably one of the reasons she died. She was D.O.A. at the emergency room. The paramedics couldn't revive her when they arrived at the hotel. Apparently, she was coming down the elevator from her room after a little trysting and was returning to the ballroom to attend the last part of her daughter's award banquet when she collapsed. She was laid out in the lobby when the paramedics arrived. I guess with all the medical personnel running around, along with all the spectators, he didn't figure it was a good time to get his toys back."

"Ben Wa Balls, huh? Your mom didn't name you after them did she?" she teased.

"I hardly think so. I doubt that she's ever relaxed enough to have climaxed, with or without a man, with or without sex toys."

"You never know. Just because she's your mother, doesn't mean she hasn't had carnal pleasure."

"Oh, I'm not discrediting my mom. It's my dad I'm discrediting."

"Oh, what a shame."

"Believe me, in this instance, the acorn has fallen a *long* way from the tree."

"Well that's terribly heartening to know."

"As a teacher, I believe in show and tell."

"That reminds me of a joke. What do you call a person who keeps on talking when people are no longer interested?"

"I don't know, what?"

"A teacher."

"Funny."

"I thought so."

"Time for you to get some sleep."

"You, too."

"I doubt if I will. I'll probably just get up and do some work on my book. But you need your sleep!"

"Yes, sir."

"See you this weekend, for sure?"

"Yes."

"Good. Good night."

"'Night, Ben."

Chapter Nineteen—Janeel's Mama Instant Messaging

Shelby: Hey, hey, hey! Guess what I found out today in Charleston.

Ben: First, why were you in Charleston?

Shelby: Well, there's this lady. This lady who owns a house by the sea. A very *expensive* house by the sea. Anyway, she's trying to sell it. It's on the market for almost a mil. Only problem is that it's about to fall into the ocean. We, (remember, this is not me speaking), feel that because of this minor, little problem, there should probably be some special disclaimer forms signed by the new buyer, i.e. 'I fully understand that I am about to throw a million or so into the deep blue sea, never to see a thin dime of it again. And, I agree that once I become the homeowner to potentially Neptune's next underwater castle, that I will not badger the federal government to bail me out, move a billion tons of sand, or even insist that they teach me how to swim.'

Ben: I thought you worked for North Carolina.

Shelby: Technically, I do. But on a lot of federal stuff we overlap duties and sit in for the experience. This was one of them. The S.C. Office of Coastal Resource Management assisted an attorney that came from Raleigh with some technical jargon and then we all went to see this house.

Ben: You have a fun job. You get to go to the ocean while I dig up bodies. So what did you find out in Charleston today?

Shelby: Since I was in the area, I took a long lunch hour and went to the straw market to ask about storytellers. I asked if anybody knew who the storyteller was that Ida from Beau Marecage talked to before she died in the late 1800s. I was shocked, somebody actually knew what I was talking about. What do the words: Fennel, Cassia, Dill, Curry, Ginger, Rosemary, Parsley, Poppy, Cayenne, Saffron, and Chervil mean to you?

Ben: That you got loose in the McCormick Spice section of the supermarket?

Shelby: Funny you should notice that they're all spices. I wasn't sure you'd see that.

Ben: I do have a doctorate you know. Go on.

Shelby: Touchy, touchy. Well anyway, I found a distant connection to the storyteller that Ida told Savory and Sage's story to. She's Janeel's grandmother's mother. If you remember, Janeel was Mareesa's friend, the dream lady who was supposed to send you a dream. Anyway, she taught her daughter the art just as her mother taught her. Their line goes all the way back to the time of the Civil War. She knows all the Beau Marecage stories from the time of earliest Garretts. Now here's the best part.

Ben: Okay, I see how you like to keep me waiting. Remember this one day when the timing is critical for you.

Shelby: Why, I don't ever know what you mean.

Ben: Okay, Scarlet. I'm on to you. No one's that innocent. Spill. The best part is . . . .

Shelby: Just as you said it would be when you recalled what Savory instructed in your latest dream; every descendant from Savory forward has been named after a spice! In fact, Savory's baby, or I guess I should say, Savory and Charles' baby was named Mace! Exactly as you said! She was called Macie.

Ben: Mace is a spice? I thought it was a weapon in the days of knights in shining armor.

Shelby: Oh Dr., Dr. How did you miss this in all of your highfalutin' education? Mace is the lace-like covering of the nutmeg seed. When dried, it is the most brilliant natural color of red known to man. Savory named her daughter after the pure scarlet color of the spice, *and,* as you said, she instructed all future generations to name their children after a spice because she wanted Charles to be able to find them if he ever came home.

Ben: Wow. That's pretty good digging. You did good. Now what? What happened to Mace? For that matter what happened to Savory?

Shelby: The story goes that Savory left Macie with a religious group on St. Helena's Island and that Macie graduated from the Penn School, now known as Penn Center. Savory is believed to have sailed to Barbados to wait for Charles. The trail on Savory is cold after that, but Macie married a man known as an entrepreneur, specifically for his investment skills with the gamecocks. They had four children. Cloves, known as Clovis, died in infancy. And Corey, short for Coriander, died separating two prized roosters. One nipped him right in the jugular. Fennel became a missionary and Dill married a seamstress for a haberdashery in Charleston. They had two children, twins; then the mother died, complications from childbirth. The twins were Cassia and Ginger and they both married sharecroppers.

Ben: Did you take notes or did you memorize all this?

Shelby: I took notes, Professor. Don't worry, I got it all down. But wait, there's more. Cassia was barren according to her sister Ginger, who had seven, count them, seven children. She actually gave two to Cassia. Gave them! In total, Curry, Rosemary, Poppy, and Parsley are the only ones who begat any children, and all of them, I repeat, all of them became teachers.

Ben: Wow! Two points for my side.

Shelby: Actually, six points for your side. Curry, Rosemary, Poppy, and Parsley had six children that survived to adulthood between them: Cayenne, Chervil, Saffron, Paprika, Sumac, and Pepper.

Ben: I lost track. What year might we be up to? Or how many generations removed from the current one?

Shelby: We're right about the time of World War II, and we're at our fondly deceased's great, great, great-grandchildren. Two more greats to go to present time. Ready for more?

Ben: Sure. Might as well get this over with.

Shelby: Thanks. I appreciate your short attention span. This took me most of the afternoon and a good chunk of the evening.

Ben: Wow! That must've cost you a chunk o' change. These storyteller types aren't cheap.

Shelby: It was gratis, because I was *interested.* Which is more than I can say for some people.

Ben: Continue. Put me out of my misery.

Shelby: All the children of the aforementioned with the exception of Saffron and Paprika died in one war or another before breeding, as they so quaintly said back then. Saffron became a nun, and Paprika married a minister. The minister was pretty randy however, because Paprika was charged with bringing eleven little spices into the world. Six died of either tuberculosis, yellow fever, or some type of influenza. Oh, and one drowned. It was rumored it was not accidental. Paprika's last child was afflicted with Downs and the good minister was not at all happy about that.

Ben: So, that leaves four.

Shelby: Very good! You *are* paying attention.

Ben: Just anxious to get this over with.

Shelby: Aren't you finding this interesting?

Ben: Oh yeah, I'm fascinated.

Shelby: I don't think you are showing the proper amount of appreciation for all my hard work and laborious note taking.

Ben: Sorry. I'll try to do better. So, where were we? Ah yes, the final four of the randy, but reverent preacher. And their names might be? We have had no Salt, Marjoram, or Cinnamon yet, mind you.

Shelby: Still don't. Paprika's four were Bay (for bay leaves, I guess), Chili (for the pepper, I assume), Cilantro, and Cumin.

Ben: Lordy, can you image the ribbing Cumin must have taken?

Shelby: I don't get it.

Ben: You wouldn't. Of course, we'll have to work on that.

Shelby: Oh, I get it. It's not pronounced comin', it's pronounced c-u-u-u-min.

Ben: Oh, my mistake. But still, Cumin? Come on, what a name to saddle a kid with.

Shelby: No worse than Cilantro, Silly.

Ben: Funny. You are too funny. Okay, finish up. I can't spend all day here. I have classes. Remember I teach. I don't go to the beach for a living.

Shelby: Oooh! Next time I see you . . .

Ben: You'll what? Tell me something I can look forward to.

Shelby: I'm going to Salt you that's what. Bay, Chili, Cilantro, and C-u-u-u-u-min, each had one child. Ceylon (I think someone went astray here, Ceylon is a place not a spice, however the best cinnamon comes from Ceylon if that means anything), Caraway, Anise, and Thyme. Ceylon ran away at the age of sixteen and hasn't been heard from since, Caraway is a law professor with three adopted children whose names were already selected before they were adopted so they are not named after spices. Anise is gay, and Thyme can't seem to find a mate. The fact that he's over 350 pounds could have something to do with that, I think. So there you have it. Charles' great, great, great, great, great-grandchildren. Unless Ceylon has a child somewhere, Savory and Charles' bloodline will be dying out real soon. Although, I believe the adopted children may have inheritance rights one day when they come of age.

Ben: You did an incredible amount of work there. I'd put you on my research team any day.

Shelby: Thank you. I appreciate you saying that. It was mentally exhausting work.

Ben: Care for some physically exhausting work?

Shelby: Are you propositioning me, professor?

Ben: Damn straight. I would like to be holding you right now and salting you.

Shelby: I think if I'm going to be seasoned, I'd just as soon it be with garlic. At least that way I'll be safe from the vampires.

Ben: When you get here, we'll 'spice' things up together. Gotta go, can't wait to see you. Later, Ben.

Shelby: Before you go, I almost forgot the best part. On the way back, I stopped to see Martha. Randall Garrett's coming to town and she's going to arrange for me to meet him!

Ben: Well, bully for you! Tell him I said 'hi!' and that he comes from good stock. Really must go now. Ben.

൪

Walking from one building to another, Ben followed the sidewalk as it crossed the grassy common area where students were gathered, smoking, laughing, and flirting.

His thoughts strayed from his class lesson and the long lecture he had ahead of him to Shelby and her twinkling, bright eyes. She seemed so excited by her discovery of Savory's descendants. Thinking about her made him happy and he realized that it had been a long time since he had allowed his mind to just wander at will for the sheer pleasure of it. Yes, thoughts of her made him smile; and a part of him, a very small part, was even beginning to make plans, to anticipate seeing her again. Touching her again.

As he walked along, he was trying to decide if this was a good thing or a bad thing. He had initially felt safe around Shelby as she didn't pose a threat. She clearly hadn't been his type. Now, he realized with chagrin that his type was changing. Damn! How had she done this? How had she worked her way into his thoughts, his moods? Hell, even his dreams were now centered around characters created in her vivid, absurd imagination.

Opening the door for a group of girls, he smiled as they giggled at his gallant attention. Freshmen. He remembered having the thrill of the unknown and the excitement of not knowing the unlimited possibilities that lie ahead. Since Anna's death, had he really shut down that much? Had he turned off the world except for the superficial, the things that couldn't go deep enough to hurt?

Suddenly it occurred to him that already, Shelby could hurt him. Unwittingly perhaps, but devastatingly, just the same. After just a few short get-togethers, followed by a series of e-mail conversations, she had managed to sneak under his defenses. She had found the chink in his armor and tunneled in. He smiled broadly as his mind's eye brought her smiling face into focus. "Just how the hell did she do that?" he said out loud, and was surprised when he looked up and saw that he was standing at the front of his classroom with his students staring back at him.

"How the hell did she do what, professor?" a student in the front row asked.

He cleared his throat, thought for a split second, and rephrased the question to pertain to his lecture. This time more forcefully, he bellowed out, "Just how the hell did the coroner know to look for traces of poison? Miss Harrison, in the back row, give me one indication."

A young woman timidly ventured a guess. "Striations in the fingernails, sir?"

"Excellent. Mr. Connelly, up front, give us another.

Chapter Twenty
Chapel Hill, NC

The weekend came and Shelby found her way to Chapel Hill in yet another economy rental car. Ben was waiting for her in front of The Bull's Head Bookshop as prearranged. The sight of him standing there, in front of the store conversing with a small group of students, one hand gesturing, the other holding his blazer askew because his hand was jammed into a pant's pocket, brought a thrill to her. There he was. And he was waiting for her. She could hardly believe that he had asked her here, to be with him, all weekend.

She parked her car in a newly-vacated slot in the second row and turned off the ignition. For almost a minute, she just sat and watched him as he continued to belabor something. *Gad, he was some kind of good looking. How did she end up being here with him?*

She was giddy with the delicious knowledge of what lay ahead for her this weekend. Although she had practically promised herself that she'd "be a good girl, and take her virginity to the marital bed," she couldn't help but want this man. In her mind, he outclassed her in both looks and social standing, and quite honestly, she didn't know if she'd ever have the opportunity again to be with someone quite like him. So . . . she had decided to make the best of it, to take what he was willing to give and give her body up for the pure enjoyment she knew it would bring. Just to be in his arms, to be the woman of the hour, if that's all it would be, would be worth it. He was everything. He was desire personified. And she knew she'd have no regrets. This was, after all, exactly the kind of man a woman dreamed of, and then waited years for, if she ever found him at all.

She tossed her wallet into the glove box, locked it, and stepped out of the car. It was something she had always done. It gave her time to think whether she really wanted to buy something, since it meant having to go to her car to get her money. When she closed the car door, Ben looked up and saw her. The grin that split his face warmed her heart. It told her that he was genuinely happy to see her. He immediately excused himself from the small, but growing circle and bee-lined it over to her.

"Hey, beautiful. You're right on time." He bent to kiss her on the cheek, whispering at the same time. "I'd love to greet you a bit more warmly but it appears we have an audience." He straightened and took her hands in his. "I am so glad you came, you just don't know how much I have been looking forward to this."

She smiled seductively up at him and murmured, "Don't do well with an audience, huh? I thought you were a great speaker."

"I do fine speaking in front of others. I just prefer to do my necking in private, if you don't mind. I don't need to be the source of more gossip than I already am. It turned out to be a beautiful day. Feel like taking a walk?"

"Sure. I've been sitting for the better part of three hours. A walk would be great."

"Good, let's go to the park." He walked her over to his roadster. The top was down in anticipation of enjoying the late summer day. "Hope you don't mind?" he asked, indicating the openness of the car.

"Not a chance. If I had a car like this, I'd be loathe to ever put the top up."

"Loathe. Now that's a word you don't hear very often."

"It means to have an aversion or to abhor."

"I know what it means, Silly. It's just an archaic word these days."

"I love it! And I love this!" she screamed into the wind as he drove down the wide boulevard. Then she looked over at him and said, "And oh, by the way, you smell just wonderful! The steel's working!"

He smiled over at her and nodded. *God, she was so genuine.* Most women he knew would be complaining about their hair being tossed this way and that, but not Shelby. She was reveling in the sensational feeling of freedom that riding in a convertible imparted. She lifted her face toward the sun and contentedly smiled to the breeze. He wished they had a longer drive so he could continue to admire her carefree spirit, but it was only a few minutes later that he pulled into the park. She lifted her head from the headrest and looked over at him and smiled.

"Having a good time?" he asked.

"I don't know why, but I always seem to when I'm with you." She didn't even have the sophistication to hold back her revealing thoughts, he told himself as he helped her out of the car. But he had to admit that what she had said was true on his part, too.

He chuckled as he drew her out of the bucket seat and seductively pulled her against his chest and into his arms. "We're going to have a wonderful weekend," he whispered just before his lips descended to hers. Her lips were warm from the sun and after a slight hesitation, very inviting. Her lips turned supple under his and he noticed that her eyes had closed. Her subtle way of letting him know she was savoring his kiss pleased him very much. He was attempting to deepen the kiss by turning her head crossways from his when he heard her moan and fire instantly leapt to his groin. *Damn! How did she do that so easily?*

"I . . . I think . . . we'd better walk," he managed to get out in a breathy voice.

"Uh, yeah. That PDA thing again. When I went to school, it was the faculty who caught you in a public display of affection, not the faculty causing it."

He was already walking beside her, his hands in his pockets. He smiled sheepishly and shrugged his shoulders. "I didn't bring my detention slips, and I hardly think anyone around would have the nerve to deny me doing something I clearly have had the need to do for well over a week." His words said that he had missed her, but in his mind he was more than just a little frustrated. *I am forever curbing myself with this woman. What would happen if I didn't have to?*

"A volcano that's what," he said aloud.

"What?" she asked, not being privy to his train of thought.

"Nothing. Change the subject for me would you? Ask me something about my work, something about history, something about anything but us."

Shelby looked over at him and quirked a brow. Was she already getting on his nerves. That wouldn't be good; she had just barely arrived. "You mentioned once that there was a particular case that brought your focus back when your girlfriend suddenly died. What was it?"

He thought for a long moment, and at first, she didn't think he was going to tell her.

"It was very bizarre. After I did the autopsy, all indications were that it was an accidental death. But something, something kept telling me that there was more. It took me two months, but I finally proved the death was a homicide. It's the first case I was ever involved in where I had to meet the murderer before I could even begin to figure out how the victim was killed."

"Wow. Awesome. So how was this person killed?"

"The person was a young woman. She was thirty-two. She died in the hospital of swelling of the brain. She was admitted with severe headaches that progressed to hallucinations. Hours before her death they had to sedate her to control her shrieking and the awful screams of relentless pain. She finally lapsed into a coma and died. No one the wiser as to how or why."

"Poor woman, how terrible for her."

"When I finally discovered how she died, I realized just how terrible her last days had been."

"How did she die? What made her sick?"

"For three weeks I asked myself that same question every single night. Over and over again, I went over the reports. Toxicology results were normal. X-rays, scans, tissue dissections . . . nothing I could find gave me a clue. Then one day, as I was examining tissue from the brain through a very powerful microscope, I found something. Microorganisms that were actually still moving. I had never seen these particular microscopic organisms before, and knowing it could take days scouring through books, I picked up the phone and called the Center for Disease Control and Prevention. I figured they'd have to know what it was, if it had killed her. Because if it had killed her, it had probably killed someone else at one time or another. Sure enough, within a week, I had my answer. The sample I had sent matched exactly to the samples they had on file for an amoeba known as Naegleria fowleri. It is a very dangerous amoeba. It causes amebic meningoencephalitis which is almost always fatal."

"Never heard of it."

"You probably wouldn't have. It's a rare disease. Only a hundred or so cases have been reported since 1965. But the amoeba itself is pretty common. It's found in unchlorinated waters, actually thrives there, in warm, slow-flowing, unchlorinated waters. It can be found all over the world, but mostly in the southern part of the United States because it's always warmer there."

"Well then why aren't more people dying from it?"

"Because it has to get into your body, more specifically, your brain. And the only way to do that effectively, is to take a direct route. In this case the direct route to the brain for this little microbe is to tunnel up through the nose. Through the cribiform plate of the ethmoid bone, the tiny spongy bone behind the nasal sinus and the easiest entrance into the cranial vault."

"The nose?"

"Yup. You have to inhale water, which most of us are adverse to doing because it hurts and makes us look foolish when we have to expel it."

"So, she was swimming and inhaled it?"

"That's what I originally thought. It would have tied things up so nicely." His features stilled and she could see from the look on his face that he was reminiscing, and not in a good way. "She didn't swim. In fact, she hated the water. Her boyfriend had a boat, but she would never even go out in it with him."

"How'd you find that out?"

"From her sister. From the very beginning she thought her sister had been poisoned. After this woman's death, the boyfriend, who actually was the victim's fiancé, became the sole beneficiary of a lottery ticket that had been given to them jointly at their engagement party. When the victim died, all the money was his. Everyone in the wedding party had chipped in to buy the happy couple a hundred dollars worth of Power Ball tickets. One of them hit; it was worth 1.3 million dollars. When I interviewed him, it was all he could talk about—the new boat he was going to get, the trip he was going to take to the Caribbean, the new Jag he had already ordered. He didn't seem to have the slightest bit of remorse about his fiancé passing."

"How could you poison somebody with an amoeba? How would you even know where to find it?"

"Well, that's the part that bothered me. She didn't swim. But because he was an avid boater, he had to know all about the local waterways. The rivers, creeks, inlets, lakes . . . he would have known if there was an area that had a problem.

"I went to the local piers, visited fisheries, talked to several river keepers, and finally, after asking around and making a general nuisance of myself, I ran into a park ranger who knew a man who owned a campground on a lake north of Raleigh. He remembered the campground owner had told him a year ago about a ten-year-old boy who had died from catching something he got from swimming in the lake. I drove up to the campsite, met the man, found out the name of the little boy and took some water samples.

"Then I called the CDC back, talked with the chief of the parasitic diseases branch and verified that the boy had died from primary amebic meningoencephalitis caused by the *Naegleria fowleri* parasite found in the lake. The samples I had taken tested positive for the amoeba. All I had to do now was figure out how the fiancé got it up the victim's nose without her knowing."

"I don't think you can put anything up someone's nose without them being aware of it. Can you?" Shelby asked.

"No, not usually. But you can make them do it to themselves, and that way it's not quite so memorable."

"He made her sniff up the water?"

"That's what I figured. So it was back to the sister to try to figure out how that could have happened."

"I can see why all this might have pushed aside thoughts of your own grief," Shelby whispered sympathetically.

"Yeah. At the time, this case kind of took over. Anna wasn't forgotten, but I had more important things to dwell on for the time being."

"So, what did the sister have to say?"

"Well she got pretty angry when I suggested her sister was snorting something up her nose."

"Uh, oh."

"Yeah. I didn't quite phrase it like I should have. By the time I finally got her settled down, we were hardly on friendly terms. But I did find out that her sister had severe allergy problems at certain times of the year and in order to combat them she had to take decongestants that tended to give her nosebleeds. So, it was customary for her to have a humidifier in her bedroom at night to combat the dryness from her electric heat pump. Also, just before going to bed every night, she would use an inhaler to moisten the delicate nasal tissues that tended to rupture so easily.

"I thought I had the answer and the connection I needed, so I went to the D.A."

"What did he say?"

"She. She said I couldn't get a search warrant unless I had more to go on."

"Shot down, huh?"

"Well, no. I enlisted the sister's help again. I had her call the suspect and ask him if she could pick up her sister's personal things, clothes in particular because he knew that a lot of them actually belonged to her. He was very agreeable, and he didn't suspect a thing. Two hours later, I had the contents of the medicine cabinet, all of her cosmetics, and her humidifier. There were two inhalers. One was brand new, still had the security wrapping; the other was a little over half full. It tested positive for the amoeba. And interestingly enough, so did the humidifier. According to the confession he gave a week later, he had tried to infect her with the humidifier first, through airborne droplets, but even with a snore guard over his own nose and mouth, he worried he would become infected also. So he just substituted the lake water for the sterile saline solution in her inhaler."

"How much time did he get?"

"Twenty-five years. He took at least fifty of hers, yet they're only taking twenty-five of his. Sometimes, in my line of work, you don't always get the reward you want."

"What reward did you want?"

"The opportunity to hold him in a headlock and make him sniff up the deadly water. Then a few days off from work so I could watch him writhe and scream as the parasites attacked *his* brain."

"Oooh. Remind me not to get on your bad side."

"You don't have it in your heart to hurt anybody."

"How can you be sure of that?"

"Babe, I've heard you bemoan the death of people you don't even know, people who have been dead for decades. I can't imagine how devastated you'd be if you thought somebody was hurt because of something you did."

"You're right. But that doesn't mean I'm a sap. Right now if Sage was standing here, I'd have no trouble turning him to pulp."

"Somewhere, he already is pulp."

"Nice thought."

"The worms crawl in, the worms crawl out . . ."

She reached over and jabbed at him. He reached over and pulled her close. "What say we go find a bodacious steak and a few brewskis?"

"You expect me to eat after all this?"

"Okay, just drink. I'll bet you're a hilarious drunk."

"Only been drunk once."

"Really?"

"Really. And don't ask what that was like because I don't remember. I was by myself one night watching a football game and drinking wine. I drank the whole bottle and have to assume I passed out."

"Why do you assume that?"

"I woke up, the game was over, the bottle was empty, and I looked like death warmed over."

"Headache?"

"Hell, yes. It lasted two weeks. Then I got a package in the mail. It was a $25 commemorative video of The Carol Burnett Show. When I called the company to tell them I didn't order it, they referred to my charge card account number and the date of that fateful night. Apparently I was still up until just shy of one o'clock, rolling with laughter at a commercial."

"Well, knowing how you are with money, I'm surprised you didn't return it."

"Nah. I thought it would be a good reminder to keep

around. Most girls worry about having loose morals when they drink. I have to worry about having a loose pocketbook. That's pretty scary for me. It keeps me straight. Plus, I love the video. Harvey Korman, Vicki Lawrence, Tim Conway–that was great stuff."

"Yeah. I kinda like slapstick, too. So, enough of me. While we walk back to the car and drive to the restaurant, tell me how you learned to be so frugal."

"My parents had always been foster parents. When I was growing up, there were at least four or five kids around the dinner table in addition to me, their only offspring. Mom was in a car accident a few months after I was born. Her internal injuries were pretty bad, so they had to remove her uterus. So, as much as she and dad wanted more children, they were stuck with just me. Mom taught me how to be thrifty. She would stretch the allotment money she got each month for the foster children. She didn't want to have to take a job outside the house, so she economized all the time. And as I watched, she taught. I learned how to cut coupons, how to wash and dry zip lock bags without tearing them, and how to make nearly everything from scratch. We never had birthday parties because we couldn't afford presents or a cake, but we played a lot of games and she taught me the value of a dollar, and we had fun."

"Sounds like you were close."

"Sometimes. I wasn't particularly happy to be stuck with domestic chores, so I usually tried to hang out with my dad whenever I could. Dad was the one who taught me about the environment. He's the one who gave me an appreciation for the coastal waters and the wildlife around us. To this day, I still look forward to going fishing with him on Lake Waccamaw."

"What a great father."

"Yeah. I miss him. He's not the same anymore. He's

gotten a little addled, as they say. Sometimes, he's not even sure which kid I am. It upsets me a little when he calls me Kyle."

"Why's that?"

"Well, Kyle was only with us for six months, but he sure managed to make an impression on everybody."

"Good or bad?"

"Bad. He was a terror. He was always leaving the freezer open on purpose, or letting the water run when he didn't even need it, and he never, ever bothered to flush the toilet. Why my parents even bothered with him, I'll never know. I begged them to send him back from the first day he arrived at our house. But Mom and Dad wouldn't hear of it. It wasn't until two years later that I learned why. Kyle's parents had been abusive. He'd been molested both sexually and physically. I didn't know at the time that he was just fighting back in the only way he could.

"Dad took me aside one day, and with tears in his eyes, told me that Kyle's parents had managed to get him back from the state. Two months later, Kyle was dead, beaten and starved as well as sexually violated. I had hated that kid, but I cried for days and days. I just hadn't understood. But my parents had. They'd had a glimpse of the child within. 'It's what's on the inside that matters' as my dad always said. They'd seen the scared, angry kid. All I saw was a monster who was rude, mean, and spiteful."

"So why does it bother you so much when he calls you Kyle? He obviously loved him."

"Yeah, but he loved me more. I always knew that he loved me more. I just want him to know who I am so he can remember that I was his favorite. His 'Pumpkin Head,' as he used to call me. He calls everybody that now. He can't remember anybody's name anymore so it's become a catchall. We're all either Pumpkin Head or Kyle. Out of over thirty kids, we were the two who stood out the most."

"It must be incredibly sad for you when you visit."

"Yeah. I don't do it as often as I used to. I know my mom understands, but I still feel bad about it."

"Is that where all your money goes, Shelby?" The softness of Ben's query, a query he was pretty sure he knew the answer to, stunned her.

"How did you know?" she whispered.

"It just figured. You seem like the kind of daughter who has what it takes 'on the inside,' plus only a 'Pumpkin Head' like you would care so much."

They were in front of the restaurant now. As Ben held the door for Shelby, she smiled wanly up at him. "I can't imagine it being any other way. They were always sacrificing for us."

As they were being seated, Shelby looked over at Ben. "So what about your folks? What are they like?"

Ben thought for a minute, and then gave her a crooked smile. "Do you per chance know who Mr. and Mrs. Thurston Howell III were?"

"From Gilligan's Island?"

"Yeah, that's them."

"They're your parents?"

"Best description I can come up with. Except that I was never fortunate enough to have them marooned on a deserted isle."

"You're kidding!"

"Nope. He's flagrant with his money and lets you know it. She's into every new bauble, trinket, and country club; but between the two of them, they don't have a clue. They live to party and entertain."

"So, they're rich?"

"He owns a bank. Some years they're rich. Other years they hide it well that they're not. It all depends on the financial upturns and downturns of the market."

"Were you supposed to be a banker, too?"

"Actually, I was supposed to be a spoiled, social-climbing, jet setter. The fact that I had a brain and wanted to do something with it annoyed them to no end. We hardly ever talk. They paid for my education, and I appreciate that, but we really have nothing in common. We never did."

"Aren't they proud of you? I'm mean you're a doctor, a full-fledged professor, a noted author."

"They would prefer it if I was the kind of doctor who could do their cosmetic surgery, not the kind who digs for bones or pokes into people's rotting flesh. As for being an author, I doubt if they've ever even seen one of my books. They're certainly not the type of books that would grace their coffee tables."

Shelby looked at him rather oddly and then took a minute to look at her menu before asking, "So, no siblings to cleave to the elite or to leave the banking dynasty to?"

"Nope. I don't even know how they managed to have me. I don't think they ever liked each other that much."

"Wow, that's pretty sad."

"Nah, not at all. They're happy. I'm happy. We're happy to see each other once a year on Ground Hog's Day and we're done with it."

"Ground Hog's Day?"

"Yeah. My birthday. If Puxatawney Phil sees his shadow, I get a diamond-studded tie tack embedded in a mink tie or some such nonsense like that. If he doesn't, I get another Murano paperweight. It's sort of my Bloomberg Report for the year."

Shelby laughed at his wry humor. Even though she suspected he had more of a fondness for his parents than he was alluding to, she was nonetheless pleased that she wouldn't have to vie against them for Ben's affections.

"Try the French dip, it's incredible," Ben suggested.

His innocent words brought an image to her mind and, try as she might, she could not get the picture of that out of her head. And the picture searing in her head right now was not of roast beef sandwiched between a sourdough roll.

"Uh . . . okay."

"Good. We'll have two," he told the waitress. When he looked over at her and winked, she thought she'd fall out of her seat. *How did she end up here, sitting across from the most handsome man she'd ever met, who sported a smile and a wink that sent her clear into orbit?*

"After the game, how about I show you my crypt?"

"Pardon?"

"That's what I call my office. You'll see why when we get there."

"I'm afraid to ask."

"You should be. It's not a pretty sight."

"Maybe we should just take in a movie."

"Not a chance. I want to show you where I work."

"Can't wait," she murmured good-naturedly as she picked up her soda and took a sip. "Can't wait."

The home team won the scrimmage, and even though the faculty seats were pretty high up, they had a good view of the action. The noise of the afternoon was followed by the still silence of the lingering day as they drove across the campus to Ben's office.

Chapter Twenty-One—The Crypt
Chapel Hill, NC

Crypt. How appropriate. It seemed everything in Ben's office somehow related to death. There were jars containing all manner of body parts, showcases with select relics, and pictures with newspaper articles referring to them. Things like bullet fragments and the piece of skull it had pierced. Graphic images of fingers torn versus fingers cleanly severed caused Shelby to turn in disgust and shield her eyes with her hands.

"This is gross! How can you work in an environment like this?"

"Guess I'm just used to it. Nothing about the body is shocking to me now. I've seen horrors untold, eyeballs dangling by their thready nerves, whole chunks of flesh eaten off of faces by beloved pets, mutilations you wouldn't believe. But I still have to investigate and look for the 'why' and the 'who.' It's my job, and I believe I do it well."

"I just don't see how can you stand the horror of all this," she said as she spun around taking in all the museum-type cases filled with one display after another.

"I don't see it as horror anymore. I see each thing as a story that needs to be solved and told. I only see the questions now. Something happened. What caused it? Why? And ultimately, who or what did this?"

"What's this?" Shelby asked, pointing at an object in an absurdly large, matted shadowbox. It was something yellowish, about the size of a softball, surrounded by an expanse of white poster board. The whole thing was professionally matted and framed.

"It's the skull of a Andamanese man. The female dries the skull of her deceased husband. Then she paints it ocher, decorates it with something akin to lace, and wears it around her neck as some kind of trophy."

"Ugh!"

He chuckled as he walked over and lightly stroked the side of her arm. "It reminds me of the vagaries of mankind. And all the weird religions requiring mutilations and human sacrifice. If it's so second nature in the primitive world to kill and mutilate, how hard must the modern man fight to go against the tide and be civilized? In my world, I deal with the remains of people who have been treated less than civilly, quite often, less than even humanely. This reminds and keeps in perspective for me, just what a species is capable of. When I think there's no way a man could chop up a beautiful woman, stuff her body into a suitcase, and throw it over the railing of a cruise ship, I walk over here and remember that, yes, under certain circumstances, with certain incentives, he can, and even has."

"I think you need to get a new job. Yours is disgusting. This has to be the worst job in the world!"

He laughed and took her by the elbow over to

a bookshelf. It was filled with text books and large reference books. Deftly, he pulled out a large binder, laid it on top of the bookcase, and flipped it open to a page heading that read, "Body Farm."

"No, these are the doctors and techs who have the absolute worst job in forensics. Yet they provide an invaluable service."

"Body Farm? What's that?"

"I'm not sure you're gonna want to know about this, so stop me when you can't bear to hear anymore, okay?"

"Oookay," she let the word draw out as if unsure of her answer.

"There's this place in Tennessee. It's the University of Tennessee's Forensic Anthropology Center, known as the Body Farm. Donated bodies are scattered over two acres of woodland, left to decay and rot naturally as if left there intentionally. They decay, they freeze, they thaw, they get gnawed on by animals. They decompose among the leaves, the snails, worms, and the rodents. Each step along the way, everything is recorded, measured, weighed. The wealth of information accumulated is invaluable. The goo that accumulates under the bodies is analyzed by career scientists. Even the chemical gases seeping out from the bodies are captured and sniffed for their stench levels. The guys who are charting these bodies through the four stages of decomposition: fresh, bloat, decay, and dry have their work cut out for them, and none of it is pretty. They see a pile of leaves in the fall and don't feel an urge to jump into it; they wonder what's underneath it, and how long it's been there. They do an awesome job. Serial killers are getting nabbed because of them. Do I have the worst job in forensics? Not hardly."

"I wish we hadn't just eaten."

"Well, that is one thing I'm careful about, when I eat and where. Come on, I'll take you into my true office, where you can relax and recuperate." He opened a door and ushered her into a semi-dark room. As they passed the threshold, he flicked on the light switch. Fluorescent lighting lit up a room that could have been the office of an accountant or an attorney. The geeky carnival atmosphere of the previous room was not carried into this sanctum. Instead, it seemed to be the place where paperwork lived and multiplied heartily. Stacks of files were piled in every corner, all of them at least three feet high. On every flat surface, more paperwork was piled. Thick reams of paper were stacked neatly in bundles crisscrossing each other as a way of assuring separation of a sort.

"Wow. You're either very behind, or you need more file cabinets."

He pointed to a stack in the far corner. "Exam case files, already graded and ready to hand back." His hand continued around the room, stopping at the next stack. "Old forensic files. Each new class gets to take one, study it, and make comments on the case and give their opinion on the general health of the cadaver. I won't need them again until January." He went to stand by the least tidy of the stacks. "Paper to be recycled. They only pick up once a month, but I could use a pick up once a week." Walking over to the desk, he sat in the brown leather chair and leaned back, putting his hands behind his head. "The rest you see scattered here and there is my new book, in various stages of editing, with all the reference sources printed from the Internet handy in case I find something that needs additional research. So actually, although it looks like a mess, it's really pretty well organized."

"If you say so," she said with a laugh, and the smile

brightening her face made him catch his breath. *She was so beautiful.*

"Come here," he said and gestured with a beckoning, crooked finger.

She walked over, but it took her a moment or two to realize that he wanted her to sit in his lap.

Tentatively, she edged closer to his side of the desk. He took her hand when she got close enough and easily drew her over to where he was, then he expertly pulled her into his lap. His eyes met hers, and as they stared at each other he murmured, "Do you know how many times I've had the urge to pull a beautiful young woman into my lap while I've been sitting in this chair?"

"No," she whispered timidly, half afraid to hear how many times he had actually done so, possibly even with his students.

"None. I have never come into this room and thought about anything but my work, until you came in. Now I don't have any desire to work, or to even think about it." His voice had lowered, and the huskiness of it attested to his words. His arm went around her shoulders and his other hand cupped her head as he lowered his head to hers. The moment his lips touched her lips, he urgently deepened the kiss and moved his mouth to cover hers completely. The pressure of his mouth on hers, the fervor of his kiss and the scandalous place where it was taking place, were all too much for her. Heat shot through her, searing into the marrow of her bones. Her arms went around his shoulders and she pulled him in close. Their mouths melded and their tongues clashed as they both sought the upper hand, the right to control and orchestrate the passion. He won. With both hands on the sides of her face, holding her lips to his, he lapped and tongued her deeply, savoring her taste and heightening his arousal.

Her fingers found their way into his hair and she loved the way it felt, coarse and thick, yet still soft to the touch. His moan encouraged her and her slim hand found its way down the side of his neck to the open vee of his oxford shirt. The crinkly hairs she found there were such an unexpected texture to her that at first, she recoiled. This was a man, a very real man, not some high school boy. He was quite obviously full-grown, surpassing her not only in size, but in his obvious command of her body. It unnerved her for just a moment to realize how mature and experienced he must be compared to her, but his kisses were doing such incredible things to her that after a few minutes, she no longer cared. The woman in her was calling to the man in him and he was responding. Her ripening and softening body was causing his to harden and she loved the power of it. Boldly, she began to unbutton his shirt.

OhmyGod, what was she doing? What was she doing? Her hand, having managed to undo two buttons, slid under his shirt and she felt his chest. Her flattened palm roamed over the large, muscular expanse. It was an incredible chest, broad and firm, and covered with thick, coarse hair. She reveled in the feel of it. As his lips caressed the side of her neck, she heard his low moan of pleasure in her bold touches. Finding a nipple in the forest of thick hair, she circled it with the pad of her finger. She thought he was going to come off the chair as his hips instinctively bucked up against her.

"Oh my God, Shelby. Jesus. Oooh." His hand left the side of her face and he finished unbuttoning his shirt for her. She was unprepared for his hand's next foray, which was to unbutton her shirt, too.

Within seconds he had her buttons undone and the plackets spread wide. Then his eager hand found first one bared breast and then the other. He alternately fondled and caressed each one, spastic in his need to caress one, then the other, as if not content to possess just one of her smooth, small mounds. Sitting her upright, he grabbed her by the waist and lifted her onto the desk in front of him. Then with both hands he captured her breasts, kneading and palming them, finally concentrating on the sensitive tips. She cried out in pleasure as his fingers closed over each nipple and toyed with it. Pulling, pinching, and stretching each dusky rose tip until they were both so hard, so pebbly, she wanted to scream from the torture.

"Please, please . . . please," she whispered, but she didn't even know what she was asking for.

He did. Ben leaned forward in his seat and took a nipple into his mouth. She gasped and slumped against him. Her head fell momentarily on his shoulder before falling back in a perfect swan-like arch of ecstasy. With her head back, and her breasts jutting forward, he was free to sample her as he willed. His thumbs caressed the tender undersides of her flesh as his lips and tongue gorged on wonderfully hardened peaks. From the sounds of her newfound delights, he knew she had never had a man suckle her breasts like this. It aroused him mightily, but it also tempered him. He knew he had a responsibility that he dearly wished he didn't. Why the hell couldn't she be as experienced and as brash as most of his students? Then he would have no qualms about stripping her of the rest of her clothing and taking her right here on his desk, among the pages of his new book, *The Things Men Do For Sex And The Women Who Die Because Of It.*

Unbidden images came into his head and he unclamped his lips from her nipple. Her head was still thrown back, her breasts jutting enticingly from her chest, the nipples gleaming from his lavish attentions.

"No, no, don't stop," she whispered. "Please, please, don't stop."

He stood up as her head began to fall forward. His hand stilled its downward journey as he reached out to caress her jaw. His eyes met hers and the flame he was trying to douse came back, triple force.

"Oh, God," he breathed as he lifted her up off of the desk and propped her against it. He wrapped his arms around her, enfolding her and bringing his bared chest up against hers. She sobbed and pleaded into the hot flesh of his shoulder, "I want you to do more to me."

Then bold beyond even her own expectations, she reached between their bodies and palmed his manhood. The strangled hiss that emanated from him only served to spur her on and she greedily began to rub her hand against his hard member. Then with all the aplomb of a seasoned whore, or a woman who definitely knew what she wanted, she reached lower and cupped his balls.

"Arrrgh!" Ben roared as he tried to move away from her and the crippling effects she was having on his self-control. "No, Shelby. No."

But she just slid away from the desk and backed him up against the wall.

"You don't know what you're doing here, Shelby. I can't take much more of this. You're driving me crazy for want of you."

"Then take me. What are you waiting for? I want it too. Please."

He took her hands. Hands that were exploring his chest, searching out the hard nubs that with only a light touch had caused him to gasp and moan, the sounds of which had probably served to boost her confidence and embolden her, turning her into the little vixen in front of him.

While he held her wrists to still them, she bent into his chest. Her tongue licked his chest hairs away from one nipple, then she took the whole thing into her mouth and sucked on it.

"Shelby, Jesus!"

"What?" she asked innocently as she moved to the other nipple and at the same time insinuated her thigh high up between his. The look in her eyes was of a woman intensely satisfied with herself. Slowly, his hands released hers; then having a mind of their own, they met behind her body. Settling firmly on her jean-clad buttocks, he brusquely pulled her pelvis tightly into his.

"Okay," he said in mock defeat. "Okay, I give up, if this is what you want. What you truly want . . ."

"It's what I want," she whispered. When her hand undid his belt and lowered his zipper, she thought she heard him whimper. Then when she released him and held him in her hand, she knew that she did.

She was fogging his brain with her touches, bringing him way too near that moment of supreme agony that his body so ached for. He knew he didn't have a prayer of satisfying her if he didn't make her stop touching him, and right now! Just when had she taken the helm, he asked himself as he sighed at her most gentle caressing of his heavy swaying sacs.

He took a deep breath and reminded himself that he was the man. He had responsibilities, especially with someone as untried as Shelby. Single-mindedly, he reached down and removed her hand. He clasped it in his and held it immobile while with the other, he unbuttoned and unzipped her jeans. Then he used both hands and inched them down until he could see she was not wearing any underwear. Fine tufts of auburn met his fingers as he stroked her lower belly.

As his eyes found the delights awaiting him at the juncture of her thighs, he sighed. Then he raised his eyes to meet hers. "Don't you ever wear any underwear?" he murmured his appreciation with a tiny smile and took her lips with his. He didn't allow her to answer his question as his tongue thrust between her lips. He took possession of her mouth as his hand took possession of her womanhood. The moan that came from her mouth into his as his longest finger spread her lips and slid into her, told him that he was back in control again.

His fingers expertly stroked her as he watched her face peak with desire. Her head was thrown back, her lips parted, her eyes closed in total abandonment to the moment. It was then that he realized he couldn't have her now, as much as he wanted to. At this moment his desire for her was as strong if not stronger than it had ever been for any woman. He wanted her badly! His bold manhood was already jutting all around her belly trying to find the place where it could sink into her and expire with delight. But he had no condom. He didn't keep any in his office. He knew many professors who did; but alas, he was not one of them. And he certainly wasn't going to encourage her to kneel between his thighs and take him into her mouth, although he could not begin to count the times he'd been offered that precise enticement by a nubile coed to either alter a grade or write a not-so-truthful recommendation. Shelby, bold as she was acting right now, was nowhere near their league.

But they were both beyond reason right now. Their bodies too hot. Their fervency too desperate to curb.

In an effort to have better access to her, he forced her jeans further down. They were now around her knees and his fingers were thrusting into her, fast and deep. He could hear the marvelous sucking sounds caused by her extreme wetness. As he continued to watch the changes in her expression and the heaving of her chest as her breathing became more labored, he reluctantly gave over to a total lack of decorum. When Shelby's beautiful face gave into the pained grimace of pleasure and her body buckled and came into his hand, he allowed himself the same release and came into his hastily-grabbed handkerchief. Both of them moaned loudly and reached for the other as their bodies spasmed, then they both sagged against the wall behind his desk and slumped to the floor.

There was silence for many minutes before Ben put his arm around her, drew her close, and ventured, "If anybody walked in right now, I'd probably never get tenure."

Chapter Twenty-Two
Chapel Hill, NC

Pretty aggressive for an ingénue, aren't you?" Ben had just come back from the adjoining washroom and was tidying his hair.

"And you're pretty . . ."

"Pretty what?"

"Pretty torturous. Are you like that with all women?"

"Yes. Remember that. Anticipation is everything."

"Not timing, as you alluded to earlier?"

"Well, perhaps that helps." Already feeling a burgeoning desire rekindling for her, he asked, "Ready for the movie?"

"I would be if I'd picked it out."

"C'mon," he said as he ushered her through the door, "It's a remake of the *Texas Chain Saw Massacre,* how much more entertaining can you get than that?"

"Remember, I grew up on *Cinderella, Sleeping Beauty, The Little Mermaid, Beauty and the Beast . . .*"

"Well, *they* all had their bad guys! And we have our own version of *Beauty and the Beast* right here. You're Beauty and I'm the Beast," he growled to make his point.

She smiled and looked up at him. "Believe me, you're the beauty. I've never seen a man turn women's heads like you do."

"Well, thank you. But while you are not turning the women's heads, you're certainly turning the men's. I think you are the loveliest woman I've ever known," he said softly.

Her eyes misted at his sincerely spoken words. "Wow, I guess I shouldn't complain about the movie you picked out."

"No, you shouldn't," he reiterated as he walked her down the sidewalk to the parking lot and his car. With a flourish he opened the door and seated her.

"You're not as innocent as I had originally thought. You're a dichotomy for sure. How is it you're a virgin, yet fairly knowledgeable in the sexual arts?" he asked as he drove through the town.

"I'm not knowledgeable at all. What you're experiencing is my discovery phase. I am very, very curious. And I want to know it all, right now, so I can please you."

"Oh, you please me all right, don't ever worry about that. But I'm wondering if you're ready for all this."

"It should have happened a long time ago. I don't want to wait any longer, Ben. I think it's time I grew up and got initiated. Can you honestly say there's a reason that we shouldn't?"

"No," he said softly and patted her thigh. "No, not if you're sure it's what you truly want."

She smiled at him as he pulled up to a stoplight. "It is. Don't worry, I think I can even handle you dumping me the day after you've had the worst sex ever."

He hooted with laughter. "Oh, that's not going to happen. And even if it does, it's my fault not yours. We'll fix the problem; but trust me, we're going to be very good together."

They pulled up to the movie theater, and Ben leaned over to kiss her before coming around to help her out of the car. Then he went to the ticket window and purchased two tickets. He kept her attention so rapt on him that she didn't notice when he seated them in the small theater that was playing *The Cut*.

When the previews were over and the movie started playing, she looked over at him with a questioning look.

"Hey, you get romance, I get the violence I crave. Everybody's happy."

She leaned over and kissed him on the cheek before taking a handful of popcorn from the bag on his lap.

After the movie, he took her for ice cream and they shared a banana split while discussing the movie. While spooning the melted ice cream from the bottom of the dish into each other's mouths, he asked her why she was so passionate about her work.

She thought for a moment before answering, carefully formulating her thoughts. Then she dove in. "Well, it's going to sound more like a lecture than a reason, but here goes. The coast is an ever-changing dynamic balance between sediment and wave energy. There are so many factors that continually change things that it's hard to keep up. And there's so much we still don't know.

"The coast is fragile. Minute changes in sea level, sand, shell debris, mud, even changes in seaweed can affect things many miles away. The Greek philosopher,

Heraclitus, once compared time to flowing water and wrote, 'You cannot step twice into the same river.' And he was right, it's never the same twice. It's constantly changing.

"And the barrier islands, which certainly are the most beautiful, have the most to deal with in terms of change; they bear the brunt of the impact from storms, hurricanes, surges, and floods. They are only isolated masses of gravel, sand, and sludge; they are completely unconsolidated and surrounded by tremendous wave energies. They are so susceptible to erosion, overwash, wind damage, and traumatic sand movements that it's mind-boggling. Add some grasses and a few vines, and sediment can be trapped. Add vegetation and concrete, and it can be tamed. At least that's what people have come to believe. But it's not true.

"The human element enters the picture, and suddenly everyone wants a jetty, a bulkhead, a rock sill, a grunt, channels dredged, inlets redirected, canals widened, dunes flattened, vegetation added or removed, unwise development, you name it. Well, it's a time bomb. The next storm can cause the whole thing to blow up, out, or away.

"My job is to educate, as is yours. I talk about topics related to geology and oceanography, but somehow the history lessons seem more important than anything else. Like the lesson learned on October 15th in 1954 when Hurricane Hazel came to town with 150-mile-per-hour winds and seventeen-foot waves. She destroyed all but three homes of the three hundred on Holden Beach.

"Did you know that scientists have discovered how to convert the energy of the warm water in the Gulf Stream into electricity? They say they can generate seventy-five times more power than all the utility plants in the United States. The process is called Ocean Thermal

Energy Conversion or OTEC. Yet people still have no idea about the seemingly limitless power of the oceans. They see the water gently lapping at the shoreline as a surfer glides through the waves and they forget. They forget its awesome power. I assess each situation I go on-site for with the law in mind, and not just the laws imposed by the regulatory commission I work for, but the laws of Mother Nature as well.

"People are just beginning to understand the danger from riptides, and that's only because people are dying in them at record numbers. So they know how strong an adversary the sea can be. I don't think they'll ever truly believe that we cannot harness the power of the ocean, that we can't force it to our will, no matter how much money we're willing to spend.

"So, when we see a storm coming, the ocean going mad and rolling fast with white caps, and we see the wind knocking down umbrellas and sending them into turtle nests, we prepare for the worst, knowing things are going to change dramatically. But little do people know, that they are changing dramatically with every single wave that comes to shore. Every tide that comes in or goes out changes everything. There is no keeper of the ocean, because it can't be kept. I am just a lowly scorekeeper, letting everyone know that we are not the favorite in this game. We are the underdog in an incredibly big way. We lose ninety times out of a hundred and we will continue to do so until we learn we're not in control.

"So, I say yea, or nay, depending on what the concession is we have to give up to Mother Nature, unless of course, my bosses have made other concessions in the courts. I know I don't have a popular job, but I take care to do it well, because I want us to achieve the harmony that balances everything and keeps the coastline safe."

"Wow. Shelby, you are amazing."

"I think the same thing about you," she said as she stifled a yawn.

"Oh, oh. I think someone's petering out on me."

"Sorry, I lost a bit of sleep this week when someone called after midnight to talk about dreams."

"Oops. I'd better get you to bed."

When she quickly looked up from swirling her spoon in the melted ice cream and he saw the hesitation in her eyes, he added, "Your bed. The one I reserved for you. Regretfully, far, far away from mine." He sensed that for all her talk, she wasn't quite as ready as she wanted him to think she was.

He stood and smiled down at her as he put out his hand for her to take. "C'mon, you've had a full day. Time to get some rest."

True to his word, Ben had reserved a small suite at the nearby Hampton Inn. Even though his body was burning for her, he left Shelby at the door to her room with only a tender kiss on her lips. He patted her cheek and smiled as he continued to fight the very persistent urge a certain part of his body had to bury itself inside her. His sense of it all, was that Shelby needed more time than he was giving her, even though she gave no indication of being scared or wanting to curb his lust, even a little bit.

As Ben rode the elevator to the lobby, he was so much more aware of his body and its hardness than he'd ever been. It was as if every cell was screaming out Shelby's name and every fiber was pulling for him to be near her, holding her, molding a sublime softness against each hard feature. He knew that he had never felt this way about any other woman. Even Anna, as close as they had been, had never caused the sensation that seemed to be his very soul burning and aching with want, with need.

As the doors opened he debated returning to her room, staking his claim, and soothing this awful burn. Good God, if only she wasn't a virgin! Then a thought occurred to him. Hell, if he didn't do it, it was only a matter of time before some cad surely would. Damn! Even the thought of her being taken by another man sent sparks of anger through him. It should be him. Damn it! It would be him! But no, not tonight. She was tired. She was in need of a good night's sleep, and she deserved better. The first time was important. It would come to her mind many times throughout her later years. He would make it special. He wouldn't rush it. He would seduce and plan, and then savor every single moment. Yes!

He bounced off the elevator with a spring in his step. Yes, a nice slow seduction. Tomorrow he would treat her to an afternoon of shopping. Then later, he would wine and dine her, slow dance with her until her body thrummed. He would take her home where everything would be in perfect readiness. And she would be his. He pictured himself naked, propped over her, his arms supporting himself as he plunged deeply into her, her dark auburn curls a contrast on the stark pillow, her head turning this way and that as she cried out her pleasure and gripped his shoulders. *Oh yes, this would be a memory seared into both their brains.*

He stopped off at the grocery store on his way home, then spent the next few hours implementing his plan.

When he overslept the next morning and woke to her call, he smiled into the receiver. "You're up early."

"The people next door were a little noisy this morning. So was their two year old."

"Ah, well not to worry, tomorrow morning you'll have no problem sleeping in. I guarantee it."

"Really? What do you have planned for today that will be so exhausting?"

"Ah, it's not only the day I've defined, but the night."

The way he whispered, "but the night," caused a shiver to go up her spine. As she lay there in her bed envisioning him in his, she couldn't help but stroke her finger tips along her inner thigh.

"Mmmm. You have me very curious."

"Too bad. Everything's a surprise. Get dressed and pack up. I'll pick you up in an hour. Then I'm going to give you a day *and* a night that you'll never forget." Before she could answer him, he hung up the phone.

She was sitting in the lobby nibbling on a croissant when he came to get her. She had gone down to the reception desk a few minutes early to check out only to find that everything had been taken care of by phone. Ben had told her that he had arranged for her to stay closer to his apartment tonight, but he hadn't told her he was picking up the tab for her accommodations. But that was just like him, she thought with a smile. He really was quite free with his money, wasn't he? Then she turned and saw him and her heart flipped.

He smiled as he came through the automatic door, took her into his arms, and lifted her off her feet. Then he kissed her soundly, ignoring the noise of her muffled shock and the curiosity of milling patrons.

"Morning doll baby. Ready to roll?"

"Uh, yeah," she said dazedly as her fingertips smoothed over her heated lips.

He led her out to the car waiting under the porte-cochère. An elderly man in a uniform was holding the door open for them. He smiled at them both and nodded at her. "Good morning, Miss."

She looked at the car, the driver, and then back over

her shoulder at Ben. Clearly she was puzzled and he was delighted to have surprised her.

"Shelby, this is Stefan. He's going to drive us around today while I take you in and out of some of the finest shops in the city. We're going to celebrate your birthday."

"But it's not my birthday."

"We'll start by celebrating all the ones I've missed. You're twenty . . . ?" he asked.

"Twenty-four," she supplied.

"Then that's twenty-four gifts we have to find. One for each year of your life that I've missed so far."

"You're crazy!"

"No. Just happy. And anxious to make up for all the birthday parties you didn't get to have. Get in. We're on a mission and we must have it accomplished by dinnertime. Stefan, first stop, South Square Mall please. East Entrance."

"Yes, sir."

Shelby scooted across the leather seat and Ben slid in beside her. Then Stefan closed the door behind them and they were off.

Two hours later, Shelby leaned against the wall of a dressing room as she tried on silk trousers. "Let me get this straight," she called out over the door, "these are my birthday presents but you get to pick them all out?"

He chuckled and tossed a cashmere sweater over the low door. "When you have a birthday party, you don't get to tell the guests what presents to bring."

"I'm having a birthday party?"

"Yes. Tonight you're having a birthday party."

"Really?" You could hear the pure joy in her voice.

"Yes. I was never invited to any of your twenty-four birthday parties because you didn't have any. Now I have to make up for all those parties we both missed out on and all the presents I didn't get to shower you with."

"I didn't know you. And you wouldn't have been invited even if I'd had any."

"That's not very nice."

She laughed at his mock sincerity as she tried the sweater on over top of the pants. It felt so wonderful against her skin. It was the softest material she had ever felt. She almost wished she wasn't wearing one of the bras he'd selected for her at Victoria's Secret. The feel of the velvety cashmere against her nipples would be heavenly; she just knew it.

When she stepped out of the changing room, his eyes lit up with delight.

"I knew that royal blue was your color. Look at you," he said as he spun her to face the triple mirror, "the blue in your eyes is mesmerizing, and look how rosy your cheeks are."

She wanted to tell him that the sapphire twinkle he was admiring, as well as the pink flush on her cheeks, was because of him. Because he was lavishly doting on her and making her feel like a princess as he admired and adorned her with the highest quality and costliest clothing she had touched in her life. It was like living a dream, a wonderful giddy dream.

"I think we should stop now. You've already spent way too much money on me."

She looked at him in the mirror as he stood over her shoulder smoothing the seam of the sweater. Their eyes met in the mirror and he bent to kiss the side of her neck. "You are a woman who deserves the finest things money can buy. I will see you dressed from head to toe before this day is over. *Then*, if you're game, I will pay you to let me remove each piece, one at a time," he growled as his hand snuck down to caress her butt. "Mmmm, silk. Shapely, firm, gluteus maximus covered in raw, Egyptian silk. Be a shame to take these off."

The incredible feel of his hand as it groped and caressed her cheek was more than she could stand and she felt herself swaying. He reached around to her front and with a hand splayed on her lower belly, he pulled her back into his body.

"Mmmm. Not sure how long I can wait to buy these back."

"What are you talking about?" she murmured, her eyes half closed now.

"I want you to strip for me tonight. And knowing how much you like to save money, I'm going to give you an enticement you can't refuse. I'll pay you dollar for dollar exactly what I'm paying for everything we buy today. And I have to tell you, I'm not calling in any markers. I'm paying full retail for every single stitch. If you play your cards right, you could be on your way to Europe with first-class plane tickets. You can forget about the hostelries, you'll be able to stay in the finest hotels." His mouth had worked its way painstakingly up the side of her neck to her newly-enhanced, diamond-studded ear lobe.

"Yes, I'm going to pay you to take off everything we just put on," he whispered seductively.

"Even the silky, lace thong?"

"Especially the silky, lace thong."

"It cost twenty-nine dollars."

"I know. It's the most important thing I'm going to ask you to remove. If you agree, I get it at a rock bottom price, compared to these," he said as his hand skimmed over to her hip and to the side zipper where a price tag hung. Both of their heads turned and looked down as his fingers grasped the tag and flipped it over it so they could see the price, $485. She gasped and he chuckled.

"Worth every penny and more," he said as he turned

her in his arms and kissed her thoroughly. A fire was consuming her and she didn't know whether to protest his blatant extravagance and remove them now for free, or just let the heat of their bodies disintegrate them.

His lips crushed hers and she was fully returning his passion when the sycophant saleswoman returned with a tray of filled champagne flutes. Reluctantly, Ben loosened his hold on her, but he didn't fully release her. He needed her to shield him, at least for a few minutes. "Ah, thank you," he sighed taking a flute and handing it over to Shelby before taking one for himself. "I thought I was going to combust," he added and winked over at Shelby.

"We're up to year nineteen, Shelby. Five more birthdays to go. Drink up and let's get over to the shoe department. I have a fondness for high heels. Very high, high heels."

"Oh, I can't walk in them."

"I mean very 'high' priced," he said with a secretive grin. "Gotta make it worth your while."

He took her over to the shoe department and bought her a pair of outrageously sexy scamps that went beautifully with the rest of the outfit he planned for her to wear that night. Then he took her to another jewelry store for a gold anklet to set off her slim ankle. The limo pulled up in front of a fur salon, but she refused to have anything to do with wearing an animal pelt of any kind, so Ben settled on a black velvet swing cape with a scarlet satin lining.

"You'll get last year's present later tonight," he whispered in her ear as the limo pulled up to an exclusive spa. It was two o'clock in the afternoon. They had spent the better part of the day shopping. Lunch had been the tidbits served in the ritzy salons as they shopped and splurged and now Shelby, a little lightheaded from the continually proffered flutes of champagne, was being ushered out of the car and into yet another glitzy store.

Ben kissed her lightly on the cheek as they approached a waiting hostess. "Shelby, these women are going to take care of you now. You're going to enjoy a nice long soak, an herbal wrap, a facial, pedicure and manicure, then a relaxing massage. You'll rest for a while before your hair is done for you. When you're ready, Stefan will be called to come for you and you'll be brought back to me. You'll dress for dinner in one of your new outfits and after dinner if you feel like it, I'll take you dancing." He bent low and brushed his lips against her ear. "Then later, I'll get my money clip out, and you can stop dreaming about that trip to Europe and go ahead and plan it. Happy Birthday, sweetheart," he whispered huskily. He kissed her lightly on the cheek and handed her off, instructing the women not to dare to change the color of her hair, and before she knew what was going on, he was gone and she was being whisked away.

Chapter Twenty-Three—
The Seduction
Chapel Hill, NC

Stefan pulled up in front of an apartment building and the incongruence of the limo to the quaint, modest-looking garden apartment complex, slapped her in the face and she suddenly felt very guilty. If this was where Ben lived, then he surely couldn't afford the lavish gifts he'd bought for her today and the spa treatments she'd enjoyed so much. Remembering that his parents were quite wealthy didn't help matters as she also remembered that they were not on the best of terms with each other.

She stepped out of the car as Stefan held the door for her. He walked her up the long sidewalk to the door of the building in front of them. "Dr. Kenyon's apartment is on the third floor, number 316. He asked me to see you inside before leaving."

"Isn't he here?" she asked.

"I believe he said he had a few errands to run this afternoon. He wants you to make yourself at home and rest for this evening. He has asked me to pick you up at eight."

As they rode the elevator to the third floor, Shelby admired the bright red lacquer on her newly-manicured nails. "You seem to know Dr. Kenyon well, am I mistaken?"

"Oh no, ma'am, you're not mistaken. I know him all right. I'm his mother's driver. Today's usually my day off, but when Ben called, I couldn't refuse him. I used to drive young Ben to school every day."

"His parents live locally?"

"Not always. They have several residences, but they often stay in North Carolina this time of the year if the weather is agreeable."

"Doesn't his father need to be closer to the bank he owns?"

"He owns several, but I don't think he's been in any of them for years. He's retired. He let's the board take care of everything now."

"Oh."

"Well, here we are." Stefan took out a key and opened the door for her.

"Thank you, Stefan."

"You're most welcome, Miss."

So, maybe he was pinched for cash, she thought as she walked through the door. She would have to insist they return everything he bought for her today.

Before the door had closed behind her, she knew without a doubt that Ben was far removed from having money problems. From the outside this might look like a middle class neighborhood; but inside, it was elite class all the way.

The living room was furnished with the most beautiful cherry furniture she'd ever seen. It was so highly polished that it gleamed in the late afternoon sun. A very masculine plaid covered the facing sofa and love seat in the center of the room. Over in a far corner was a grand piano that sat in resplendent repose, a music book open above the keys waiting for the master's return. On every glossy surface there was a cut crystal vase filled with roses, a dozen pink on the sofa table, a dozen white on the coffee table, tea cup roses on each end table, and a gigantic arrangement of red bud roses sat on the piano.

She had hardly taken it all in when a tiny woman in a maid's uniform appeared from a room to the left of the piano.

"Hello, Miss Shelby. I am Anita. Mr. Ben asked me to wait for you and to show you to your room. He suggests you rest before your dinner."

"Oh, okay. I am a bit tired."

"I'll show you to your room." She led her through a formal dining room and an immaculate kitchen to a long hallway. At the first open door Anita stopped and gestured her inside. "He instructed me to prepare the guest room for you. If there's anything you need, please ask. I am also here to help you dress should you need any help. Can I get you anything now? Some tea, perhaps?"

"No, no thank you. The women at the salon had fruit and cheese platters along with little goodies everywhere, I'm not even sure I'm going to have room for dinner."

With a timid smile and a slight nod, Anita turned and retreated down the hallway and into the kitchen.

Shelby walked into the room and looked around. It was a delightful room, full of whimsy and inviting touches. The heavy, bold furniture, although solid white, was enlivened by pale yellow and vibrant blue striped linens. The love seat in the sitting area was upholstered in complimentary colors but in a floral pattern instead of the stripes. On the walls and ceiling, white trompe l'oeil puffy clouds floated across a pale blue sky. The roses on every surface in this room were yellow. Four dozen of them. She walked over and sat on the fluffy bed, bounced on the mattress a few times, and then laughingly threw herself back, her arms spread wide. What a glorious day this had been, and now, here she was in Ben's home! And it was truly and magnificently all Ben; sleek and classy, clean lines with no froufrou, yet homey and comfortable and very, very nice.

She put her hands behind her head, conscious of not flattening her new sleek do and closed her eyes. She wondered what Ben's room was like. Maybe, just maybe, with a little luck and the right stripper moves, she'd have a first-hand opportunity to see it tonight. The thought of being in Ben's bed while he was in it, sent delightful shivers through her. She kept her eyes closed and mentally pictured him naked under the sheets, pulling her into his arms and capturing her mouth with his. She actually heard herself moan, and cautiously opened her eyes to make sure she was still alone.

A card sticking up from the arrangement of flowers on the nightstand drew her eye and she sat up and reached for it. "Your birthday presents are in the closet. Remember to put them all on as I'm dying to watch you remove each and every one of them for me. Ben."

Oooh, this was heady stuff. She felt something warm puddle in her stomach and then fire fanned through her. Was this the way it was for everybody, or was she just nervous? She reached for the crystal water carafe that was on the night table and poured water into the matching glass. As she downed the contents, she continued to look around. On the walls were pictures of North Carolina lighthouses and the few knickknacks that were on the dresser were very detailed miniatures of those exact same lighthouses. It was a great room, neither feminine or masculine, but certainly not reminiscent of the man whose anteroom to his own office was known as the crypt.

She walked over to the closet and opened the doors. Then she fingered and admired again all her lovely birthday presents from Ben. Clutching the ultra-soft cashmere sweater to her chest she went over and gingerly laid down on the bed. Within moments of her head snuggling into the pillow, she was fast asleep. She dreamed Ben was caressing her naked body by rubbing it all over with her new cashmere sweater. As she lay asleep dreaming under the clouds, she moaned his name and licked her lips.

CR

Ben sat at her hip, slowly drawing the long sleeve of the sweater along her cheek and down her neck. God, she was so lovely. And fresh. Her skin glowed of health and youth. His fingertips touched her smooth hair. He missed her floppy curls, but this look would be more in keeping with his image of a sexy vixen. A sexy vixen who was going to do a striptease and remove all her clothes just for him this very night.

He bent over and kissed her lightly on the lips and then he eased himself off the bed and left the room.

Walking into the kitchen, he addressed Anita. "Why don't you give her another fifteen minutes and then wake her to get dressed."

"Yes, sir."

"And Anita?"

"Yes?"

"Make sure all the roses are moved into my

bedroom before you leave tonight, if you don't mind."

"Yes, sir."

"Thank you. Tell my mother thank you also. I appreciate you helping me today."

"You're welcome, sir."

He picked his glass up off the counter and downed the bracing Crown Royal in one greedy swallow. It wasn't often that he drank hard liquor but tonight, for some reason, he felt he needed something to take the edge off a little. He left the glass in the sink and walked down the hallway to his bedroom and to the adjoining bathroom where he turned on the shower. As he removed his clothes and stepped into the steaming mist, he had a moment of guilt. Here he was pulling out all the stops, dressing her for sexy role-playing, setting up a romantic candlelight dinner, preparing to tease her body with mind-numbing dances . . . all for one thing. The exclusive right to be her first, to take her on his terms. He didn't even know if this was what she truly wanted. He only knew that whenever he held her, it felt so right. Never mind that he was long past ready, was she?

He ducked his head under the spray and tried to drown out his thoughts of her: her under him, her over him, her center core welcoming him as he wormed his way into her body. *Damn! Despite all his planning, he wasn't sure he was going to be able to go through with this.* A few moments later, as he toweled himself off, he came to a decision. He would just take his cues from her. If she balked, just once, he would back off all the way and take her back to the hotel.

❦

Shelby stood in front of the mirror while Anita

fastened the clasp of her new necklace. It was a single diamond floating in an off-center heart and it matched the diamond studs in her ears. She reached up and smoothed a strand of hair. Her hair was much longer without the curls, hanging past her chin it gently curved under and swayed provocatively. It was a lovely style, but one she doubted she'd ever be able to do on her own. The stylist had blow dried it as she pulled on it and curled it under for the better part of half an hour to achieve this look; but Shelby knew that for practicality's sake, as soon as she stepped out of the shower tomorrow morning her curls would be back, short, full and unruly, once more.

"You are lovely, Miss Shelby. Dr. Ben will surely enjoy escorting you to your birthday party."

"He told you about the party?"

"He just told me it was your birthday and you were having a private party. But the way he has been fretting, I know he cares very much for you."

"You really think so?"

"I have never known Dr. Ben to use the limo or to have me wait around for flowers to be delivered while he made everything perfect for anyone."

"What else has he done?" Shelby asked.

"I cannot say. But I think you will be very happy. You must go now. Mr. Ben is waiting."

"Thanks, Anita." Impulsively, she gave the tiny woman a hug and a gentle squeeze.

"Happy Birthday, Miss Shelby."

ᏦᎡ

Ben was sitting at the piano when she walked into the living room. As soon as he saw her, he began playing a boisterous rendition of "Happy Birthday to You."

Shelby smiled through his slightly off-key singing and then blushed as he jumped off the bench and kissed her on the cheek.

"Stunning. Positively stunning," he said as he stood back to look at her. His fingers itched to touch the cashmere sweater in the places it hollowed out as it draped against her. He knew that smoothing the material over her torso would be thrilling for them both. He took in her short, show-stopper silk skirt with the little ruffle flounces around the hem, her sheer black hose that he knew were being held up by a stop-your-heart garter belt, and her new shiny black sling backs. She was everything sexy and everything innocent all at once and he decided that he desperately wanted to make love to her. Tonight. As long as it was all right with her. And he had certainly seen to it that it would be, he thought with chagrin.

"Ready? Our chariot awaits."

She gave him a big smile. "Yes. Wine me, dine me, then strip me," she whispered in his ear.

"Would that I could reverse that order," he teased as he ushered her out of the apartment. "I'll see you next week," he called out to Anita just as the door closed.

"She's your cleaning lady?"

"Well, actually, she's my mother's maid when my mom's in residence here. She comes by once a week to tidy up for me."

"You have a lot more money than you let on."

"I do okay."

"You're being modest."

"I guess it's just hard when you come from money to get away from it."

"Nice problem. Never had it."

He chuckled as he placed his hand at the small of

her back and ushered her into the elevator. Then as the doors closed, he leaned down and whispered in her ear, "I'm not above paying for something if it has value to me, and the things I bought for you today are about the most valuable things I think I've ever purchased."

"That's because they're going to cost you double," she teased.

He grinned and winked back at her. "Even if I only pay for them once, I don't believe I have ever had the pleasure of seeing someone so happy with any gift I've ever given."

"I had a wonderful time. You were way too generous though."

"Nah." Ben opened the door and they walked out into the beautiful night. The stars blinked erratically in an inky black sky as a big moon struggled to pull itself up off the horizon. At the end of the sidewalk ahead of them, they could see Stefan holding open a door and waiting for them.

"Where are we going for dinner?" Shelby asked.

"I had originally thought to take you to a little out of the way place so I could have you all to myself, but after seeing you in those clothes today, I knew I had to take you somewhere where I could show you off. So we're going to Barton's."

"Never heard of it."

"It's pretty exclusive. At least the prices they set make it seem that way."

"Evening, Sir. Miss," Stefan said as they slid into their seats. He closed the door behind them and this time Shelby noticed that the screen had been raised.

"I don't want to share you anymore than I have to," he said huskily as he lifted her hand to his lips and kissed each knuckle. Shelby was glad she was sitting; she knew her knees would have given out if she hadn't been. The way he painstakingly drew his lips over each fingertip, then licked his way down to her palm, caused her to tremble.

When they reached the restaurant, they were seated at a table that had a view of the private gardens in the back. Special lighting enabled them to see the blooming rose and camellia bushes. Strands of Spanish moss were draped majestically in a tall Live Oak that was lit from the ground. It was a beautiful setting. Shelby thought an impish wood nymph darting from tree to tree would have fit very nicely into the scene; it was that surreal.

Ben ordered for them and soon they were sipping a fragrant wine and feasting on dainty scallops wrapped with bacon served in a delicious cream sauce. Lobster tails and filet mignon followed, and over a chocolate crème brûlée, they sipped rich coffee and counted stars.

"I am so full," Shelby protested.

"Good. Then I know you have the caloric intake needed to keep up with me on the dance floor."

Ben signed for the check and they left for the piano lounge where, by special arrangement, a trio was waiting to play prescribed dance numbers Ben had selected.

They sat at a small table on the edge of the dance floor and sipped a cordial while the band warmed up. When the beginning strands of "You Belong to Me" started, Ben stood and offered Shelby his hand. As the soloist crooned, "See the pyramids along the Nile . . ." Ben pulled Shelby in close and led her across the dance floor. Soon, their bodies moved as one; it was as if they had fused together. Every hard muscle in his body had sought out her corresponding softness and held fast. He never wanted this moment to end. Holding her like this, breathing in her enchanting freshness and feeling this incredible, sensual bond was heady. Even though he had yet to finish a glass of wine, or even the cordial at the table, he felt drunk, intoxicated with her.

She looked up at him and smiled. As he looked down into her upturned face, a stupendous realization dawned on him. He was in love. Sweet Jesus, he was in love with this woman.

A warm feeling washed over him, flushing his veins, and he reeled with desire. He loved this woman. He *really, really* loved this woman.

Now he didn't know what to do! He'd gone about seducing her, but look who got seduced instead! He was momentarily stunned, enough that he mis-stepped. When she lifted her head from his shoulder to question his movements, he fell full and hard into the depths of her eyes. Hell, why fight it, he asked himself, and bent his head. His lips took hers wholly and intently. It was a kiss that commanded, as well as celebrated, and the people at the tables along the edge of the dance floor had to acknowledge that as far as kisses went, there wasn't a movie that had done one better. This woman was definitely being swept off her feet.

When he joined the soloist and whispered the final words of the song, *You belong to me*, into her hair, he knew he had never meant any words more.

❧

Ben sat in the overstuffed chair, one leg crossed over the opposite knee, a brandy snifter sloshing sherry around the high edges in his splayed hand. The grin on his face was as broad as it could possibly be. "Now, remember, you can stop anytime you want. Whenever you think you have enough money, just say so. You don't have to take anything off unless you want to."

On the table beside him was a pile of receipts, next to that, hundred-dollar bills were fanned out beside fifties and twenties.

"Who picks the item to be removed?" Shelby asked.

"You do. I look it up, see what I paid for it and when you hand it to me, I give you the money in exchange."

"Sounds . . . easy."

"Oh, believe me, it's pretty good work if you can get it."

She leaned on the arm of his chair, took the brandy snifter from his hand and took a bracing gulp. "Fortification," she murmured and then handed it back to him. She had already had a fair amount of fortification if you considered the wine at dinner, the after-dinner cordials, and now hefty gulps of his vintage sherry.

"And where do I stand?"

"Right in front of me, so I can get a good look. Not too close, not too far. That's good, right there."

"Is there music?"

"Oh, yeah. I almost forgot. Push that button over on the CD deck. Yeah, the red flashing one. Now the one right below it." Instantly, the soft, low, belting sounds of the traditional stripper's song came through the speakers that were hidden in the corners. *Ba da ba ba, ba da, ba ba . . . .*

Shelby's eyes danced and she gave a sexy little shimmy as she slowly strolled toward him, taking out her diamond ear studs. "Gee, I was getting pretty partial to these," she said as she admired them rolling around in her palm before handing them over to him.

He took them from her, fished through the receipts

for the one from the jewelry store, and counted out $460. She took the money, grinned big as life, and waved it in front of her face. "Hey, this is fun."

"Continue," he murmured, in a most commanding voice.

Next came the necklace at $740. She put her hands behind her neck and unclasped it, then dangled it in front of him before dropping it into his lap.

Shelby added the money to the small pile she already had. "I should stop now," she whispered. But then she eyed the large pile of money still on the table beside Ben. "Nah."

She got a little caught up in the music and did a few bumps and grinds for him. He laughed because they looked anything but sexy.

Deftly she bent from the waist, which was impressive in its own right, and removed first one shoe and then the other. Swinging them by the straps, she walked over and deposited them at his feet.

"One slightly used pair of wonderful dancing shoes," she said. "You didn't even step on my toes once so they're only used on the bottom."

"$280."

"Wow, that's a lot for shoes."

"I would have bought you a pair of Manolo Blahniks if you'd wanted them. They were $800."

"Oh my!"

"So, you're a cheap strip as far as I'm concerned."

"You won't be saying that soon. I'm going to get all that money," she said with a big smile as she waved her hand a little drunkenly at the money on the table. "Just you wait and see."

"That's what I intend to do. See. So show me."

He was beginning to notice her tipsiness and, for a brief moment, considered whether he should let this go on. He certainly didn't want to take advantage. But then she looked coquettishly at him, winked playfully, and blew on her red fingernails. She rubbed them against the cashmere sweater to polish them, then reached for the hem and slowly inched the sweater up her slim torso and over her head. She swung it over her head twice and then released it. It hit him square in the face. When it fell to his lap, he stared at the black lace bra that hid just her nipples. And even though her breasts were encased in the smallest cup size bras came in, his body went hard in half a second flat. Oh, she was playing with fire and he thought she damned well knew it.

"I believe that sweater was $320," she prompted.

He clamped his mouth closed and blinked his eyes. "Oh, yeah." He counted out the money and handed it to her, all the while ogling her unabashedly.

She was alternately blushing and trying to find ways to innocuously cover herself and brazenly flaunting her sensationally slim body.

"More," he said.

"You want more?" she asked teasingly. "I'll give you more." With a flagrant hand motion, she ceremoniously unzipped the side zipper of her skirt; it fell to the floor as soon as the zipper was undone and sooner than she had expected it to. She started a bit then stooped to retrieve it. "Oops."

His mouth went dry and his tongue slack as he saw her long, slim legs encased in black-on-black stockings attached to garter clips. Raising his eyes, he saw the juncture of her thighs outlined by the lace edging of the slim, hip garter panty.

"You don't know how hard it is for me to remain sitting here," he gritted out.

"How hard is it?" she asked innocently, sending him a sideways smile, chiding him.

"It's plenty hard. Come see."

"I don't think I'd better. Pay up for the skirt."

"Gladly."

He dished out $180.

The music had stopped now and there was silence as he counted it out to her. She was so close to him now that he could see the fine, downy hairs leading from her navel into her panties.

She was idly flicking the garter strap and it was driving him wild as it repeatedly slapped against her thigh.

Then she turned and pranced away, apparently completely forgetting she was wearing a thong-type garter panty. He practically fell out of the chair watching her smooth, tight buttocks sway back and forth. He sighed rather loudly. Then she remembered and tried to cover herself with her hands as she spun back around.

It would have been pretty comical, only nothing was funny right now. He was damned near in pain.

"It is odd how the most revealing items are bringing the least reward," she ventured.

"Then stop."

"I don't want to."

"The money's that much of an enticement?" There was a touch of disappointment in his voice.

"Oh, no. It has nothing to do with the money. I like what this is doing to you, and I don't mean making you broke."

"You could strip for me every night like this without breaking me."

"Well, that's good to know." Boldly, she said, "I want $20 for each stocking."

"They only cost $20 for the set."

"Do you want them on or off?"

"Here. Here's a hundred."

She sat on the ottoman that had been pushed aside and began to slowly roll down a stocking. She made a big deal of unfurling it and letting it drop before going to the other one. Then she stood up and hooked her fingers in the elastic band of the garter panty. "Now I don't remember if I put anything on under this, so don't get upset if I have to hurry and pull them back up." She pulled them out and peeked into them. "Well, if I did, they're pretty tiny. I don't see anything down there." She started pulling them down and his heart did flip-flops before running steadily like a diesel motor.

As they cleared her hips, she smiled and said, "Oh, yeah, that black stringy thing you liked so much." Sure enough, as the garter pants went further down her thighs, he could see the tiny, black, string-bikini-thong panty he had bought her.

Then she was standing there in only a very skimpy pair of underpants and a nearly see-through bra.

"I think I have enough money now," she whispered.

He stood up and slowly walked over to where she stood nervously fidgeting with her hair. With one hand deftly on her back, he unsnapped her bra and popped it open. With the other, he pulled on the tiny side ribbon of her thong and untied it. With his eyes totally focused on her luminous, wide eyes, he slid the straps of her bra down her arms and let it drop to the floor. The bikini he was holding in his hand by the ribbon followed.

"I didn't know they did that."

"I did."

"Oh."

"So, you think you have enough money?"

"Mmmm Hmmm," she hummed a bit uncertainly.

"I don't think so. You can never have too much

money."

He leaned in to kiss her softly on the lips as his hand moved to cup a breast. "Tell me now if you intend to make me stop," he whispered.

"Not a chance," she answered.

He bent and lifted her into his arms, then he carried her through the kitchen, down the hallway, and into his bedroom.

"You're not going to leave money on the nightstand in the morning are you?" she asked as he laid her in the center of his bed.

"If I have to," he replied as he stood above her and began loosening his tie. He took his money clip out of his trouser pocket and placed it on the nightstand. "Take it all. I'm sure I'm going to get my money's worth one way or the other."

"There are more ways than one?"

His booming laugh echoed in the room. He had just unbuttoned his shirt and was pulling it off. He looked formidable and even a little frightening with all that dark male hair and bunching muscle. He removed his belt, shoes and socks, but left his pants on as he laid down on the bed and covered her with his body. "There are more ways than I can count. We'll just try a few tonight if you don't mind. I've had a tiring day shopping." His lips closed over hers as the heat of his kiss and the heat of his body burned into her veins.

His lips moved down her throat and he moaned, "Just don't judge me too harshly. It's been a long, long time since I was with a woman, and never one quite like you." When his lips moved down her chest and he took a crested peak into his mouth, she sobbed her pleasure and he knew she was going to be his undoing.

His warm, hulking body moving over hers was doing incredible things to her. As his body hair brushed against her smooth skin, her breath caught. This was heady. She could barely stand the sensations as jolt after jolt of unfathomable pleasure rolled over her. This was it. She was going to do it. This man arching over her and pressing his hips firmly into hers was going to finally make her a woman. Her sexual curiosity would finally be appeased. The fact that she had such strong feelings for him not only took away any doubt she might have had, but reaffirmed her desire to give this special part of her to him. Only him. Ben.

When his hand moved down her side and he grasped her hip, pulling her even closer to his strident, pulsing hardness, she felt her body opening, eager, even anxious for his assault.

"Please Ben, hurry. I need you."

"Aw, honey, I need you, too. I need you so badly I'm going fucking crazy here. Open your legs. Let me get you ready."

"I *am* ready."

"Trust me, honey, you're not. Not just yet. But you will be," he moaned as his fingers found her cleft and separated her lips. "Mmmnghh," he grunted. "Soon," he added as his hips thrust against her thigh while his finger burrowed further into her. "Yeah, maybe you are at that." She felt warm and slickery, but incredibly tight around his finger. His one finger. Shit. She was going to hate this. When she stretched to accommodate him, she was not going to like this at all. But as her muscles clenched around his finger, he found rationalization in his absolute knowledge of the human form. She *would* stretch. She *would* take him fully in. And it would feel like the most wonderful thing on earth. To him.

"Shel, I keep forgetting to ask, are you protected or do I need to use a condom?" he asked as he prepared her for him.

"I'm on the Pill."

"That's wonderful news," he whispered as he removed his fingers and began circling the top of her slit with the pad of his thumb. He felt the bud he found there growing as she moaned and arched her body up to meet his hand.

"Ah, sweet Jesus. Forgive me, Shel, nnngh. Arghh, I can't wait. Must . . ." his voice trailed off as he hurriedly lifted off her, unzipped his pants, and together with his underwear, pulled them down and stepped out of them. His ardent manhood leapt out of a triangle of dark, curling hairs as he lay back down and led it to her. She had only a glimpse of the angry-looking appendage that lifted against his belly before he moved back to her. In a panic, she realized that it was triple the size she thought would fit. Until Ben, the flaccid penises she'd seen in art galleries were all she'd had to go by. Then the moist tip of his penis touched her as he thumbed it down and poised it at her opening. He hesitated for just a split second before allowing his hips to guide the jutting hardness in. She held her breath.

Her barrier greeted him almost immediately and without reservation, he pulled back and plowed through it. He was fully seated, his eyes on hers, when her eyes popped wide open and filled with tears.

"Home," he said simply, as he filled her and looked down into her beautiful face.

"Home? As in home base?" she asked weakly, with a grudging smile.

"No, home as in haven. And exactly where I want to be," he murmured as he backed out and gently thrust back in. "Home, as in dwelling." He pushed his hips forward again, more firmly this time. "Home, the place I want to crawl up into so badly."

His breathy words came to her mingled between loud grunting noises. And although it sounded like he was laboring tremendously and in great pain, she sensed that he was not, as she absolutely was not. On their own, her hips began to rise up to meet his. Stride for stride she arched her body into his as he rode her and held her tightly to him. Then just as she thought that this was futile, that this rubbing and sliding feeling was doing nothing but creating a hollow emptiness that continued to grow, as it intimidated and taunted, she felt something happening way beyond the normal scope of her body. She was sure that if she couldn't touch it and grab hold of it, that this desperation would never leave her, that she would be left wanton and aching forever. Just as she despaired of dying, wanting something totally unknown to her, her body stretched, reached, and caught a ride on the most wonderful, golden moonbeam. She felt herself slide down as the gold sparked into a kaleidoscope of rainbow colors. She crested and exploded from within and felt the earth disappear out from under her. Spiraling, falling, and then slowly drifting, she found herself encased in a velvet blackness as her body collapsed and then thrummed steadily. Vaguely she heard Ben call out and with both hands roughly grasping her buttocks, he thrust hard into her.

For Ben, dark thunderheads were gathering, huge charged clouds of lust and energy. They built one onto another, darkening and growing steadily until finally, like a jagged thunderbolt snaking across the sky, everything erupted inside him and with shooting sparks exploding everywhere, he emptied into her.

For long, agonizing moments, he held her tightly to him as his teeth clenched and his head turned inside out. Then he managed to raise himself up on his elbows as he caved his head into the pillow beside her head. "Home," he whispered and then he fell fast asleep.

Shelby entwined her fingers in his short curls as he lay half on top of her, sleeping. So this was it. This marvelous "thing" called sex. This "thing" men and women have done together since the beginning of time; this "thing" that controlled and determined fates; this "thing" that carried emotions so intense people never could get enough of it. So now, even she had been initiated. It truly did feel like she had just joined some kind of club. She stroked the side of Ben's face and turned her head so she could look at him. Even in complete repose, his nose and lips misshapen into the pillow, he was incredibly attractive. She was glad she had a few minutes of quiet to savor this moment and all that was Ben, for she knew that as desirable as he was, he wouldn't be hers for long. A man like this could have any woman, so why would he continue to want her?

Chapter Twenty-Four—
The Inner Sanctum or
Beyond the Crypt with Ben's
Favorite Fantasy

When Shelby woke the next morning, Ben was in the shower. She stretched languorously and wondered if she should join him or not. She decided against it just seconds before she heard the taps turn off. Afraid she looked a fright, she grabbed the top sheet and ran for the guest room bathroom.

Ben came out of the bathroom toweling his chest and grimaced. He should have known better than to leave her here alone. She must have become self-conscious, he thought, as he dropped the towel and started dressing. He looked down at his pulsing manhood. He was so up for being inside her again.

After a leisurely breakfast at a popular pancake house, Ben took Shelby back to his office. He had forgotten to give her a book he had picked up on the South that was filled with Gullah traditions. She was going to be leaving soon to go back to Holden Beach and he was going to have to get back to work reading some term papers. Their blissful, long weekend was coming very quickly to a close as classes resumed on Tuesday; and Shelby, stalwart and loyal as ever, could only be talked into taking one day off from work.

As soon as Ben had unlocked the door to his inner office and let her precede him in, he came up behind her and caressed her backside. She was wearing a soft, jersey skirt that outlined her ass quite nicely. "You have a very, very nice derrière," he murmured. Then, as if he'd just that moment decided on a new course of action, he turned and went back to the open door, closed it, and locked it.

Shelby turned and gave him a puzzled look.

"You know for a long time, I've had this very wicked fantasy. It attacks me at the most inconvenient times and distracts me terribly. It occurs to me that maybe by acting it out with you, I could be cured of it. Have you ever had any acting experience?"

"A little. I was in two plays in high school and had a bit part here and there in college."

"Are you game?" he asked with a boyish grin.

She smiled back at him; she just couldn't help it, he was so irresistible.

"I could be. Tell me about it."

"Well, it involves a student. A particularly sexy student," he said as he strode over to her.

"I thought you didn't mess with your students."

"I don't. That's why this is fantasy. Pure fantasy. Indulge me?"

"Tell me more about this 'particularly sexy' student."

"Seems she's managed to get herself a failing grade in a very important class and she comes to see her professor to inquire if there's any way she can improve it."

"Mmmm. Interesting. Does she have a name, this student?"

"Pick one."

Shelby thought for a moment and whispered naughtily, "How about Monica?"

"We're off to a really good start already," he said with a sideways smile. Her alluding to the infamous intern was *definitely* a good sign for what he had in mind.

It took her a moment to realize the significance of the name she had chosen. The poor woman's name was almost synonymous for fellatio. "Oh," she said and blushed.

"So, Monica, what can I do for you?" he said in an extremely husky voice. Shelby noticed that his demeanor had changed. He had become somehow distant, yet his eyes were intense and dark as he stared deeply into hers.

This must be his business demeanor, she thought. The steely, unwavering professor he became when he went into the classroom. Uncomfortable as she felt with the idea of play-acting with this man who suddenly seemed like a complete stranger, she trembled slightly with anticipation. The playful imp in her curved her mouth into a sultry smile as she decided to go for it, to work herself into his fantasy and give him what he craved. Maybe if she could satisfy him in ways that others hadn't, she could keep him a while longer.

Pouting her lips and assuming a provocative pose, she grumbled, "You gave me an 'F' on my project. When my father finds out, he's going to kill me. I wanted to know if there was anything I could do to improve my grade." She licked her bottom lip and ran the pad of her middle finger over it. "I would do anything to keep Daddy from finding out about my bad grade."

"Anything?" Ben asked.

"I have a good chunk of my rather sizable allowance still left. Wouldn't you like a plasma TV or a case of wine?"

"Actually," he said as he moved her finger aside and replaced it with his, "I have no time to watch TV and the sulfites in wine give me a headache."

"There's nothing else you'd like?"

"Oh, there's something else I'd very much like."

"Name it. It's yours."

"Show me your tits."

Shelby feigned shock and stepped back. "Professor!"

"You've got an 'F.' That's how you can work it up to a 'D.'"

"Daddy expects better than a 'D.'"

"We'll work on your grade one step at a time, Monica. Let's start with getting you a 'D' first." He ran his finger over the tops of her breasts. They were encased in a demi push-up bra that jutted them out against her white, oxford shirt.

Shelby met his eyes and saw the lust growing in them. He was getting very excited and it was quickly rubbing off on her. Timidly, she reached her hand up and slowly unbuttoned her shirt. When she opened the shirt wide, slid it off her shoulders, and let it drop to the carpet, he moaned softly. Then he said. "Very nice. Very, very nice, Monica, now the bra."

Shelby, as Monica, reached behind her and easily undid the single hook letting the bra slide slowly forward on her arms, baring her breasts. The bra fell off her hands and found its way to the carpet.

"Mmmmm, mmm, mmmm," he sighed appreciatively. He stepped closer, and while his eyes bored into her chest and feasted on her, his fingers reached for her.

He gently pinched the nipples and pulled on them. "So tell me Monica," he murmured, "Do you show these beauties off much?"

Shelby was nonplussed for a few moments. Was he talking to her or to Monica? Did he really think her breasts were beauties? He sure was acting like he was very much enamored with them. And oh, what he was doing to them! He was turning her stomach inside out and her knees to silly putty as her center core liquified. She managed to stammer, "I . . . I have a boyfriend."

"He must love looking at these." He bent, took one pebbly, hard nipple into his mouth and sucked. Then he stood and looked down at the wet tip, "And tasting them, too," he added.

Pretending a nervousness that she actually felt but was trying to hide, Shelby asked, "Do I get my 'D' professor?"

"You do, indeed. Now, if you'd like to go for a 'C,' you could lift that skirt and show me your sweet little pussy as well."

Shelby thought she was going to fall to the floor in a heap. No one had ever said anything even remotely close to those words to her. At first even the meaning of them escaped her as she trembled from the deep timber of Ben's voice. Then realizing what he expected of her, or Monica, she shuddered. She felt a heavy, slick wetness move through her nether regions, coating her. The exact same region that Ben, the professor, now wanted to view. Just by his words, he was flooding her underpants, big time.

He patiently waited out her indecision, then prompted, "Well, are you going to be going for a 'C' or not?"

"Yes sir," she mumbled, then slowly began inching her skirt up.

Ben thought he was going to die from the pleasure

of watching Shelby as Monica, blatantly showing off her charms to her "professor." The lust building in him was becoming massive and monstrous in its intensity as he watched her skirt rise and her panties come into view. His erection was jutting out from his trousers and it was like granite. It seemed his passion had reversed his blood flow to the extent that he was lightheaded with his desire for Shelby, or Monica, or whatever the hell this tantalizing woman in front of him was called.

When she had her skirt raised to her waist, she held it with one hand while with the other, she inched her panties down to the top of her thighs. Her auburn tufts came into view as her hand moved away; then she was standing in front of him, topless and with her panties pulled down to her thighs.

His eyes feasted on her as she stood there nervously trying to figure out what to do with her hands. He could just barely see where her cleft began through the tight curls. And oh, how he needed to see more of her.

Her thighs were slightly apart, he could smell her musky scent rising and causing his nostrils to flare. When he stepped close to her, he reached out with his fingers and touched her. He looked into her face and watched as she nearly swooned.

"'C' minus. Unless I get to see more." He pushed her gently back until the backs of her thighs met the edge of his desk, then he lifted her onto the edge and pulled her panties completely off.

"Spread your legs wide for me and we'll make this a solid 'C' plus." He didn't wait for her to comply. Taking a thigh in each hand, he separated them himself. Then he knelt between them and unabashedly examined her. "Has this boyfriend of yours looked at you like this, too?"

"Well, uh, no," she managed to mutter.

"Well, he should, this is beautiful. You're beautiful. Everywhere. Your skin is so soft." His hands stroked her thighs and then moved up her torso to caress her breasts, to tug on her nipples as his eyes continued to feast between her legs. "Even your nipples, when they're hard, are soft," he murmured in amazement. When both hands fell back to the juncture between her thighs and his thumbs spread her wide for his gaze, she thought she would die from embarrassment. But as invasive and intimate as this was, it was also very sensual and she loved the sounds of praise he made as he examined her so carefully.

Shelby shuddered as he touched her and she could feel herself creaming his fingers as they explored and opened her to his gaze. With infinite care, he inserted one finger and followed its progress with his eyes; then, withdrawing it, he joined it with another and reinserted it. Fingers from both hands moved all over her, touching her everywhere, stroking, pressing, and spreading her wide for his inspection. Her head fell back and the tips of her breasts pointed to the ceiling when he leaned in and kissed her at the top of her moist slit. His tongue laved the hard nub that quickly appeared, and when it grew large enough that he could slip it between his lips, he sucked on it. Moments later her thighs spasmed and she convulsed against his tongue. Her low, mournful moan sent his rock hard penis into violent spasms of its own as it searched out a place to find its own release.

When her head lowered and her eyes met his pleading ones, he said, "An 'A' if you'll suck on me, a 'B' if I can just fuck you right now."

Shelby went right back into her character, "As appealing as the 'A' sounds, I don't think my daddy would believe an 'A.'"

Instantly, Ben stood, dropped his pants, stepped between her spread thighs and entered her.

As he held her on the desk by gripping her flanks, he thrust into her with all the vigor of a decathlete. The slick slamming of their bodies as he repeatedly rammed into her made whipping and thumping noises. He plowed into Monica, er, Shelby like a madman possessed. Then he locked his knees, gave one final thrust, arched his back, and howled.

He had never known an orgasm could be like that. It was not only the most powerful he'd ever had, but the longest in duration. It left him weak in every muscle and sapped not only his energy, but his brain waves were also askew as if misfiring. He didn't know exactly where he was for a moment or two. Then he remembered and smiled. He would remember this moment until his dying day; this incredible coupling would be embedded in his gray matter forever. He doubted that there'd ever been one like it in the history of the universe; there surely hadn't ever been for him.

"You okay?" Shelby asked.

"Marvelous. Simply marvelous," he sighed.

"What can I do for extra credit?" Monica was back.

He moaned. "You can go home. I can't keep up with you. Come back next semester and I'll tutor you for the final."

Chapter Twenty-Five
Instant messaging

Shelby: Well, I met good ole Randall. He's a jerk! Oh, he was polite enough, and he seemed to listen to me, but it was with one ear, you know how some people do that? It's quite obvious to me that his mind is made up to sell. I met him at the Plantation yesterday. He came there to hand out some awards and support some fundraising, but he didn't really seem into it. There are rumors that he plans to sell out to a developer, which means pretty soon everything will be subdivided and developed into homes, or condos, or some such nonsense.

Ben: People need places to live.

Shelby: They also need places to go to see our heritage, to learn about history. I'm afraid I was a bit harsh with him. I hate that all he's seeing right now are dollar signs.

Ben: You don't know that. Be kind.

Shelby: You weren't there; you didn't see how distracted he was. It was very clear to me that he didn't even want to be there. He kept holding his stomach like maybe he had too much to drink or something. I'm sure he's quite the Lothario. Probably comes down here to all the girlie clubs and parties between all his speaking engagements.

Ben: This is not like you. I've never seen you this judgmental. Aren't you letting your gung-ho-for-the-environment attitude bias you a bit here?

Shelby: Ben, he wants to sell out!

Ben: It's his Shelby, he has that right!

Shelby: It's everybody's history, not just his! I'm going to find one of Macie's heirs and put a stop to him.

Ben: Shelby, don't make this man your nemesis. Let it go.

Shelby: No, I can't. I'm going to find someone who can challenge him. If I can find the rightful heir, he can be challenged. Maybe it won't mean anything in the long run, but it will stop him until somebody else can.

Ben: This is not your war.

Shelby: Of course it is. I fight for the environment everyday. Everybody should. I am surprised you aren't in agreement with me on this. Didn't you like the Plantation? Didn't we have the most marvelous time there? And what am I supposed to do about those dreams? Charles wants to go home!

Ben: Let's not turn this into something it isn't. This is not about me and you. You know I enjoyed the Plantation immensely, and you in particular. I have very fond memories of our first kiss there; and although I can see your point about it being preserved for future generations, we don't have the right to impose our will on the man who legally holds the title.

Shelby: Then I must find a way for him to not own the title legally. And I think I have it. I'll find an heir. We'll get the DNA tests needed to prove legitimacy, well, maybe not actually legitimacy, but the connection, and we'll go for reparations. There's a commission set up for just this kind of thing. We'll force Randall to be fair, or at least we'll keep him in court until we wear him down.

Ben: I don't know who the 'we' is in this, but count me out. I'm on Randall's side. I don't think what you're talking about would please C.E.G. at all and frankly, I'm surprised at you. Where's the sweet girl I spent time with this weekend?

Shelby: You mean Monica?

Ben: Well, yeah, I kind of miss her, too.

Shelby: I'll just bet you do!

Ben: Hey, it's real hard grading papers now. Seems nobody deserves an 'A' anymore.

Shelby: I got a 'B.'

Ben: Yeah, next time we'll have to work on that 'A.'

Shelby: When will that be? It's your turn to come here.

Ben: I think I can get away the weekend after next. Think about what you'd like to do in the meantime.

Shelby: I already know what I want to do.

Ben: This is not a secure line. I'll call you later tonight and you can elaborate on that for me. Got a meeting I have to get to. And don't worry about Charles, I'm looking into final resting places for him now. B.

Chapter Twenty-Six
Beaufort, SC

Shelby sat at the table in the small diner playing with the straw in her iced tea. She had been mildly arguing with the woman Mareesa had arranged for her to meet. "You're wasting my time. I hate like hell to think that I drove all this way for nothing."

"I do know something. But I'm not parting with it for free."

"I can't pay you any money Janeel, I already told Mareesa that."

"I don't want money. What I want has to do with your job."

"And I can't compromise my job either. If you need sandbags or a seawall, you'll have to apply through the same channels as everybody else, but I *can* help you with the paperwork and walk it through for you."

"That's not the kind of help I need. What I need is somebody like you who's knowledgeable and passionate about the coastal environment to set a fire under our younguns."

"Huh?"

"Our kids. They don't care about taking care of the fragile coastline. They don't care about what's here now, and they sure as hell don't care about what happens to it for the next generation. I thought that maybe you could give a series of lectures, bring it home to them how easily all this can be wiped out." She gestured grandly out the big picture window with both hands and Shelby had to smile at her enthusiasm.

"You're interesting, you're a heck of a lot closer to their age, and it's obvious that you care. Just the fact that you're here about Beau Marecage tells me you're perfect to be the one to talk to them."

"And if I do, you'll hook me up with . . ."

"The latest spice girl," Janeel said with a knowing grin. "Or as you call her, 'the heir.' Maybe you're right, maybe we do need an heir to step forward now. So, z'it a deal?"

"Yeah. I think I can handle a few seminars about the ever-changing, dynamically-balanced and fragile coast. I can certainly lead field trips to the N.C. Maritime Museum on Front Street and to Blackbeard's Storeroom over on Gallant's Channel."

"Cool. That ought to buy our fishermen a few more years of unloading a good catch at the docks. C'mon and I'll give you the name of a man who can hook you up with Cindy."

"Cindy?"

"Cinnamon. One of the heirs, remember?"

"She's here?"

"No. She's in Barbados."

"Barbados?"

"Yeah, you're not the only one searching out skeletons. She's been trying to find out what happened to Savory for over a year now."

"Really?"

"Yup. Got a burr in her butt and she just had to go off and try to find out what happened to her kin."

"Has she had any luck?"

"She found a tombstone that had Savory's name on it, but I'll let her tell you all about that when you meet her."

"You don't know how much I appreciate this Janeel."

"Yea ah do. Yea ah do."

Shelby laughed as she followed the swishing muumuu covering Janeel's broad backside over the beach access.

Chapter Twenty-Seven—
Randall Wyatt Garrett
Baltimore, MD

Randall stood in the foyer of his townhouse staring down at the latest letter from his attorney. Criminy! Would the noose of this inheritance ever come out from around his neck? Now a twit of a woman named Cinnamon, of all things, was suing him for reparations!

Well as far as he was concerned, she could have the blasted place! It was more trouble than it was worth. Hell, at last report, it wasn't even turning a profit for the Historical Society! He walked down the hallway and into his study before tossing the letter onto a pile of envelopes, all with similar letterheads. They all pertained to Beau Marecage: notices of taxes soon to be due, clarifications of intent regarding the upcoming lease, which really should have been handled by now, solicitations from real estate specialists in the field of restored Southern homes, developers eager to subdivide and build either tract houses, mini-estates, or timeshares, and now this, a legal action that could, and most probably would, stop any and all actions on any of the preceding missives.

He ran his long fingers through his thick sandy brown hair as he walked over to the bar. He just wanted to be done with it! Get rid of this albatross that had been around his neck for the better part of his life. Since before his father had passed, the damned place had been nothing more than a money pit and a huge waste of time.

He poured himself a healthy dose of Crown Royal, splashed in a bit of soda water, and took the drink over to his favorite easy chair. He sat heavily into it, the glass dangling in his hand over the side as he heaved a great sigh.

Well, to be honest, as a child he had loved the place. Each tree had been a challenge to climb. Every inch of encroaching swamp a new place to explore. Even later as tourists milled about and explored on their own, he had enjoyed the solitude and serenity of the place. Mentally he pictured himself swinging back and forth on one of the tire swings placed especially for him by Tillen, one of the "faux" servants for the reenactments. A hearty black man with an eager smile for anyone under ten, he had been a good friend and a laughable character actor as a former slave. When he tried, Randall could recall a clear summer day and see up through the branches to the clear Carolina blue sky, the green leaves mingling with the cerulean sky and the yellow brightness of the sun, as he swung back and forth and around and around. Yes, he'd had some wonderful times there, in his youth.

But now, now when he returned, all he felt was pain. A sharp wrenching pain in his gut accompanied him as soon as he stepped out of his vehicle onto the drive and looked up at the house. It was curious, for sure. It had first started happening about two years ago; and now, on every subsequent visit, it returned like clockwork. So, in addition to the constant hassles of quasi-ownership as lessor, being on the board for the Historical Society which required quite a bit of his free time, and endless money outlays for one thing or another, the big old house on the hill was giving him one big-time bellyache.

It was all very curious. He had wondered if he might have an ulcer, aggravated only by visiting the centuries-old homestead. His friends had told him that, nah, if anything was going to give him an ulcer, it certainly wouldn't be the house; it would have to be his fanatical approach to his photography career. That he was a perfectionist, and as anal as could be, was no secret to anyone, least of all him. In fact, at this point, it was his trademark. In a town with many photographers to choose from, discerning patrons found him to be the ultimate. No wedding, Bar mitzvah or cotillion was worthy of note unless Randall Wyatt Garrett attended with his assortment of cameras slung around his neck and a ready assistant by his side. Every week there was one or more of his photos on the society pages depicting new brides or anniversary couples posing above his customary initialed logo.

Yes, his passion for photography certainly should have been the cause for an ulcer, had there been one; but there hadn't been, he'd checked. The doctor had assured him that nothing was abnormal anywhere along his digestive tract. He suggested that the cause of the shooting pains might be psychosomatic, that perhaps he should consider relieving himself of the burden of owning the Southern plantation that had such an uncanny ability to twist his gut at first sight. To that end, Randall had started soliciting bids and inquiring as to the best way to get rid of Beau Marecage and along with it, the history of a family with whom he no longer had any real connection.

The end of the line. Yup, he was it. It would all end with him anyway. Might as well sell it off now and not have to scramble to find the money for those damnable taxes. Oh, he had it, he'd just have to sell something– some stocks, a few CD's, maybe liquidate that warehouse on 12th that a moving company was so interested in. He *could* come up with it, if he wanted to. Problem was, he was growing more sure with every passing day that he didn't want to. He was ready to end it, get on with life and stop those dreadful trips down South where all he could look forward to was gastric distress.

He lifted the glass that he held by just his fingertips and took a hefty swallow. Yeah, that's what he'd do, sell the damned place as he'd been thinking. Bringing the amber liquid to a height level with his eyes, he stared at it and wondered just who the hell this Cinnamon was and just what he'd have to pay her to drop her suit and go back where she came from. He took another swig before picking up the phone on the side table. He punched in the number for his attorney and best friend, Ron Pascarelli.

As he waited for someone to pick up, he kicked off his shoes. Man, it had been a long day. Six shoots, five of them women in white gowns who were determined he make them look like the most beautiful creation ever to wear a tulle veil. He was mid yawn when Ron's secretary, Deb, came on. He cut her off just as she had managed to finish pronouncing the six connected names that made up Ron's law firm. "It's me Deb, Ron in?"

"Oh, hi Randy. Yeah, he's in, but I gotta warn ya, he's not in the best mood."

"I'll chance it. Put me through."

"'Scarelli."

"Hey, you get this letter about somebody named

Cinnamon?"

"Can we talk about this later? I got a deposition in ten minutes."

"Did you get the letter?"

"Yeah, I got the letter."

"So, is it gonna hold off a sale?"

"It can."

"For how long?"

"For however long it takes. This is heavy shit. Reparations . . . gee Randall Wyatt, looks like whoever your ancestor screwed is screwing you. This could be in the courts for years, and you could conceivably even lose. This is human rights stuff. There's actually a commission on this. I think it's called The National Coalition of Blacks for Reparations in America."

"What are you talking about?"

"It's politically correct now to pay the slaves back for what they lost and what they had legal right to. If this Cinnamon is on the level, she could be entitled to compensation for what her ancestors lost in probate all those years ago."

"You're kidding!"

"No, I'm not. If she's family and she can prove it, she's got a case."

"Which means the courts will give her Beau Marecage?"

"Probably not, but something . . . she'll get something."

"What would you recommend?"

"Find out what she wants. Otherwise you're gonna make me a very rich man. These things can go on and on forever."

"You already are a rich man," Randall said drolly.

"Yeah, but if this gets hung up in the courts, I'll have all your money as well as mine! Now I really have to go. Find out what you can about this Cinnamon lady, and we'll get together and have a sit down with her attorney."

"You're my attorney, why don't you find out about her?"

"Then I'd just have to bill you for a P.I. Her address is in that letter. Why not send her a handwritten invitation to that annual fundraiser you have down there next month? It wouldn't hurt to see what we're dealing with here and find out how hostile the enemy is."

"Yeah, then I can point out all the things that need fixing around the old place."

"Don't go there. You and I both know that the land is far more valuable than that house will ever be."

"Good point."

"It probably would be better to approach the whole thing as a sentimental fop, you know, all the memories, you could never possibly sell . . ."

"If she's stupid! She or her attorneys probably know we're already entertaining offers."

"Well, just watch what you say buddy boy, let her do all the talking, don't give away your hand. Later."

The offending click on the other line left Randall feeling alone and uncertain at best.

What a crock! How did he get himself in these messes! He pushed himself up from his chair and went to the bar to refill his drink. Standing at the end of the long cherrywood bar he'd had installed, he lifted his head to the ceiling and rubbed the back of his neck. Originally, he thought he'd have lots of friends stopping by when he'd purchased this townhouse a few years back. They had before, when he'd lived in a two-room apartment and had only a ragtag place to pour drinks and set out snacks. The continually-cluttered, miserly two feet of kitchen countertop that had served as the makeshift bar for the guys who always dropped by on their way home from work had been quite the hangout. But then they all got married. One by one, they all fell over the cliff, proposed, and sent out white vellum invitations.

He, however, had been too busy to date. Going to weddings wearing three cameras against his starched tuxedo shirt didn't make him much of a candidate for his own solemn ceremony. Not that he was eager to be married; he wasn't. But it would be nice to have someone to talk to, someone to come home to, someone to eat dinner with now and again. As he stared at his surroundings he wouldn't exactly admit that he was lonely, just a bit tired of listening to himself and wishing he had someone else to pour drinks for.

He took his refreshed drink and walked behind the bar. He dipped his fingers into a huge crystal vase that was shaped like a beach ball and ran his fingers through the matchbooks he had amassed. Certainly the size of his collection attested to his penchant for fine dining, although he had to admit that they represented far too many solitary meals. Then he looked into the mirror on the back wall and saw himself. He tried to analyze just exactly who it was he saw staring back at him. He saw a rather tall, sandy-haired gentleman who was getting ready to either lose his family homestead or fight for it, a man who worked so hard that he no longer knew what mattered to him anymore. He leaned in and looked into his own fiercely green eyes. "So fella," he began, "what is it you want on this go around? To win, lose, or draw? And why? Just what the hell's the difference anymore? I don't want the damned place. It makes me sick to even go there anymore. Literally," he added with a self-deprecating chuckle.

He assessed his lips, then smiled brightly, as if to convince himself he was all right. "You're in a rut, big guy. Nothing makes you happy anymore. You've got a handful of friends who are too busy with their own lives to give a damn about yours, and you've got a townhouse you've spent a fortune decorating that you can't stand to come home to."

He picked up his drink and, watching himself in the mirror, downed it all at once. Then he stepped back and put his hands on his hips and declared in a put-on Southern accent, "I'll tell you what, we'll go down to Charleston, find this Cinnamon, and put her in her place."

Just then a thought occurred to him and he scrunched up his face, his eyes intent. That woman, that Shelby Laine lady . . . the one he'd met who insisted he not sell out to the developers. She had been pretty adamant. Could there be a connection here? She seemed like the sort of rabble-rouser that could get everybody into a tizzy. Who did she think she was anyway? And what was it she had said about Charles Garrett? He squeezed his eyes shut. Was it about burying his body or something like that? He could not remember, he'd been in too much pain at the time to pay that much attention to her.

His eyes blazed as he stared back at the man in the mirror. For the first time, he saw something quite strange in the reflection that bounced back. He saw a resemblance that took a moment to place. Then he remembered. The portrait over the mantle in the dining room at Beau Marecage. Charles Edward Garrett. By God, he would not let these women take away the legacy he'd acquired from his how-ever-many-times great, great grandfather! He dumped the ice from his drink down the drain in the sink and spun on his heel. Then he stalked down the hall and brusquely pulled opened the hall closet. He pulled out two big suitcases, took them into his room, placed them side by side on his king-sized bed, and turned to open all his drawers. He packed furiously and with an energy he hadn't had for quite some time. He would show them. He was Randall Wyatt *Garrett*. Beau Marecage belonged to *him*.

He snapped his fingers as another thought occurred to him and he hurriedly ran to his darkroom to gather the necessary equipment. He would photograph Beau Marecage. In all the years he had visited, he had never so much as clicked a shutter there. He stopped shoving lenses into cases to consider that thought. Just why was that? Why had he never showcased Beau Marecage? Why had he never looked at it through the lens of a camera? Excitement filled him as he readied himself to travel. He called his assistant and instructed her to rearrange his schedule so he could be away for two weeks, then he reread the letter he had earlier discarded on top of the pile of letters having to do with Beau Marecage.

Putting aside the legal jargon, it was basically stating that this woman, Cinnamon, was a descendant of a child born in 1864 to a woman named Savory. The papers attested to the fact that the child's father was Charles Edward Garrett of Beaufort County. And that because of her birth, she was entitled to a share in the estate of Charles Edward Garrett. It went on to say that the right of succession had been skewed from the offset as the child, Mace, should have been the rightful heir instead of Charles' brother. It went on to list the order of succession deemed proper according to that supposition, from Mace, daughter to Charles Edward Garrett and Savory Garrett, noting Savory's last name to be coincidentally Garrett as she was owned by the Garretts, all the way to Cinnamon Ballyou, daughter of

Ceylon, now thought to be residing in New Orleans. The signatures of Cinnamon's aunts and uncles, Ceylon's siblings, were also included in the petition: Caraway, Anise, and Thyme. Curiously, Ceylon's signature was not included.

He read it twice. Then thoughtfully considered that if all this was true, what was Cinnamon to him? Was she a cousin? Since she was supposedly the descendant of a slave, she had to be black, didn't she? Or at least part black. He remembered some old adage about never knowing what was in the woodpile. He chided himself for being biased because he wasn't that way at all really. Then he wondered what she looked like. *It figured, he muttered to himself, it just figured. The illustrious history he'd always heard about, always reveled in, repeated whenever the opportunity arose, was tainted.* Well, why not? His wasn't the only family being accused and found out for such dishonorable acts in the past. Certainly what was considered acceptable and even condoned behavior in the late 1800s would be abhorrent now; but really, was there truly a way to right this wrong, if indeed it had happened this way so long ago? And why was it his job to own up to it and right it? Why was it falling to him?

He threw a pair of dress shoes and a pair loafers into the last case, snapped it shut, and stood up to his full six-foot-two height. *Well, Cindy, baby, you'd better have some really good proof, that's all I can say.*

Chapter Twenty-Eight
Beau Marecage, SC

I'm so nervous, Shelby. I've never been to a ball like this."

"It's not really a ball, Cindy, just think of it as a dance. A dance where everybody tries to be social and formal when they'd all rather be at home propped in front of the TV."

"I don't know what to say to him!"

"You will. When it's time, you will. Just remember, don't talk about money. Everything is sentimental to you. Gush over every little thing. Make even the most inconsequential things seem significant. Ask questions like: Do you think our ancestors actually leaned on this particular tree? Do you think the moon reflected off the swamp water in this exact same way so many years ago? Which ancestor do you think picked out this wallpaper pattern? Stuff like that. Make him think you're interested in the history of the place above everything else. Sentimental. Remember that."

"Thank you, Shelby. I don't know what I would do

without you. You came right out of the blue just when I needed you most. The good Lord knew I needed a way, and he provided it. I thank him everyday for you, Shelby. And Janeel, she's real grateful to you for talkin' with the kids. They're organizing a beach walk to pick up trash this weekend. They want to talk to you about a river keeper program similar to the one you talked to us about. You've made such a difference in those kids I can hardly believe it. But what's truly wonderful is that you've given me the courage I needed to speak up for Savory. She didn't deserve the way they treated her."

"No, she didn't."

"I'll never be able to thank you enough for understanding and listening to me . . . and for giving me a heritage I can claim as my own."

"Now, shush. We're all in this together. Beau Marecage is just too special to become the latest Hilton. Smile pretty and you'll have no trouble at all. You are going to be the most ravishing girl at the ball."

"It *is* a ball!"

"Dance. Just a dance," Shelby reiterated as she adjusted the flounce on Cindy's gown.

"Go now, everything's set. They'll all be wondering who you are before the evening's out."

"And when will we tell them?"

"You'll tell *him*. I'll come get you for that part. You just smile and look pretty and do try not to get introduced by name to him before it's time. Just be friendly. Be friendly to everyone. These people are here to raise money for Beau Marecage. Remember, it could be your home one day."

"Oh, never. I could never . . ." she said as she looked around in awe. "It's just too grand."

"So are you," Shelby said as she gave her a quick kiss

on the cheek before pushing her out the bathroom door. "Now get out there and wow them, Randall especially, got it?"

"Got it," she replied with a smile. *Got it*, she repeated to herself as she made her way to the ballroom. She waited in line at the ballroom door until it was her turn to go in, and then she lifted her head high and strolled into the room.

There was a receiving line, just as she had expected. As she waited her turn to meet members of the Historical Society and Randall Garrett himself, she hummed a tune she had picked up in Barbados.

What a wonderful place Barbados had been to run off to after leaving college with her history degree. She had just barely started teaching when she had suddenly become obsessed with discovering her own history and had fled to Barbados to do some research. As she pushed the modern-day version of Barbados out of her mind and tried to envision what it might have been like in the late1800s when Savory had finally made it there, she cringed.

Still frowning, she forced herself to picture the primitive island as it must have been back then as opposed to the vacation mecca it was today. It certainly hadn't been the safe haven that Savory had sought. During her time in Barbados, Cindy had only managed to find out a few things about Savory, and none of them had been very encouraging. There had never been a Savory Garrett recorded in any of the logs or registers Cindy had managed to find and research. But finally, she found a slave listed in an old church record as Savory Grant. The handwritten ledger showed Savory Grant married a man named Ernst Smyth in 1869 and buried him just three years later. All indications were that he had been a much older man, especially as he hadn't sired any children on her. On his passing, his small tenant farm and orchards were settled on her. The small church where she was a devout member had kept meticulous receipts. It appeared she had tithed her full ten percent faithfully for almost fifty years before passing herself.

Cindy had not known for certain that she had found the right Savory until she had discovered the simple tombstone now surrounded by decaying wrought iron fencing within view of an old home site. Quite weathered, its facing bleached almost completely white by years of harsh sunlight, the tombstone stood proudly erect. The only thing that could be read easily was her name. If you looked closely and felt with your hands, you could just make out the words chiseled in script underneath her name: *Mother to Macie Garrett.*

She thought about her own mother, Ceylon, who had given birth to her when she had also been just sixteen. How she herself had been taken as a toddler to a Gullah family in Beaufort to be raised as one of their own when Ceylon had caught the eye of a young white man just finishing law school. To this day, Ceylon would not take the chance and acknowledge she'd even had a child before meeting and marrying James Arthur Anderson, especially one that others would consider black. Ceylon, fair-skinned and small featured, would forever live in the world of those passing for white. In her prominent, upper-class mansion far removed from reminders of the black race, she seldom thought of the daughter she'd once had whose skin was not as light as her own.

Lost in her thoughts, Cindy hadn't noticed that the man in line behind her was talking to her until he tapped her on the shoulder. Ignoring his comment, since she hadn't heard it, she moved forward and found herself standing directly in front of Randall Garrett who had just finished welcoming another guest. He turned and smiled at her.

"Are you a patron?" he asked.

Not knowing what patron he was referring to, but sure she probably wasn't one, she shook her head.

"I didn't think so. I would have remembered seeing a woman as attractive as you had you attended one of the meetings."

"Thank you, what a very nice thing to say."

"Are you just visiting?"

"Well, actually," she said as she took in her surroundings and remembered the words of her new, dear friend, Shelby, "I am hoping to make my home here one day." She finished off her wistful chant by giving him a bright beautiful smile. She could hardly believe she was here, in this grand place, standing in line being introduced to the man of the hour. Shelby had not told her how handsome Randall was.

Randall Garrett had never seen a woman quite as beautiful as the creature who now stood before him. Her dark green eyes were warm and sparkling, her red full lips wide in a magnificent smile. Dark chocolate hair graced her face and framed the most lovely caramel complexion before falling nearly to her tiny waist. She was exotic, but yet not. Possibly Indian, he thought. Or maybe a touch Spaniard? Tahitian? He did not know. He only knew she was divine, from the tip of her unadorned head, to the flowing gold lamé gown that clung to enticing curves, all the way down to the tiny gold sandals on her dainty feet.

When he found his voice, he automatically intoned the same thing he had said almost thirty times previous, "Randall Garrett, so nice of you to come."

"Oh, I am delighted to be here!" she said breezily and Randall couldn't help smiling at her enthusiasm.

"Well, good! We are equally delighted to have you."

Cindy blushed under his scrutiny and met his hot eyes with her shuttered ones. She was used to men admiring her, at least this one was now focusing on her face. "You have a lovely home."

"I'm afraid I can't take much credit for that. The Society sees to the decor. I'm only called when there's a plumbing or a heating problem," he quipped.

"Well, it feels just the exact right temperature in here, so apparently you do your job quite well."

She was an absolute delight. He didn't want to have to pass her on down the line. "And your name?" he asked.

"My friends call me Cindy."

"Oh, well Cindy, I look forward to talking to you some more."

"I'll be around," she said over her shoulder as she waved just her fingertips at him.

"Save me a dance?" he called after her.

She returned a coy smile and turned her attention to the woman now in front of her. *Not bad looking at all.* She wondered why Shelby hadn't mentioned that. Twenty minutes later when she had finally finished making all the introductions she cared to, the dancing started. Not anxious to dance yet and quite aware that Mr. Garrett was being entertained by three young giggling ladies, she sauntered over to the punch table. The man who had been behind her in line approached her just as she took a cup.

"Care to dance?" he asked.

"No, not right now thank you," she said, giving him an encouraging smile. "I'm a bit thirsty, maybe in a few minutes?"

When the man wandered off, she turned to find Randall Garrett looming over her, "Care to dance?"

"How'd you get away from them so quickly?" she asked as she put down her cup and took his arm.

"I told them I was positively parched. I'm delighted you were keeping tabs on me enough to notice."

"You were surrounded by a rather loud group of women, it was hard not to notice."

"That is their mission, I believe. But you are quite different. You stun with only your beauty and your engaging smile."

"Those are very kind words."

"I meant it. You are by far the most beautiful woman in this room. In fact, I feel confident in saying that I believe you are the most beautiful woman I have ever met in my entire life."

Cindy's knees buckled slightly just as he was turning her to face him on the dance floor. He didn't notice her loss of footing, nor her quickening heartbeat as he took her into his arms and led her across the dance floor. Although dancing wasn't her favorite activity, she had some aptitude for it. Soon she found herself caught up in the dreamy music and the comforting feel of his strong arms. A few times he pulled away slightly to look down into her face and she looked up into his, but they never said anything. After a few quiet moments, he tucked her back against his shoulder and held her to him as he continued to lead her across the dance floor. When the song was over, he kept her for another, and then another, until the inevitable happened. He was given the cut by the man she had first refused.

They ate finger food at separate tables, continually keeping an eye on each other. When he felt it was appropriate to leave his table and his companions, he sought her out. "Is there a chance you might allow me to show you the gardens, Miss . . .?" he asked politely in front of the group at her table.

"Why certainly Mr. Garrett, I would be honored to see the gardens with you," she countered, purposely avoiding his question as to her last name. When they had passed through the door and out into the night, they turned to each other and laughed hilariously at the forced formality. It was obvious it wasn't natural for either of them to be this polished.

She shivered in the cool air as he took her arm and led her away from the house. Without hesitation he quickly removed his jacket and draped it lightly across her shoulders. The large coat fell with a heavy weight as it encompassed her. The heat from his body lingered and emanated from the lining deep into her skin, warming her from within. She didn't know when she had felt so warm and secure, and incongruently, at peace with everything.

She should have been nervous with this man, but she wasn't. Although she tried to remind herself that she was supposed to be angry with him, or at least with his family, she didn't want to be angry anymore. She just wanted to enjoy this incredible feeling of lightheartedness.

As they walked, he bent low and whispered in her ear, "A penny for your thoughts."

Her thoughts right then had more to do with finding a way to get him to hold her in his arms again than they did anything else, but she certainly couldn't tell him that. Maybe it was time to get on with Shelby's program.

"Do you ever think of your ancestors walking along this path, or leaning against this very tree?" she asked as she broke from walking beside him to press her back against the bark of a tree growing beside the worn pathway.

When he came to stand directly in front of her and

propped his body by his open hand on the tree trunk just above her shoulder, she realized she had made a tactical error. With his arm bent at the elbow, he leaned over her and his eyes looked intently down into hers. Their lips were unbelievably close. In the meager light, she could see his eyes twinkling as a tiny smile came to his lips. "This tree probably isn't as old as I am and I doubt that any of my ancestors would have even envisioned one being here. This pathway was installed by the Historical Society not twenty years ago."

"Oh," she said.

"Forgive me," he whispered against her cheek as his head lowered, "I just can't resist." She felt his forefinger tilt her chin up slightly just before she felt his lips touch hers and she fluttered her eyes closed so she could fully enjoy his kiss.

A thousand flashing visions suddenly swam in front of her eyes as he continued to kiss her, and she knew without a doubt that she'd been kissed by this man before. Scenes of a dark body and a light body entwined in a loving embrace against the backdrop of tall grasses flicked through her mind like cards in a nickelodeon. A hunger borne out of nowhere seized her as she wrapped her arms around his neck and kissed him for all she was worth. An intense longing that she hadn't been able to place or credit, yet had been forced to carry deep inside her for so many months, had finally found its release. No primal urge or pheromonal chemistry could explain her actions; yet somehow, she knew this man. She knew him intimately, and always had.

The moan that came from him as he swept her into his arms and brought her tightly against him was so filled with both anguish and passion that it momentarily stunned her. But as she felt his arms surround her as he pulled her to his chest, she rejoiced in the uncanny familiarity of his embrace. As his lips moved hungrily over hers and his tongue breached her wet lips, he moaned again. Then, as if slaking an unquenchable thirst, his frantic tongue delved deeply into her mouth, over and over again. She stood on tiptoe to receive his eager tongue as his splayed hand moved from the small of her back to a fully-rounded buttock. With his large hand he gripped her and pulled her in close as he shoved his fully-engorged manhood into her soft belly.

He suddenly broke away to look questioningly into her bright eyes. The confusion on his face was evident, his eyes unseeing, his brow furrowed as he tried to understand what was overtaking him.

"We've been here before," she whispered as her hands framed his face. "Don't stop kissing me. Please, I need you."

That was all he needed to hear. Even though nothing of what she said made any sense, her words telling him to continue were all he needed to hear just then. His lips captured hers again and this time there was no gentling them, he was desperately hungry for her. A strange desire filled his loins with heat and all his body wanted to do was make her his, only his. As he kissed her, he moved against her, rubbing his heavy, swollen member deep into the creases of her gown.

It was the sound of the door opening behind them that brought him out of his sensual stupor. "Jesus, what are we doing?" he whispered against her neck, holding her clasped tightly to him, quite reluctant to let her go.

"I don't know," she replied breathily. "I guess we just got carried away in the moment. Only I think the moment we were in was in 1863."

He set her away so he could look at her. "What are you talking about? How could we have been caught up in a moment in the past? But there's something about you . . . . It's never been like this for me. This is scary. It's almost as if I couldn't stop kissing you for fear I'd never get to do it again."

"Well, if I have anything to say about it, I'll make another opportunity. Believe me, I'd like to make lots of other opportunities." She punctuated her words with a most sensual sigh as she smiled up at him.

He smiled down at her and stroked a long silky tress that hung down her shoulder. His eyes followed to where it continued past her bosom. He lifted it and used the tip to brush the area between her cleavage.

"You have beautiful skin, warm and glowing . . . flawless," he murmured.

"I'm very careful about the sun."

"Good for you. You're a smart lady. I want to see you again, Cindy . . ." he remembered that he didn't even know her full name and wasn't able to address her as he wanted to. He chuckled. "By the way, now that I've practically gnawed off your lips, what exactly is your name?"

Her brows lifted as she recalled Shelby's warning not to let him know her name until it was time. She probably shouldn't have even let him know her first name. "I liked what you did to my lips." She stood on her tiptoes and brushed her lips against his. "I have to go now. Someone's waiting for me." She spun away from him and dashed around the corner of the house.

He stood stunned for a moment, staring at tree bark where her body had just been. Then he turned and ran to follow her. But she was gone. His eyes swept the ground around him as if looking for a clue to help him figure out who she was and where she went. Like Cinderella, she had run off into the night and disappeared. She had said that someone was waiting for her. The idea that she might have a man in her life sent shards of jealousy through him, tearing at his insides like huge razors.

He walked completely around the house and was preparing to search the outbuildings when one of the Society patrons approached him. "They're looking for you inside. It's time for your speech."

"Oh, that's just grand!" he muttered as he turned and stalked up the hill.

Inside, he was ushered up to a podium where he spoke for a few minutes on behalf of the board thanking everyone for being so involved in the community. As soon as he could, he moved away from the crowd. Determined to find her, he was making his way to the front of the house while requesting a flashlight from one of the caretakers. He would hunt for the elusive woman he had been so earnestly making out with just a few short minutes ago. He would search until dawn if he had to.

He was, needless to say, shocked when he turned and practically fell into her in the hallway just outside the restrooms.

She smiled brightly and backed him into the foyer. She was holding a large box in her hands. "Here, I brought this for you." She held her hands out to him.

Still stunned that she had reappeared so suddenly, he reached out and took it. Then he looked down at it.

"What is it?" he asked as he stared down at the ornate wooden box.

"Open it."

He smiled at her and looked back at the box. His hand felt for the catch and he lifted the cover. Nestled in the center of blue velvet was an old revolver, quite old, yet somehow familiar. He looked up and, at his puzzled expression, she chuckled. "It's yours now. It's the matching Navy Colt. Shelby thought you should have it."

"Shelby?" he asked, feeling the first wave of uneasiness drifting through his consciousness.

"Yes, Shelby Laine. She found it in the sand on Figure Eight Island. It was Charles Garrett's. It belonged to your great ancestor. It matches the one in the case down the hall. He had it with him when he went to sea. It has just recently been recovered, along with his body. Although his body was recovered at a separate location."

His voice grew thick but he managed to choke out, "How do you know Shelby Laine?" The dread was apparent in the tone of his voice.

"She's a friend of mine. She's helping me with my reparations suit."

"You are Cinnamon Ballyou?" he choked out, already knowing the answer.

"Yes," she said simply.

"Why didn't you tell me?"

"I wanted to, but Shelby advised against it."

"What else has she advised you against?"

"Nothing really. She just thought it would be better if we met before you knew who I was."

"I thought you weren't coming tonight. The R.S.V.P. I received from you said you were unavailable tonight."

"Shelby thought it best that I meet you when you weren't expecting me."

"And just where is Shelby now?" he asked through gritted teeth.

"She left. She knew you'd be angry."

"Oh, I am. I am that."

"Do you like the present? Shelby says it's very valuable. It's an antique and a genuine war souvenir."

He looked back down at the gun in the box and gave

a great sigh. His attorney's words came back to him. He tried to remember if he had said anything tonight that he possibly should not have. Then he remembered the one thing Ron had instructed him to do.

"What do you want Cinnamon? Why the big show?"

There was silence as everyone around continued to listen and wonder at their strange conversation.

"I want Savory to finally be accepted by your family. I want her to have some peace about all this," she gestured with her hands indicating the grand staircase just off to the right with its gleaming crystal chandelier. "She was locked in a bedroom up there with the baby she bore for Charles. Nobody cared about her or her baby. Nobody would listen when she told them Charles had intentions of making her his bride. She had to run away. She had to leave her child behind!"

There was a profound silence as everyone in the room held their breath waiting to hear what would come next. Randall stared at Cinnamon as tears started streaking her face and then ran unchecked to the polished wood floor.

"It's just so sad!" she said on a final sob before turning and running out the front door.

Randall stood there, too stunned to move, still holding the box in his hands. Someone came to take it from him, and he nodded his acquiescence as it was lifted from his hands. Then he stood staring at the door through which Cinnamon had left, knowing that even if he could manage to come up out of this quagmire and walk to it that she would be long gone, spirited out of his life just as she had been spirited in.

Chapter Twenty-Nine
Baltimore, MD

I thought she was Asian or Indian, even Hispanic! I knew her skin was darker than most, but honestly Ron, it never occurred to me that she was part black!"

"Well, now you know. She apparently is. An octoroon I believe she would be called, one-eighth black, at least. But that's neither here nor there. What did you say to her that could compromise you?"

Randall paced on the oriental carpet in front of his friend's desk, running his fingers in deep trenches through his thick hair. "Well, that's the interesting part. We really didn't talk all that much."

"I don't understand."

"Well, most of what we said was . . ."

"What?"

"Nonverbal," was the most he would commit to.

"Come again?"

Randall spun abruptly around and placed his palms flat on the desk. With angry eyes, he vehemently spit out,

"We tangled tongues! I felt her up! She led me on!"

"Oh."

"Yeah, oh," Randall said as he straightened and began walking over to a chair.

"I didn't know you went that way," Ron ventured, tongue-in-cheek.

Randall spun around so fast, and with so much fury in his face that Ron pushed out of his seat.

"Okay, okay . . . I won't go there."

"Don't ever!" Randall bit out.

"So, I think we're okay. She probably doesn't know any more than she did before. Although I am puzzled about the fact that she gave you that gun. You say it's easily worth four or five grand?"

"Easily."

"Well, that's quite an investment. She must be hoping it'll pay off in the long run. Did you get any idea what she wants out of all this?"

"Yeah. She wants to avenge Savory."

"In what way? Monetarily?"

"I have no idea! She said something about acceptance and peace. To be honest, what I remember most about her little speech was that she'd had the most incredible crocodile tears falling onto the Heart of Pine flooring we had just put in."

A puzzled look came over Ron's face as he slowly got out of his chair and walked over to where his friend sat sprawled in his. "Hey, buddy, she get under your skin?" Then he quickly walked backward with his hands raised. "Hey, no pun intended; it just came out."

Randall gave his friend a contemptuous leer and shoved himself out of the chair. "I've got work to do. Two weddings and a graduation. Let me know when we go to court on this."

"We're supposed to work something out, remember?"

"Forget it! I don't want her to get anything."

"Well then you might as well add my name to your stock portfolio."

"At least I'll be giving my money to someone who's getting it honestly."

Ron gave a loud whoop of laughter. "You must be the only one on the planet who thinks attorneys earn their money honestly."

"Well, shystering is better than whoring."

"How far'd you go with those tongues anyway?"

"You could say too far. Or not far enough, depending on my mood."

"Hey, cheer up. You're still the best-looking bachelor in Baltimore, but I'll tell you what, I'm gonna stop telling the girls I fix you up with that you own a gen-u-ine Southern plantation."

The sound that reverberated back to Ron's ears was the slamming of his heavy wooden door as it shook against the frame.

"The man can't take a joke," he muttered as he slumped into his seat.

Chapter Thirty
Walking the Streets of the City

As Randall walked down the street, his hands deeply thrust into his pockets, he was oblivious to the glances he received from women on their lunch break. Normally, he would have eyed them up and down just as they were doing him; but now, coming on to a woman was the last thing he had on his mind.

The angry gray cloud that he towed with him hunched his shoulders and caused him to have an uncharacteristic frown. *How dare she?* He kicked a food wrapper away that had attached itself to the front of his loafer. He'd had all intentions of staying on in Beaufort County and taking pictures of Beau Marecage, but because of all the turmoil, he had hightailed it back to Baltimore the very next day. He had lied when he told Ron he had work to do. Everything had been rescheduled; he had no pressing work.

He noticed the sidewalk had changed beneath his feet. He was walking on old cobbles right now. He looked around, and being unfamiliar with the area, he looked up at the doorway he was standing under. Baltimore County Library. He shrugged his shoulders. What the hell, maybe he could do with a good book. Lord knew he could use the distraction. Either he was wide awake mad as a hornet at the woman who had used him, or he was tossing in his sleep remembering the incredible feel of her body and her wildly passionate kisses.

He pulled open the heavy door and walked into the semi-dark interior. It took a moment for his eyes to adjust, and since he'd never been in this building, he did what most people have a tendency to do—he walked to the right.

He walked among legions of science and history books, most having to do with World War II, until he came to a section labeled "Southern History." Flicking his fingers down the spines, he stopped when he saw the title on one of the books.

It said simply, *Blockade Runners*. He remembered that Shelby Laine had spoken briefly about a particular blockade runner, the one his ancestor's body had supposedly been found under. He tried to recall the name, but could not. He took the book off the shelf anyway and went to sit at a table where he thumbed through it. Within minutes he was absorbed as he read the fascinating history of the blockade runners.

CR

The British territories of Nassau and Bermuda, with their close proximity to the U.S., became the chief depots of the blockade runners. Steamers, loaded with baled cotton in Wilmington sailed to Bermuda where the captain sold the cotton for guns, gunpowder, lead, woolens, blankets, and chloroform, as well as other military supplies and contraband.

Most of the captains were from Smithville, N.C., now called Southport. For one trip from Wilmington to Bermuda and back, the captains would receive $3,500 to $5,000 in British gold, the medium of exchange in Bermuda, payable half in advance. A Chief Engineer commanded $2,500, a Chief Officer drew $1,250, second and third mates $750, crew members and firemen $250, and the pilots $3,500.

The South's cotton, worth four to seven cents a pound stateside, sold for fifty to seventy cents a pound in Bermuda. An average bale weighed 500 pounds and the average cargo per vessel was 800 bales, with some larger ships able to carry 2,100 bales; this was a very lucrative business. Profits on a single voyage for a blockade runner ranged from $150,000 to $525,000.

Skippers in the trade made this toast famous, and it was especially popular with the British:

"Here's to the Confederates that grow the cotton, the Yanks that keep the price up by blockade, the Limeys that pay the high prices for it—to all three, and a long war."

Equally as important as cotton and commodities that brought high prices in Europe, were tar, pitch, and turpentine—commonly known then as naval stores. In an era where wooden ships prevailed, these items were indispensable. Prior to 1861, Wilmington was the largest exporter of naval stores in the world.

Imports from Bermuda, in February 1863 alone, included: 80,000 Enfield rifles, 27,000 Austrian rifles, 2,100 British muskets, 2,000 Brunswick rifles, 354 Carbines and 129 cannons.

Between November of 1863 and December of

1864, runners brought in 8,500,000 pounds of meat and 500,000 pounds of coffee.

Over and over, river pilots from Smithville guided the "runners" up the Cape Fear River into Wilmington where their cargoes of military supplies were transferred to trains and sent north to Richmond and General Lee's Army of Northern Virginia.

Wilmington, 220 miles south of the capital of the Confederacy in Richmond, was 150 miles from Charleston, South Carolina and 370 miles from Atlanta, Georgia. The principal operations of the blockade runners converged in this coastal city with its sheltered harbor and long inland river. In total, 397 vessels successfully ran the blockade and made their way up the Cape Fear River.

Most of the low silhouette, short-masted boats had only minimum rigging and a shallow draft of no more than nine feet so they could easily get over the sand bars at the harbor mouths. Painted so they were harder to see, they also used Welsh coal as the preferred fuel because it gave off very little smoke when the vessel was pressed for speed. Canvas strips were draped around the paddle boxes to deaden the sound of the wheels. The typical early type of vessel pressed into this type of service had a speed of eight knots and displaced 1,000 tons. The later, more advanced models displaced 1,700 tons and had a speed of eighteen knots. The Bermuda to Wilmington run was the longest at 674 miles; Nassau to Charleston was 515 miles; and Nassau to Savannah, the shortest run, was 500 miles.

The last miles of the blockade runner's journey were the most treacherous as they came across the horizon and slipped into the southern ports with their swift, lean, light-draft ships that were designed just for this service. They were painted all black or misty gray so they could slip by the Federal fleet undetected.

The *Banshee II*, one of the most revered and profitable of all blockade runners, made eight trips and paid her owners a 700 percent profit despite her capture. On one trip alone, she brought in 600 barrels of pork and 1,500 boxes of meat, enough to supply Lee's army for a month. Her sister ship, the *Banshee,* almost met her fate when a white Arabian horse being imported from Egypt for Jefferson Davis neighed while the runner was slipping by the Federal fleet. The enemy opened fire, but the all-black blockade runner managed to escape in the darkness. She eased over the bar and sped up the river to unload her precious cargo.

The *R.E. Lee* made twenty-one round trips, carrying 7,000 bales of cotton worth some $2,000,000 in gold. She brought in war supplies to pay for herself many times over.

In all, the Federals took 1,149 ships as prizes. Another 355 burned or were run aground. The total loss to the Confederacy was 1,504 ships captured or destroyed, valued at $7,000,000. By conservative estimates, the cargoes condemned were worth $22,000,000. But so many valuable cargoes were thrown overboard that it's hard to know the true loss the South suffered. A Confederate officer once stated that all the approaches to Wilmington Harbor were thickly paved with valuable merchandise.

The night of January 15, 1865 marked the beginning of the end for the blockade runners. Fort Fisher was forced to surrender after being overwhelmed by 10,000 Federal troops and a naval armada of 628 guns.

The next day at Old Inlet, the men at Fort Holmes on Bald Head Island destroyed the works and garrison and evacuated. Across the mouth of the Cape Fear

River, Fort Caswell and Fort Campbell did the same, along with Fort Pender, also known as Fort Johnston, at Smithville.

Union troops marched toward Fort Anderson, constructed on the site of Brunswick Town, the last defense for the town of Wilmington. The Federal monitor Montauk moved north up the river. Along with it was the wooden gunboat *Pequot*. The *Mackinaw* followed, as did the *Maratanza*, the *Lenaha*, the *Bassicsu*, the *Pontusuck*, the *Huron* and the *Chippewa*. The fort was badly shelled, yet the entire garrison managed to escape under cover of darkness and burned the bridges to the city behind them as they left.

The Union Army was forced to fight their way through rice fields and creeks as the Confederates retreated northward. On February 11, 1865, the Union Army entered the city of Wilmington and the lifeline of the Confederacy afforded by the blockade runners was severed.

CR

Randall sat upright in his chair as he closed the book. His ancestor had been one of those men, one of those men who had fought to keep the South in the war so they could preserve their way of living. Incredibly, he felt proud. For the first time ever, he felt pride in the fact that his family had lived through some very trying times and had still managed to survive. The fact that Beau Marecage was intact seemed more a miracle now than it ever had. Inspired by the history he had just read, he checked out a few more books pertaining to the war and the South in general, and walked the amazing twenty-four blocks back to his car. At this rate, he was going to have to replace these loafers soon, he thought as he slid onto the seat of his car.

Chapter Thirty-One
Instant Messaging

Ben: I can't believe you did that!

Shelby: She's entitled!

Ben: Shelby, you know there's not a chance in hell she'll take that plantation away from its legitimate heir.

Shelby: She's a legitimate heir, too.

Ben: She's an *illegitimate* heir!

Shelby: That's not her fault! Charles wanted to marry Savory and he would have if Sage hadn't killed him!

Ben: You're being ridiculous. None of these so-called reparation suits ever pan out.

Shelby: That's where you're wrong. A few

have. Even if this one doesn't, just keeping it in the courts will keep Randall from selling Beau Marecage.

Ben: It's his to sell!

Shelby: No, it isn't! Charles was the heir, *his* children were next in line!

Ben: Shelby, you are not going to be able to upset six generations of legacies. It just won't happen.

Shelby: I cannot believe you are not supporting me on this!

Ben: I not only am not supportive of what you're doing, I'm on Randall's side! He owns it, he should be able to do whatever he wants with it!

Shelby: He just wants to make money! He wants to subdivide and sell lots, putting stupid houses all over!

Ben: What's wrong with that? People need houses to live in.

Shelby: Not at the expense of a historical estate like Beau Marecage.

Ben: Thank God you're not that type.

Shelby: What type?
Ben: The type that puts 'an' instead of 'a' in front of historical.

Shelby: Don't change the subject! Beau Marecage is *an* historical site and it should be preserved!

Ben: Okay, now you've really made me mad.

Shelby: Good, because I'm mad too!

Ben: I'm going to call Randall and tell him I'm rooting for him.

Shelby: You'll do no such thing. I swear to you that if you do, I will never speak to you again!

Ben: I think this is getting out of hand.

Shelby: I should have known you'd side with the moneygrubbers, given your family and all.

Ben: Hey, that's not fair!

Shelby: Sure it is. You moneyed people stick together. Well, us environmentalists are a pretty insurmountable bunch. We wield more power than most people think!

Ben: Shelby, I know the coalitions you can pull together, but really, is this the best thing for Cindy?

Shelby: Cindy wants a little settling up on the family history. It was her family that got the shaft. She's happy to participate and help us right everything.

Ben: Shelby, please. Let's not be at odds over this.

Shelby: Well, apparently Ben, you haven't been paying attention, because we already are! I needed to know whether you were capable of caring for people in more than just a superficial way. Well, I guess I got my answer! And believe me, I'm not at all thrilled to have been used by a 'master' such as yourself!

Ben: I'll just give you a few days to calm down. I think you're being a touch irrational. By the way, I'd hate to make the drive for nothing, so please let me know if you're still up for me heading east this weekend.

Shelby: Don't bother!

Chapter Thirty-Two
Chapel Hill, NC

Ben opened the door to a man who looked almost as haggard as he was. "Yeah?"

"I'm Randall Garrett."

Ben started to close the door on the man. "I'm not allowed to talk to you."

Randall pushed back against it with his hand, "I beg your pardon, you didn't even know I was coming. How is it you're not allowed to talk to me?"

Ben gave him an exaggerated smile and crooked his finger indicating that Randall should follow him. He led him down the long hallway and into his home office. He walked over to his chair, spun it around, and pointed for him to sit.

With a puzzled grin, Randall did as he was instructed and took the proffered seat. He watched as Ben moved the mouse around and opened an e-mail program. When Ben found the particular missive he wanted, he stood up and intoned, "Read."

Randall sat forward so he could see the screen

better and read the last series of instant e-mail messages that Shelby and Ben had sent back and forth. They detailed Shelby's involvement in Cinnamon's reparations case and Ben's adamant replies that she not get involved, followed by his wholehearted support of Randall's plight.

"Oh," Randall said simply when he was finished reading the series.

"Yeah. Oh."

"She's a pistol."

"That she is."

"I want to strangle her."

"Me, too."

"You got any scotch."

"Twelve years old."

"That'll do."

Ben walked out of the office and down the hallway to the kitchen. Randall followed. "So, how'd ya find me?" Ben asked. "I don't know anybody who knows I'm seeing Shelby."

"I didn't even know. I was looking for the pathologist who took apart my many-times-removed great-uncle. I called the man whose card was in the gun locker Cinnamon *presented* to me and found out from him that they'd found a body under a blockade runner at Sunset Beach."

"The *Vesta*."

"Yeah, but that wasn't his ship if what I've been reading is accurate."

Ben found the bottle he was looking for and poured them both a healthy dose. "Boy, do I have a tale to tell you. But I have to warn you, some of it is pure conjecture. See I've had these weird dreams lately . . ."

Two hours and many scotches later, Ben gave

a great sigh, "And that, my new friend, is how I met Shelby and all the other crazy people who won't let me sleep at night. Speaking of which, do you have a place to sleep tonight?"

"Thought I'd just find a hotel," Randall said, slurring his words.

"Nah, you can stay here. The guest room's down the hall. Help yourself."

"That's mighty white of you," Randall replied, then laughed his head off.

"Waz so funny?" Ben asked.

"Don't know. Wonder where that s'pression came from? 'Mighty white of you.' I gotta watch what I say now that I'm in love with a black woman."

"You are?" Ben asked in a high-pitched voice.

"Pretty sure I am. I ain't never felt this way before, and I've known a lot of women."

"Yeah, me too."

"You love her, too?"

"No! I've known a lot of women. Shelby's different though."

"Shelby's the cause of all my troubles."

"Mine, too."

"I think I need to use the bathroom."

"Me, too."

☙

The next morning, heads heavy, Ben and Randall scowled at each other over the breakfast counter. Between the two of them they had managed to make coffee, pour orange juice, and toast some bagels.

"I don't have to be in the office until eleven this morning. Why don't you follow me over? I want to show you something."

"Sure. It's not my ancestor's remains is it? Because I'm not sure I could stomach that on any given day, let alone today."

"No, it's not Charles I want you to see."

There was silence while they both sipped their coffee and crunched on overdone bagels.

"So, what do you know about Cinnamon?" Randall asked offhandedly.

"Not much really. The day Shelby e-mailed me about somebody named Janeel hooking her up with Cindy she was quite excited. At the time, I had no idea she'd get this far, or I would have tried harder to stop her."

"Where'd she find her?"

"Barbados."

"Barbados?"

"Yeah. She was trying to find out what had happened to Savory. Apparently a few months ago, she became obsessed with finding out about her ancestor."

"What did she find out?"

"I don't know really. That's when Shelby and I had that communication breakdown."

"Oh."

"I know she teaches history somewhere on St. Helena."

"Well, that's a help."

"Why? Are you going to try to find her?"

"I don't think I have a choice. I can't sleep, I can't eat, and I can't even begin to think about my work."

"Well the reason you can't eat is because these bagels are pitiful," Ben said as he dropped his on his plate.

"That explains breakfast, but not every other meal I've tried to eat this week," Randall said with a rueful grin.

"So, you got it bad huh?"

"I don't know what I have. I just can't stop thinking about her."

"And those crocodile tears?"

"Those, and a few other things," he muttered as he reached for his coffee.

"Well, I could call Shelby and find out how you can get in touch with her, except she's not real receptive to me right about now."

"You could say you've reconsidered. That you've changed your position. You're all in favor of the reparations suit."

"What? Are you crazy?"

"Maybe I am. Just because you say you're in support of it doesn't mean I'm going to lose. At least this way, I don't have your failed relationship hanging over my head."

"Shelby and I don't have a relationship."

"Oh, really? Then what is it you have? According to those e-mails, I sensed something serious going on."

"Nah. Not serious."

"Yeah, right. Okay, but I gotta tell ya, I think there are some strange forces coming into play here. And no matter how hard we fight it, I don't think it's going to do either one of us a bit of good to be in denial, least of all me. I know that if I don't see her again, I will spend the rest of my life regretting it."

"All this from seeing her one night?"

He smiled broadly over at Ben. Then he closed his eyes, nodded, and sighed. "One very memorable night."

Ben shook his head then pushed away from the table. "Grab your gear and follow me over to my office."

Randall stood and helped Ben tidy up as he thanked him for his hospitality.

"Are you heading back to Baltimore today?" Ben asked.

"No, I think I'll take my camera and walk around Beau Marecage. I'm in the mood to lose myself in something that doesn't matter."

"Doesn't matter?"

"In terms of pleasing others. Portrait photography is not very rewarding at times. It's one criticism after another. I swear, I'm accused of creating wrinkles where there are none, causing shadows that make double chins, and making people look old, tired, and overweight. Even the most beautiful brides are hard to satisfy. The camera sees all, but the customer doesn't appreciate it much."

Ben chuckled as he grabbed his briefcase by the door. "At least in my job, the customer rarely talks back."

"You are a lucky man," Randall said as he went out the door after him.

Chapter Thirty-Three
Ben's Office

B en tossed his briefcase on his desk and opened the center drawer. He took a key from the tray and walked over to a tall file cabinet. He unlocked it and bent to open the bottom drawer. Then he pulled out a canvas bag and laid it on the corner of his desk.

"I don't know what the protocol is in this case. There are probably a few channels I should be going through before I give these to you, but I have no idea what they are, so here. These are Charles' effects. All the things I found on his person."

Randall touched the bag and ran his hand over the strap that held it closed. Uncertain as to whether he should open it here or take it somewhere else, he hesitated.

"Go ahead, take a look. You may have some questions."

Randall took the bag and began emptying it, one item at a time. As he did so, Ben identified each item.

"Bone buttons. Rifle bullets. Marble toys. Real

hand-blown glass. I think there's a comb of some sort inside that knife. That piece of linen had homemade soap in it. I believe it was made on the Plantation. Ah, and that's the locket. The thing that started all this."

Randall took the small package in his hand and looked questioningly up at Ben.

Ben watched as Randall slowly and carefully unwrapped it, then reached over and showed him how to open it when he began fumbling with it. As Ben sat perched on the corner of the desk, he watched as the locket popped open and Randall stood staring. There were no words said for many minutes as they both looked down into the pictures. Then Randall tilted the locket and read the inscription:

Everlasting Love

"He really loved her."

"I believe that he did."

There was more silence and then Randall took a deep breath. "Then Cinnamon is right, she deserved better."

He snapped the locket closed. Put it in his pocket and stood. "I guess I'll get going. I've taken up enough of your time."

Ben stood and shook his hand. "Next time you bring the scotch."

Randall smiled back at him and picked up the canvas satchel. "Thanks, you've been a good ear."

"I do have one question for you before you go. Since you're the next of kin, what would you have me do with Charles' remains? I have a call into Oakdale Cemetery in Wilmington. A lot of Civil War soldiers are buried there. In fact, they have a sort of mass grave in a special section of the cemetery that the town bought for them way back when. It's guarded by a bronze statue of a confederate soldier. I think they may be able to find a place for another son of the South, and a blockade runner at that. I have a few more places in mind I can check on, in case that doesn't pan out. He's in cold storage for the moment, patiently waiting for a final resting place of honor."

Randall stood at the door staring off into space, then he snapped back to the present and said, "I'll make the arrangements. I'd like to see him buried at Beau Marecage. It's time for him to come home now."

"I think he'd like that."

With a wave of his hand, Randall acknowledged Ben's approval then walked out the door, closing it silently behind him.

Ben stood staring at the paneled oak door for a moment then he turned, sat down at his computer, and started typing.

Chapter Thirty-Four
An e-mail to Holden Beach

Ben: I know you're probably at work right now, but I didn't want to wait any longer to apologize. I've had some time to think and reconsider. If this reparations suit is that important to you, then I'm all in favor of it. I will be supportive of you and Cinnamon in your endeavors to right the wrong that was done to Savory so many years ago. Please forgive me for being so argumentative and also for being so unenlightened. I would love to see you this weekend which, by the way, starts tonight. I'd like this weekend to be special, so I've decided to book a room at the Sunset Beach Inn. Meet me in the Vesta Suite (how appropriate, don't you think?) at eight and I'll show you just how much I've missed you. Don't bother replying, I won't have access to my computer after three. If I've been forgiven, I'll see you there. Ben.

Later that night, Ben sat behind a row of cars waiting to go over to the island of Sunset Beach. He'd run into more traffic than usual and was running a few minutes behind time. Shelby was probably already at the suite. He had wanted to arrive before her so he could lay out the strawberries and champagne and prepare a soothing hot bubble bath in the huge Jacuzzi tub. When he'd called this afternoon to arrange everything, he had spoken directly to the owner, Dave Nelson. He had met him the first time he stayed there after being summoned to take care of the body from under the blockade runner. It had been important to secure the Vesta Suite since that was how they had met. He was going to tell Shelby that he was ready for an exclusive relationship. He wanted her to agree that they were now officially a couple.

CR

Shelby sat on the love seat facing the window that looked out over the Intracoastal Waterway. Half a mile away she could see the lights of the bridge as dusk settled over the island. As she sat and watched the boats go through, it finally occurred to her that the bridge was not closing for car traffic. After several more minutes of watching, she got up and went out onto the screened-in porch to see if she could determine what was going on. The bridge definitely wasn't moving. It had been over twenty-five minutes now, of that she was certain. She grabbed the room key and went down to her truck to get the binoculars she always kept there. Then she walked behind the inn to the sloping hill leading down to the marsh, and from there to the Intracoastal. She put the binoculars to her eyes and scanned the area. Sure enough, the bridge tender was out of the small house that served as the control tower for the ancient swing-bridge. He was frantically waving his arms to several men standing on a crane platform twenty feet from the bridge. Following the gestures the man was making, her eyes fell to the pilings that were bridge supports. They were leaning at an odd angle. Dread filled her as she realized what must have happened. The workmen had somehow hit the supports and now the bridge could not be closed. The cars lined up on the other side could not come over to the island. Ben was in one of those cars stuck on the mainland.

She let the binoculars fall to her side and with a dejected demeanor, turned and walked slowly back up the hill. When she got back to the room, she walked out onto the porch and focused the binoculars again, trying to see if she could spot Ben's little roadster. Suddenly the phone rang and she jumped because of its unexpectedness. Realizing that it could only be one person, she ran to answer it.

"Ben?"

"Yes, it's me. I'm stuck at the bridge. It's out. They say it could be morning until they get it fixed. There's something wrong with some bridge supports. They can't close it."

"Not even for people to walk across?"

"They say it's not safe, and they don't want to make things worse. D.O.T. in Wilmington's been called, but no one expects to see anyone for several hours."

"Great. I'm here, you're there. What a way to start our weekend!"

"I'm pleased you're upset. I take it I'm forgiven?"

"Yes," she whispered, and the huskiness of the sound caused Ben quite a bit of anguish.

"I'm going to try to get over there."

"How? The only way is by helicopter or boat. You don't have either."

"No, but I have the most incredible hard-on, and I'm determined not to let it go to waste."

"You going to drive to Myrtle Beach or something? Try to pick someone up at Thee Doll House?" she chided.

"No, I'm going to plant this hard-on inside *you!* Sit tight. I'll find a way."

She heard the phone click as he disconnected. Now just how was he going to find a way across the Waterway? She walked back out onto the porch and watched as the lights on the bridge became brighter as the sun set further. It was conceivable he could rent a boat or even a kayak for that matter, she thought. It would be a simple matter to put it in at the bottom of the slope at Twin Lakes Restaurant, paddle across the Intracoastal, and bring it up at the boat ramp just past the bridge. But where would he rent one this time of night? Even the places that rented jet skis were closed by now. Nobody wanted their rentals out at night when it was too dark to see where you were going. She propped her feet up on the wooden footstool and watched the boats going up and down the Intracoastal. At least they were enjoying a night of unimpeded travel.

She had almost dozed off sitting and watching the wood storks gliding into their roosts for the night when something moving on the side of the road caught her eye. She sat up straighter and tried to focus, then she stood and walked to the screen. She put her hands around her eyes to take away some of the glare from the room lights behind her. Then she saw him. Ben. Walking along the road at a fast clip. When he spotted her, he started sprinting.

"Shelby!" he called.

"Ben!" she called back.

"Fix a hot bath for me would ya, honey? I'm

freezing!"

Oh, my God. He swam across! She ran to turn on the taps, then ran out the door and down the stairs to meet him.

She ran into his arms and he swung her up into the air in his. "Shelby, Shelby . . . I couldn't wait until tomorrow. I had to see you tonight," he whispered against her neck.

"Oh, Ben!" she sobbed. "You fool! You could have been killed!"

"Well, there was this sailboat that was moving pretty fast, and I wasn't quite sure he'd see me in time to turn, so I had to dive for the bottom and swim underwater for a bit. I was lucky, I came up by a jon boat and they shielded me until I got to the other side."

She slapped him on the shoulder as she screeched at him, "Don't ever do that again! That was stupid!"

He put her down and framed her face with his hands. "Yeah, but I'm here."

She smiled up into his face as he lowered his to hers. "That you are."

Even though he was drenched and his hair all but dripping, she thoroughly enjoyed his kiss. He was gentle and very tender as he let his lips close over hers. When he shivered, she didn't know if it was because he was chilled or as taken with her as she was with him.

"C'mon, I've got a bath running for you, it wouldn't do to have it overflow."

"You getting in with me?"

"Do I have a choice?" she asked.

"No. I swam across the Waterway to get to you. You can certainly get in a bathtub with me. You got any problems with that?"

"I'll lead the way," she said with a big grin.

CR

The next morning, the bridge was repaired and they were able to spend the weekend doing all the beachy things tourists do. They drove around, shopped, and visited Silver Coast Winery, and a local gallery and gift shop called The Sea Gallery. They spoke with the owner, Chasen and his grandfather, Miller, and Ben bought a few watercolors by the local artist, Terry Buckner. Shelby bought a photograph by Ken Buckner of the old swing bridge that had broken down, forcing Ben to swim to her. Later they dined at Twin Lakes, enjoying every kind of seafood imaginable. They went into an-upscale dress shop called Island Breeze where Shelby splurged and bought a flowing tropical-print dress that complimented her eyes. They licked ice cream cones from How Sweet It Is and sat in the beautiful garden by the quaint little gift shop and talked about their jobs.

Shelby explained to Ben what the difference was between "shore" and "coast," shore being the edge of the water, coast being the edge of the land. Then they walked hand-in-hand back to the island and Ben related the little known story about how the word "coroner," came about.

"In England, in the early1500s, the king sent an official known as the Crowner to tally up how much money was due to the Crown from an estate when someone died. Later, that same official was called upon to determine the cause of death. The title 'Crowner,' soon evolved into 'coroner.' And there you have it, the history of the name and how the job came into being."

"Very interesting," Shelby said with a smirk. "You and your ilk have gone from figuring out estate taxes and dunning grieving people for money to telling people that the glove didn't fit."

"Oh, don't even get me going on the disastrous O.J. story!"

He squeezed her hand and lifted it to his lips as they made the turn off the causeway to the gravel path leading back to the inn. His tiny kisses were warming her when she felt him yawn against her hand.

"I'm sorry. I don't know about you, but I sure could use a nap. What do say to taking a few towels down to the beach where we can stretch out and make up for some of the sleep we lost last night appeasing our passion?"

"Are you sure we're appeased?" she teased, caressing his cheek while deftly inserting her thumb into his mouth. He sucked on it while her other hand stole down his chest and idly stroked a nipple. When he closed his eyes and groaned, she arched away from him and started walking backward up the steps to the Inn.

He gave her a wicked grin and reached for her but she was too quick for him. She spun and darted through the door, ran past the desk and out to the breezeway connecting the rooms to the main house. He gave chase and caught her at the door to their room where he squelched her laughter with a searing kiss.

He pushed his body into hers, flattening her against the door. "I *know* I appeased you, but it seems I'll just have to do it again. It apparently didn't take." His hot breath fanned her throat as he licked and nipped a series of quick kisses down to her collarbone. His leg insinuated itself between her thighs and she felt the hard ridge of him straining against his shorts.

"And again, and again," she whispered as she reached behind her back and opened the door. He continued pressing hot kisses into the side of her neck as she allowed him to back her up into the room and out of her sandals until her knees hit the back of the bed. Then he abruptly broke off kissing her and met her passion-filled eyes with his. He placed a splayed hand on her chest and pushed. She fell to the bed and he followed her down kicking off his own sandals.

Chapter Thirty-Five
Chapel Hill, NC

The bone-deep satisfaction of their coupling stayed with him until mid-morning of the next day when after the first few calls, he finally had to accept the fact that he was back at work.

When the phone rang again, Ben answered with a cheery, "Dr. Kenyon."

"Ben, I need your help on something."

"Randall?"

"Yup."

"What's up?"

"I need to know what I have to do to get a body brought stateside from Barbados."

"Savory?"

"Yup."

"You'll need her next-of-kin's help."

"Cindy's the only kin I know of, and I want to surprise her. I don't want her to know until it's done."

"Done?"

"I want to put her beside Charles at Beau

Marecage."

"What a great idea! Both Shelby and Cindy will be thrilled! But that's going to be difficult without her help."

"But it can be done?"

"Yeah. It'll take some money."

"Got that. Who do I need to call?"

Ben told him the best way to arrange everything and finished up with, "So are you and Cindy back together?"

"Not yet. You and Shelby?"

"Yeah. We just spent an incredible weekend at the beach."

"Must be nice."

"It'll happen for you."

"Well, at least I found her."

"You haven't talked to her?"

"No."

"What are you waiting for?"

"Building courage."

"Well, don't wait too long; it won't get any easier."

"Got any ideas?"

Ben thought for a moment then asked, "You got access to the plantation at night?"

"Yeah, I got the keys."

"Get her there on the pretext of working something out on the legal issues, then wine her and dine her all alone in that big impressive dining room. That would turn any girl's head."

"Hey, that's not a bad idea. I can hire a caterer. Even get a band for dancing."

"Hey, hey, hey! Don't get too carried away. You want to be alone with the girl, remember?"

"Oh, yeah."

"Well, good luck. Let me know how you fare?"

"With Cindy? Isn't that kind of private?"

"Not that! With the re-internment!"

"Oh, yeah. I'll let you know. Maybe we'll have a ceremony."

"A memorial?"

"Yeah, you didn't think I meant a wedding did ya?"

"I never know with you."

Randall laughed heartily as he disconnected the call.

CR

Ben smiled at the receiver as he placed it back on the hook. The man was a goner. He certainly was looney tunes over that woman. He got up from his desk and made his way through the building to the cold storage section where the paperwork was waiting for him to sign. Charles' body was being readied for its final journey. He nodded at the students who were completing their assigned tasks on cadavers and walked over to the back loading area where a casket was being offloaded.

"This is quite some casket. Cypress isn't it?"

The driver smiled and lovingly ran his fingers over the top. "Sure is. You don't see too many like this any more. It used to be the only kind of casket white people were buried in a hundred years ago, while the coloreds got the plain old pine boxes. Now we have mahogany, cherry, oak, you name it. We made another one just like this last week. Strange. One delivered here, one delivered at a funeral home in Beaufort. Must be nice to have money to bury like that."

Ben just quirked his lips and nodded. He had a hunch who that other cypress casket had been ordered for.

He signed the paperwork for the driver and supervised the loading of Charles Edward Garrett's body from the stainless steel gurney into the velvet-lined coffin. Judging by things, Randall had spared no expense for his ancestor's burial.

The hearse that was to take the coffin to Beau Marecage was running late; the driver had called just a few minutes ago to get the directions again. Ben dismissed everyone saying he would wait and see the body delivered to the driver. When he was alone with the casket, he lifted the lid one final time.

"Well, here you go Charlie. At the end of the road this time, at least you'll get to lie beside your beloved–for all eternity. Or to use your own words, *Everlasting Love.* I wish things had been better for you. I truly do." He closed the coffin lid and patted it twice.

Then he sat in a chair by the door waiting. As he sat, the sun streamed in through the window in the door and warmed his face. Within minutes, he was fast asleep.

As he slept, he dreamed that Charles stood above him talking to him in a quiet, thoughtful voice.

Ben, you are indeed fortunate. You can have your love. You do not need to hide her away from the world. You can take and hold her and cherish her in full view. You can live in this wonderful country, the country I died fighting for, in a home that you choose with your love. You can plan for a family and live happily together without fear of either of you being condemned for it. Don't waste your life. Don't waste your love. Savory and I never had that opportunity. We had the love, the most beautiful, intense love, but it did not have the promise that it should have. We should have had dozens of children and many, many years of happiness. Learn from my life. Do not let your love be squandered as ours was on its very bloom. Cherish her. Cherish the time. It is fleeting, even if all goes well for you.

The sound of harsh knocking on the metal door startled Ben out of his reverie. He shook his head to clear his mind of the words that still lingered there. Wondering if he had just had an introspective moment or if he had really dreamed he heard Charles speaking to him, he stumbled over to open the door.

"I'm here to pick up a body."

Ben stared at the lanky apprentice who was chewing a big wad of gum. He reached behind him and grabbed a trashcan and held it under the kid's mouth. "Spit," he said and watched as the confused kid looked between him and the trash can before spitting out his gum.

Ben replaced the trash can and turned back to the man. "This is not just a body, son. The man in this coffin is a war hero, a devoted son of the South, who passed on a great Southern heritage. A father and a man who loved deeply. Don't ever think of a body as some kind of cargo. It's a life that touched many."

"Yes, sir."

Ben signed the burial transmit permit and watched as the kid and two assisting firemen who had been waiting at the curb carefully loaded the coffin into the hearse, closed the door, and locked it. Then he turned and headed back to his office.

Whether the words tumbling around in his head were of his own making or whether something supernatural was conveying a message to him from beyond the grave, Ben knew it didn't matter. The words were true. He was lucky and he knew it.

Chapter Thirty-Six
Beau Marecage

Cindy knelt at the prayer rail in the old Praise House on St. Helena's Island. She'd had the day off and had decided to spend it somewhere she knew Savory had been. Thoughts of Savory had been on her mind all week. She could not shake the feeling of melancholy she had whenever she thought about the young woman who had lost so much.

It had bothered her before, but now that she knew what love was, it devastated her knowing that Savory had spent her life without the man she was devoted to.

Just how the hell had she fallen in love with Randall so quickly? These things were supposed to take a while and intensify over time, weren't they? At this rate, if things intensified any more, she'd combust next time he touched her—if there was going to be a next time. It sure seemed like he had taken her subterfuge as betrayal. She was sure he hadn't tried to find her. She'd made sure she'd be easy to find if he were looking.

She stared up at the cross hanging on the wall and

prayed for her heavy heart as she begged the Good Lord to deliver her from these feelings. If He was going to make you fall head over heels in love with somebody, the least He could do was make them come around!

She remembered reading once that when you fell in love, your brain produced a chemical called phenylethylamine. It picked up your heart rate, increased your energy level, and gave you a happy, dreamlike feeling. Why, since she was sure she was in love, didn't she have any of that? She only had the dread of unrequited love. That must be the difference, she thought. At least Savory had known her love was returned. At least she had known Charles had loved her. Even if no one believed her, she'd had that to hold onto through the lonely years.

Well, chocolate had phenylethylamine in it too, she told herself as she stood up and prepared to leave the Praise House. I'll just go suck down a chocolate sundae and forget all about Randall Garrett! When she turned to walk down the center aisle and saw him standing in the shadow of the doorway, her heart leapt. With the late afternoon sun behind him, silhouetting his outline, it might have been easy to mistake him for someone else, except for his height and full head of wind-blown hair.

"I was told I could find you here. I hope I'm not disturbing you."

"Who told you I was here?"

"Everyone I asked. I started at Penn Center and was told you were here. Then everyone I passed on the way here told me, 'She's in the Praise House.' How do you suppose so many people knew I'd be looking for you?"

"I told them you might be."

"How did you know?"

"I didn't. I had to hope though."

He closed the twenty feet between them with long,

easy strides then gently tugged the huge sunbonnet off her head. Letting it fall behind her back, he fisted the ribbons in his hand and drew her into his chest. "I've missed you. It was like I lost my very soul the night you ran away from me. Tell me you missed me, too."

"I was just kneeling here wondering if Savory had found any chocolate on the island of Barbados."

"Aren't they known for having the cola nut there?"

"Well, I'm greatly relieved to hear that. You've eased my heart tremendously."

"One day, you're going to have to explain this strange conversation to me. But right now, I need you to come with me."

"Where are we going?"

"Beau Marecage. I need to show you something." He stood back and put his hand out and she took it. He led her out of the church and into the last rays of the setting sun.

Cinnamon sat beside Randall in the Lincoln Town Car as he drove down the highway.

"My attorney would be furious if he knew we were together like this, but I just wanted us to talk. I think we can come to some kind of agreement without either your attorney or mine. I've been doing a lot of reading and a lot of thinking. I have a few things I want to show you. I am not the selfish, money-grubbing person that Shelby Laine has led you to believe that I am."

"She doesn't think that about you; or if she does, she's sure never let on about it to me."

"Really?"

"She'd like nothing better than to see Beau Marecage preserved, but she's not the type to be mean-spirited. She's never said one bad thing about you to me. Not one."

"Well, that surprises me. She sure as hell tore into me a few weeks ago, made me feel like a snake because I was considering selling my own property!"

"Well, that's Shelby for you. She speaks her mind and isn't afraid to confront someone, but she's above malicious gossiping. Even if she didn't like you, I doubt she'd use me as a way to get back at you. All she cares about is preserving the history and the culture. I'm sure her purpose for finding me had nothing to do with you personally."

"Well, she certainly had a purpose for you!"

"Yeah, she saw me as a way to keep you from selling Beau Marecage, at least for a while anyway."

"You knew that?"

"Of course I knew that! I don't want to see it torn down either. Did you think I was in this for the money?"

"Well, yeah, I guess I did. The legal briefs I read were all about money and restitution and monetary rewards."

"That's just what you have to do to get people's attention these days. Money talks."

"Your words or hers?"

"The attorney's."

"Just who is your attorney?"

"Janeel's husband. He said he'd draw up the papers, but anything more and he'd have to charge."

"So, you don't have any plans to go any further with this?"

"Oh yeah, if we need to, we'll keep fighting. Beau Marecage is too beautiful to destroy."

He reached behind him on the backseat and grabbed a large photo album that he laid lightly on her lap. "Yeah, I have to agree with you there."

Cindy looked over at him and saw his wry smile. She

smiled back and gingerly opened the cover. Inside was page after page of wonderful photographs, all taken at Beau Marecage. There were pictures of trees, swamps, wildlife, the manor house taken from every conceivable angle, the outbuildings, the fields in fallow, and an odd assortment of rusty farm equipment amid hayricks.

"These are lovely. Where did you get them?"

"I took them."

"You took them?"

"Yes. That's what I do for a living. I'm a photographer."

"Oh, I never knew. For some reason, I thought you were a developer."

"No, I only develop film."

"These are great. You should sell them."

He gave a great hoot. "I intend to. They're some of my best work."

"You don't need to sell Beau Marecage for the money?"

"No, it was never about the money."

"So, why did you want to sell?"

"I'm not sure, but it all started with what amounted to a stomachache. It grew to become an incredible pain in my gut. I only got it when I arrived at Beau Marecage. I would sometimes be so doubled over with the pain that I could hardly drive. Then when I pulled through the gates to leave, it was gone. I can only equate it with the horrendous pain that Charles must have felt when Sage ran his blade through him. I'm sure I didn't suffer anywhere near what Charles did—at least not in severity—but certainly, I needed to put an end to it. My doctor said it was psychosomatic since it only happened here, so I thought selling the place and just getting rid of it would solve my problem. It finally solved itself though," he said as he reached over and took her hand in his. "The night I met you, I was in awful pain. But the very moment we met, the pain went away, and it hasn't returned. I've come back several times since then, and there's been nothing. No more pain."

"Well, that's good news. So, have you changed your mind about selling?"

"Have you changed you mind about suing?" he countered.

"I could."

"I could, too."

Randall pulled off the highway and drove down the long, narrow lane leading to the house. When they turned off the lane into the circular drive and parked in front of the impressive front portico, Cindy suddenly noticed the lack of cars in the parking lot several yards away. As he turned off the car, everything around them went dark.

"Where is everybody? Are we the only ones here?"

"Yes, it's just us. Does that bother you?"

"Should it?" she asked, her eyes searching out his in the semi-dark.

"Yes," he whispered as he took her hand and brought it to his lips, "it should bother you very much."

A shiver went down her arm. Oh, this was just too heady. He was everything she had dreamed about since she could remember dreaming about boys. He was handsome, gentle, with a great sense of humor, and he had a way of touching her that filled her with heat while still making goose bumps rise on her skin.

He came around to assist her out of the car. Then he took her by the hand and pulled her up, admiring her long, long legs showing through the slit in the side of her dress. It was a soft summer dress with tiny flowers all over it; the plunging neckline was outlined with lace and attached to a lacy collar. "Your dress is very lovely. Very feminine," he added as he admired the hint of cleavage. Her skin had a burnished glow in the meager light coming from the car's dome lamp. It was golden in places, light copper in others.

"Why thank you, but doesn't it look a bit turn-of-the-century to you?"

"No, not really. Should it?"

"Well, it's from a vintage consignment shop. This week was Plantation Week at the school where I teach and I like to dress the part. It makes it special for the kids. I love the period stuff. I really get into it."

He chuckled as he drew her alongside him. "Is that one of the reasons you like it here?"

"Maybe. It's just so beautiful here. Whenever I come here, I feel like I'm coming home, like the place is welcoming me back. I used to come here as a child all the time. The family I lived with worked here. While they were in the fields, or in the kitchens, I used to climb the trees or scoop out frogs from the ponds. I used to pretend that one of the ducks was the ugly duckling. I would imagine it turning into a lovely swan and flying high over the marshes on its way to the sea. At the time, I didn't know that swans prefer ponds to oceans. The beauty of this place never ceases to amaze me. There's always something new to see, something special that was never here before."

"It's funny, but I never quite saw that here until I met you."

"Really?"

"Odd, isn't it? But you seem to put 'spice' in everything for me. Since that night, I see a lot of things differently."

They walked into the house to find everything lit by candlelight and the wonderful aroma of roasting meats permeating the air. In the dining room a sideboard stood ready with several chafing dishes filled with seafood, selections of pasta with accompanying sauces, several vegetable entrees, and four choices for dessert.

"Oh, my!" Cindy exclaimed.

"I wasn't quite certain what you liked so I signed on for a variety."

She laughed as she walked around the room admiring the table linens, the shiny china plates, the cut crystal water goblets and wine glasses. The caterers had thought of everything and the display was sumptuous. "I like it all. Everything looks delicious. This is very kind of you, Randall."

"I don't want you to think of me as kind," he whispered by her ear as he handed her a plate.

"What would you have me think of you as?"

"Sexy, handsome, charming . . ."

"I'm beginning to think you have lured me here for the purposes of seduction."

"You would be right. How am I doing so far?"

"Well, let's see—all alone, dining by candlelight, red roses on the table, chocolates for dessert . . . where are the violins?"

"They're on a CD in a player on the patio where I shall take you for dancing later."

"Then I would say you have all the bases covered. This appears to be more of a date than anything else."

"You're catching on. I had to see you again. I don't like that the last memory I have of you is with tears streaming down your cheeks."

She piled her plate high, taking a sampling of each item, then he took it from her and carried it to the table. When she joined him there, he pulled her chair out for her.

"So proper you are."

"You won't say that later," he snickered.

She gave him a raised eyebrow as he seated himself across from her.

"Tell me, have you any boyfriends that I will need to beat up?"

She gently shook her head and said, "No, haven't had much luck in that department, I'm afraid."

He put his fork down as he stared at her. "And now why would that be? You are positively beautiful–stunning in fact."

"Well, thank you. But there has been some difficulty because of my heritage."

"In what way, might I ask?"

"Well, I'm not really black, per se, and not quite white either. It's been a bit confusing trying to figure out where I belong. My own mother gave me up because I was darker than she was."

His eyes met and fully engaged hers as he said emphatically, "Well, your heritage is the same as mine. We're related, you know. I won't disown you. In fact, I want to *own* you. You've been waiting for someone special. Me. You can belong to me now."

She stopped eating and put her chin in her hands as she leaned over her plate. "Truly, can I?" She teased.

"Most assuredly."

"Well, I can tell you that's a relief, for although men of both ethnic backgrounds seemed to be attracted to me, they only wanted one thing. And that wasn't courtship. Apparently, I wasn't good enough to take home to momma for either race."

Randall laughed delightedly at her, then quipped, "What a dilemma. Charles couldn't have Savory because she was black, and now you can't have a black man because you're white."

"I'm not really white."

"Nor are you black. I thought you to be a tad Asian or Indian when I first saw you. But your nationality or race mattered not; I thought you were the loveliest creature I had ever seen."

"I'm just a strange mixture, I guess."

"A very lovely mixture," he said with warmth.

She lifted her wine glass and smiled at him. "Thank you for this evening. This is truly lovely."

"It is by no means over, my dear. I have a lot of wooing yet to do. Finish your dessert and I'll take you for a walk around the garden."

"This sounds a bit familiar . . . ."

"Yes, well, it worked rather well last time."

"I practically devoured you!"

"Yes, and I'm counting on you doing that again."

"Randall, we must stop this kidding."

"I'm not kidding. I'm going to take you out and show you this most marvelous tree I found yesterday."

"I don't do well with trees."

"You do extremely well with trees."

"Randall–"

"Cinnamon–"

"We can't do this."

He came around to her and pulled her from her seat. "We must do this," he whispered. Looking into green eyes that were flecked with topaz, he kissed the tip of her nose. "I have known from the very first moment I saw you that we were meant to be together. There is a connection, and I know that you feel it too. I am in love with you. I think I always have been; I just couldn't find you. And there's no way in hell I'm losing you again. Black, white, brown, I don't care about the color of your skin. We belong together. We always have. And I promise you I will never let anyone say otherwise. Never, ever, again."

"Again?" she asked.

But he refused to elaborate. How could he tell her he felt like he'd had these feelings before, when even he knew that he hadn't?

"Come be my love," he whispered, "come walk in my garden."

Mesmerized, she walked beside him. He led her down an oyster shell pathway, then behind some hedges and finally down a sloping hill to a gigantic weeping willow. Its fronds were sweeping the edges of the marsh. The night was still and quiet with only the sounds of faraway crickets intruding.

"It's magnificent," she whispered.

"Yes, isn't it?" he whispered back.

He turned, took her in his arms, and kissed her boldly.

Cindy realized that she was all alone in the moonlight with this man who was not much more than a stranger to her. When she pulled away from his embrace, he gingerly took her hand and lifted it to his lips. He placed tiny little kisses on each fingertip before turning to face her and looking into her bewildered eyes. She was stunned by his attentions. Things like this simply didn't happen to her. But they were. Incredible things were happening to her. Her insides felt like they were melting and with each touch, he was sending a new electric current through her.

"There are so many things I want to tell you. I want to take you places all over the world and do things with you. Wicked, wicked things, things that will make babies for us; things it would be better doing married. Cinnamon Ballyou, would you do me the honor of becoming my wife? Joining your family with mine for all time and taking the name of Garrett, as Charles desired

Savory to do?"

"Marriage? You want to marry me?"

"With all my heart. On the souls of my ancestors, I promise to cherish you always and to be your everlasting love even unto death. I love you, Cindy. Somehow, I always have and I know without a doubt that I always will."

"But marriage? So soon?"

"It's not so soon. I have thought of nothing but you these past weeks. To quote the French sage, Comte DeBussy-Rabutin: 'Absence is to love what wind is to fire—it extinguishes the small, it enkindles the great.' My love for you is fierce, and I can no longer stand the separation. This should have happened a long, long, time ago. It's like Savory and Charles have been granted another chance, and we're the ones who get to live the lives they missed out on. Come, I want to show you something."

He led her around the massive tree to the other side of the yard. Behind a cluster of Live Oaks you could see freshly-painted iron fencing with fancy scroll work. Inside the black, wrought-iron fence were two headstones sitting side by side. The one for Savory, she recognized as the one she had touched so many times in Barbados; the other was brand new. Cinnamon leaned over the fence and read: Charles Edward Garrett, father to Macie.

Tears were streaming from her eyes when Randall turned her to face him. With his thumbs, he wiped her cheeks. "You haven't answered me. Cinnamon Ballyou. We all have one destiny. You're mine. Will you marry me and become the new mistress of Beau Marecage?"

"Yes," she whispered. "Yes, I have to. I couldn't stand living without you twice."

His hands framed her face as his lips descended to

hers and he kissed her with all the love and passion he felt he had been saving for an eternity. Then he cupped her cheeks with his big hands and looked into her face. "Just think, a woman descendant from one of the slaves who worked here so many years ago, is now going to be one of its owners. If this doesn't fulfill some kind of destiny for Charles and Savory and bring history full circle, I don't what does. I love you, Cindy Ballou."

As the moon rose above the swamp, he lifted her into his arms. His silhouetted form joined that of the magnificent willow's as he carried her back to the house on the hill against the backdrop of the marsh and the full moon.

Chapter Thirty-Seven
The Piano

H e knew she'd come. She just had to. He'd sent her a dozen peach roses with a card that read: "Did you know that peach roses say, 'I want you, I desire you, you excite me?'" Included with the flowers had also been an invitation. Then he sent a car, one he had bought especially for her. But he wasn't about to tell her that just yet. She'd just argue and refuse to accept it.

He sat at the piano, his chin propped on one hand as the other lightly tickled the keys on the low end. Anticipation was thrumming through him, and even though he was determined to play this song without the sheet music, he was loathe to practice it anymore. He could not remember a time when he was this afraid that things might not turn out his way. Then the doorbell rang.

He jumped up to answer it, a big smile ready on his lips. But it wasn't Shelby. It was a delivery man with roses. His heart sank. She *wasn't* coming after all.

Politely he greeted the man, signed the receipt

314

pad, and reached into his pocket for a tip. But the man stopped him.

"No, no, no. Not necessary, I've already been tipped. Besides, it's not every day you get to deliver a dozen lilac roses to a man. You must've done something right, buddy." And with that he turned and left.

Ben took the roses into his apartment and started unwrapping them, looking for the card. They certainly were lilac all right; a most unusual color for roses. He found the card and read it. "Did you know that lilac roses say the sender is enchanted with the recipient?"

He smiled as he walked into the kitchen to look for a vase. He had just placed the roses on the counter when the doorbell rang again. Thinking the man had returned for something, he went to answer it.

And there stood Shelby dressed in a pale lavender, linen dress. The dress contrasted beguilingly with her dark hair and deep blue eyes. She looked so lovely that she took his breath away.

"Hi! You requested my presence?" She sported a big smile and an arched brow, as if unsure she had gotten the message right.

He took her by the arm and pulled her into the apartment. Then he closed the door, leaned her against it, and enfolded her into his embrace.

"That I did," he said seconds before his lips descended to hers. "Mmm, and not a moment too soon," he murmured as he went back for more.

When he finally let her breathe, she let out a big sigh and whispered, "You're supposed to say I'm enchanting since I'm in lilac."

"You're enchanting," he breathed huskily and took her lips with his yet again. This time his kiss was fiercely passionate, and it didn't seem that he ever wanted to end it.

With her hands, she pushed lightly against his chest and lowered her face into his shirt so she could catch her breath again.

"Your message said something about tying up loose ends? What was that all about?"

He put his arm around her shoulders, led her into the living room, and then seated her on the sofa. He strolled over to the bar and opened the bottle of champagne that had been chilling in a sterling silver ice bucket. While he updated her on Cinnamon and Randall, he poured the golden liquid into two tall flutes. He chuckled and walked over to hand her one. "Seems Randall has become a slave himself, a slave to love. They're getting married on the twentieth of next month. And get this, he wants me to be his best man!"

"Now, why would that be? He hardly knows you."

He sat beside her on the sofa and told her about the night he and Randall had met, finishing with, "So, Charles' body being discovered when it was, and *you*, being so set on finding out his story and then being so doggedly determined not to let Randall sell Beau Marecage, led to Randall and Cinnamon meeting and falling head over heels in love. You have single-handedly managed to avenge Charles and Savory. Their families are finally uniting, and it's all because of you. Cheers! The loose ends are all tied up!" he said, saluting her with the last dregs of his champagne. Then he stood, took her glass with his, and refilled them both.

"What I don't understand is how they fell in love so quickly."

"Mmmm," he said as he thought about her question. "Maybe I can shed a little light there. As a man, your ideals, your fantasy woman–for lack of a better name, is developed in early puberty. All the things you are exposed to make up a sort of criteria of all that you begin to think of as sublime, heady, sexy, or sensuous–if you will. They're 'love maps' created to define whatever arouses a person sexually. Or pushes them into certain patterns of sexual behavior. Men begin developing them around the age of eight and most men don't ever deviate too much from the ideal they've invested themselves in. Once a butt man, always a butt man. Big on tits? Then most likely you'll always like big tits. Gotta have those long, long legs? Then you probably will always envision long, limber legs wrapped tightly around your hips.

"Take me for example. I thought I knew what my erotic criteria for a woman was–I liked big tits, large hips, and jiggly thighs. Until I met you. Then I found that I craved your small, nubile, tender nipples more than I craved breathing. I yearned to feel your slim hips in my hands as I pumped myself into you, and I dreamed of your tight little ass, and firm, smooth thighs. I had apparently been making women fit into an established pattern I had conceived in my head, instead of finding the woman who truly appealed to me the most.

"So, from a man's point of view, all I can tell you is this: if you're lucky enough to find her, you'll know her when you see her, even though all along you thought she should be something else. I totally thought I was predisposed to an entirely different type of woman than you are. But boy, was I wrong. You're not at all like the dream women I have heretofore pictured in my mind's eye. Even during moments of extreme arousal, I now know I was just settling. Somewhere along the way, I had shifted my true ideals to conform; but I think I always knew that there was something missing. But now, I can't for the life of me picture anyone else fitting the bill quite like you do."

He took both her hands in his and looked deeply into

her clear blue eyes. "I have never had the completeness and awestruck wonder that I experience with you when we make love. You absolutely dumbfound me, in addition to wiping me out," he added with a chuckle. "So yes, I can understand how Randall and Cindy found each other so quickly. You can say the path was cleared for them many, many years ago, or that it was fate, or destiny. But truly, I think it is just a matter of meeting the one you're supposed to be with. Look at the odds. The world is full of people, and there's only so much time. The odds are not really in favor of that one true meeting, as much as we'd like to think so." He leaned in and lightly kissed her on the lips.

"Come here," he commanded, then stood and lifted her into the circle of his arms. He led her over to the grand piano on the other side of the room. His sultry eyes met and held hers as he positioned her against the side of the piano. He left her and slid onto the smooth bench, then he began to play.

She recognized the melody right away. It was the first song they had ever danced to, "You Belong to Me." As she followed his fingers on the keys, her mind began forming erotic images. "See the pyramids along the Nile . . . ." He wasn't singing, but she could hear the words as he played. She watched his fingers rock back and forth between a series of keys, then flutter along the keyboard quickly before his head tilted and he smiled up at her. She was mesmerized, and incredibly turned on as his shoulders shrugged slightly upward in his beautifully tailored sport coat, lending emphasis to the hands flying over the black and white keys.

His fingers moved as if trained to play without conscious thought, the melody leading them. He was stroking the keys with long delicate fingers, first softly, then more purposefully. Lost in the soul of the music, his hands spoke to her.

She looked into his eyes and he returned her heated gaze, and it was as if he was completing her thoughts. *Yes, my hands are that good. They can do incredible things to your body. I know it and so do you.*

She shuddered from the sensuousness of the mental word play, leaned toward him, and was almost tempted to answer, "Yes. Yes."

Lost deep in her consciousness she drifted as she continued to watch him masterfully control each and every digit, and in turn, each and every key, making the music flow so beautifully that it brought tears to her eyes. His eyes locked on hers again, and his piercing, hot eyes told her, *You can see how skilled my fingers are. You know I can touch you in secret places with a rhythm that will complete you and send you to the moon.*

After the last refrain of "You Belong to Me," his fingers trilled up and down the keyboard making each key dance in its turn, flashing up and down as his fingers lightly stroked them individually. *See?* His smile asked. When he stopped, she was sure she had to be blushing.

Neither had said a single word the whole time he had been playing, yet she could swear they'd had a whole conversation, all about the sensuousness of his hands. The way he had commanded those keys was the way he commanded her, her heart, and her body; and his expertise staggered her.

He stood and took her into his arms. Looking down into her passion-filled face, he whispered, "You *do* belong to me."

"Do I?"

"Don't you?"

Tears streaming down her face, she simply nodded.

He lifted her into his arms and carried her into his bedroom.

Chapter Thirty-Eight
Holden Beach

That sure was the oddest thing, Shelby said to herself as she walked along the beach in front of her rented beach house. She and Ben had been walking, kicking at the sand, and laughing in the wind as they chased a crab back into its hole. And then they had stopped to watch a toddler chase some sandpipers in little circles. His high-pitched sound of glee had made them both turn and smile at each other. Then she had found a way to make him bump into her just because she wanted to feel his thighs on the back of hers. Her hand had slipped up to lightly cup him and he had groaned his pleasure. Then he had taken off running, calling over his shoulder that he had to go to The Lighthouse, a giftshop on the Causeway and that he'd be right back.

She sat at the water's edge feeling the water lap her toes as she rested her head on her knees. When had she been this happy? This content?

She'd always loved her job and now even more so, since hurricane season was almost over. The new drugs her father was on were improving his memory. The last two times she'd visited, he actually knew who she was. And Ben. Ben made everything wonderful. They spent every spare moment together that they could. The only thing that marred it was the distance. Although it wasn't quite the hardship on her part that it once had been since Ben had bought her a brand new car. In exchange, she had offered to take pole dancing lessons for him. Her body had never been in better shape. She probably *could* eat a whole box of benne wafers now without gaining a single ounce.

Once a month they agreed to meet Randall and Cinnamon at Beau Marecage to relax and enjoy their friendship. They were also helping them establish a foundation for scholarships for the Gullah children who wanted to study their heritage. Yes, she was happy. She was very happy when she was with Ben.

She visited the gravesite at Beau Marecage every time they went there. Once, she put a lily on Savory's grave and a glass cat's eye marble on Charles'. Another time, much to Ben's surprise, she had opened a grocery bag and liberally sprinkled the contents of two dozen spice jars over both plots. As the spices had mingled and their individual and combined essences had floated on the breeze before gently wafting to the ground, Shelby had tightly closed her eyes, breathed in an aroma so heavenly it had humbled her, and cried.

She heard the sound of sand crunching behind her and looked over her shoulder. Ben was coming back. He plopped down on the sand beside her.

"Where'd you go?" she asked.

"The Lighthouse. Just like I said."

"Why?"

"Had to get something."

"What?"

"This," he said as he pulled his hand out of his

pocket and uncurled his fingers. There, in the center of his palm was a sand art beach scene complete with shells. Deftly, he used the fingers of the same hand to turn it over. Glued on the back, was a two-inch by two-inch magnet. With his other hand, he reached for her hand and pulled it forward. Then he placed it firmly in her palm with his hand covering it.

"You understood me. You knew I was afraid of committing, even to the one woman who made being in a relationship fun and exciting all the time. Even though our feelings grew stronger and more meaningful with each passing day, you didn't press. You knew I didn't want to settle down."

"Why spoil a good thing?" she said with a smile. A smile she didn't feel. "You're not the marrying kind, I've always known that."

"No, that's not true at all. In fact, it's just the opposite. I want the whole marriage, parenthood package. I want it so badly that I have to talk myself out of it and constantly refuse the idea, because I can't stand the thought of having it and losing it all again, losing the dream, the purpose for living. I had it right there one minute, and the next, it was gone. And it could happen again, just as easily as before. My rationalization, until you, was that it was better not to risk it. But you tunneled under the wall and now every day I look at my refrigerator expecting to see a grocery list stuck up there with some cute magnet telling me we need something equally as weird as Wilton Clear Vanilla Extract.

"But you didn't push it. You gave me the time I needed, more time than I needed actually. I was beginning to think that it was something you didn't want. That you were so career-minded that there wasn't room for a husband and children, or that you were the only female in her late twenties with a sundial instead of a ticking biological clock. But the moment I became attached to you, I lost my liberty–voluntarily. I no longer have the desire to keep it. For liberty now means just the opposite of what I want. I don't want the solitude of being alone anymore. I want to be with you, all the time. So here, I didn't get a ring, I got this instead." He removed his hand from hers.

She looked down at the magnet in her hand and just stared.

"I'm not afraid of seeing a grocery list on the refrigerator anymore. I know now that there are worse things than reminders of a lost love, like finally finding out what you truly need and then not having it. If need be, I'll go to the grocery store everyday of my life for you, as long as you're going to be home when I get back to help me put everything away. Deal?" He bent over and kissed her tenderly on the cheek. "In Roy Clark's words, 'Be wife to me, be life to me, be mine.'"

"You want to marry me?"

"Hell, yes."

"Why?" He hadn't said the words she needed to hear. Yearned to hear.

"I figure sex like we have would cost me at least three or four hundred a night. Not everybody has their very own stripper and pole dancer you know. This would sure be a lot cheaper."

"Oh gee, thanks, you twit."

"Oh? Did I forget to tell you that I love you?"

"You do?"

"More than I would ever have believed possible. The everlasting kind. The kind where you're buried in the sand for 150 years and you still find a way to get back to your woman."

"He did that, didn't he?"

"With your help, he certainly did. They're side by side now."

"Poor Charlie. He gets killed, dragged under a ship, left to rot for 150 years. Then you cut him up and freeze him. At least there's finally an end to the brutality his body has endured."

"Yeah, now he's in a box, buried where he can decay naturally among the denizens of the dirt."

"Man, I do *so* want to be cremated!" she said with a grimace.

"Yeah, me too. At least whatever's left that the organ harvesters don't want."

"How do we keep getting on such morbid subjects?"

"Could it possibly be the fact that death is my business?"

She smiled over at him. "Yeah, but what do you like to do when you're not working?"

"I think you know. Come here, sit on my lap. As one very much alive body to another, let me show you a few things about your own body you may not even know."

"I doubt that there's anything about *my* body that I don't already know."

"Bet me. But first answer my question."

"I would love to put your magnet on my refrigerator."

"You don't have one."

"Oh, that's right."

"I'll get you a ring."

"I'll wear it."

"Is that all you're going to say? You know what I'm waiting to hear."

"I'm sorry . . . are you talking to me? You who made me wait and wait and wait."

"Say it, damn it!"

She smiled coyly over at him, and ran her tongue

over her bottom lip. "I'm not sure I'm ready to give up raunchy sex to call it *love*making."

"Say it or I'll push you down and take you right here."

"There are children on the beach."

"If you don't say it, we could be making one of our very own within the next few minutes." He pushed her down into the sand and rolled his body over hers.

His hand went under her cropped sweater and he palmed a firm breast. "Say it right now or I'll bare it," he threatened.

She looked around and noticed that suddenly there was absolutely no one on the beach.

"Where'd everybody go?" she asked.

"I sent them to get their cameras."

"You're bluffing."

"Say it."

"It."

"Okay, now you're asking for it." His hand left her breast and moved to her waist where he began unmercifully tickling her.

As she writhed and laughed and giggled, he continued to demand that she, "Say it." Over and over he instructed her to say the words he desperately needed to hear.

And finally she did. Softly she whispered, against his neck, "I love you, Ben."

His big hands framed her face as the wind whipped at her hair. His eyes met hers and both of them just stared. Then with tears brimming his eyes, he took her lips with his in a kiss that was a prelude to their everlasting love.

Benne (Sesame) Cookies
The Traditional Charleston Recipe

3/4 cup butter
1 and 1/2 cups brown sugar
2 eggs
1/4 tsp. baking powder
1 and 1/4 cups all-purpose flour
1/2 cup toasted sesame seeds*
1 tsp. vanilla

Cream butter and sugar and mix with the other ingredients in the order given. Drop rounded teaspoonfuls onto a parchment-lined cookie sheet, three inches apart. Bake in 325-degree oven for 30 minutes. Yields 7 dozen.

* To toast sesame seeds, stir dry in a heavy pan over medium heat until browned.

Benne Seed Cookies

This recipe results in a lighter, buttery wafer. It's a bit more challenging to make, but really delicious.

1 cup (about 5 ounces) sesame seeds
1/4 cup butter or margarine, softened
1 cup sugar
1 egg
1 teaspoon freshly squeezed lemon juice
1 teaspoon vanilla extract
1/2 cup all-purpose flour
1/4 teaspoon salt
1/4 teaspoon baking powder

Preheat oven to 350 degrees. Spread sesame seeds on an ungreased baking sheet. Stirring occasionally, bake 5 to 8 minutes or until golden brown. Cool completely on pan.

In a medium bowl, cream butter and sugar until fluffy. Add egg, lemon juice, and vanilla; stir until well blended. In a small bowl combine flour salt, and baking powder. Add dry ingredients to creamed mixture and stir until a soft dough forms. Stir in sesame seeds. Drop teaspoonfuls of dough 1 inch apart onto a heavily greased baking sheet. Bake 6 to 8 minutes or until edges are lightly browned. Transfer to a wire rack to cool completely. Store in an airtight container. Yield: about 5 dozen cookies.

CPSIA information can be obtained at www.ICGtesting.com
Printed in the USA
BVOW010722081211

277737BV00001B/25/P